MW01712155

A Secret Close to Home

BY IDA LINEHAN YOUNG

NON-FICTION

No Turning Back
If I Cry I'll Fill the Ocean

FICTION

Being Mary Ro
The Promise
The Liars
The Stolen Ones

The Room Upstairs

A Secret Close to Home

A Secret Close to Home

IDA LINEHAN YOUNG

FLANKER PRESS LIMITED
ST. JOHN'S

Library and Archives Canada Cataloguing in Publication

Title: A secret close to home : a novel : inspired by true events / Ida Linehan Young.
Names: Linehan Young, Ida, 1964- author.
Identifiers: Canadiana (print) 20230586333 | Canadiana (ebook) 20230586368 | ISBN 9781774571927 (softcover) | ISBN 9781774571934 (EPUB) | ISBN 9781774571941 (PDF)
Subjects: LCGFT: Novels.
Classification: LCC PS8623.I54 S43 2024 | DDC C813/.6—dc23

PRINTED IN CANADA

MIX
Paper | Supporting responsible forestry
FSC® C016245

This paper has been certified to meet the environmental and social standards of the Forest Stewardship Council® (FSC®) and comes from responsibly managed forests, and verified recycled sources.

Cover Design by Graham Blair

FLANKER PRESS LTD.
1243 KENMOUNT ROAD
PARADISE, NL
A1L 0V8

TELEPHONE: (709) 739-4477 FAX: (709) 739-4420 TOLL-FREE: 1-866-739-4420

WWW.FLANKERPRESS.COM

9 8 7 6 5 4 3 2 1

Canada Council for the Arts — Conseil des Arts du Canada

We acknowledge the [financial] support of the Government of Canada. *Nous reconnaissons l'appui [financier] du gouvernement du Canada*. We acknowledge the support of the Canada Council for the Arts, which last year invested $153 million to bring the arts to Canadians throughout the country. *Nous remercions le Conseil des arts du Canada de son soutien. L'an dernier, le Conseil a investi 153 millions de dollars pour mettre de l'art dans la vie des Canadiennes et des Canadiens de tout le pays*. We acknowledge the financial support of the Government of Newfoundland and Labrador, Department of Tourism, Culture, Arts and Recreation for our publishing activities. Also, we acknowledge the support of Celebrate NL, a Crown corporation within the Department of Tourism, Culture, Arts and Recreation for its support of arts organizations in the year 2024, Year of the Arts.

Truth is like light. Though altered in refraction, the same event can be perceived differently but is still the truth to those who tell it.

Dedication

For Willie and Celie: may we carry on with the foundation you laid so firmly beneath us and the love you had for one another as a guide, as we embark on our new journey, picking up where you left off.

1

Spigot Harbour, Newfoundland
1905

Jimmy Bailor paused for—if he'd counted—the hundredth time before his stiff form stumbled onward through the burgeoning thicket. His plodding gait, as he traversed the long way home from the two-room schoolhouse, was getting to be as much a habit as a habit could be. His attempt to avoid the more frequently travelled routes scoring the water's edge and near the main wharf in the bustling town wasn't working out as he'd hoped.

With fists clenched by his sides, he grumbled to conceal the crunch of his leather soles and to take his mind off his frustration for thinking avoidance wise in the first place. Even the scad of snow made it harder. He tripped in hidden tree roots and holes formed by the underlying moss that had risen with the frost of the previous week.

Boughs on the thick spruce whipped him as he pushed past. He couldn't find the more pronounced path through the trees. The taunting forest added to his grievances against nature in general, his small-for-his-age, waiting-to-sprout form, and the overall unpleasantness of the day.

The last panic-driven forward thrust deposited a dusting of snow down the back of his neck. He stumbled onto the roadway panting and, admittedly though it was next to impossible, fearful of becoming lost. Jimmy looked around and got his bearings before making a dash to a house a little more distant than he'd anticipated. A well-timed gust in the trees at the head of the trail that he should have been on mocked him with a flurry of snow that momentarily blinded him. He staggered as he passed.

Despite his woes, there was something to be said for the time engaged in being lost. His schoolmates were all home by now waiting for supper, and he wouldn't come across any of them. Darkness would be on the harbour soon to perfectly match his dismal mood. With his head down, he entered through the house door, avoiding the shop entrance. His mother would be finishing her daily business obligations—as she called them—when he got home.

Jimmy hoped to raid the pantry for a fistful of cookies and escape to his room. He didn't need any warnings they would spoil his supper, because experience proved this not to be true. He knew this to be a comfort afforded the privileged. At least that was what his schoolmates were ever eager to point out. They wore stains that came with feeding hens, cows, or goats and filling wood boxes before school, while he arrived with impeccably pressed trousers.

Raised voices coming from the kitchen startled him, and the door banged louder than he intended. He grimaced. With slow, quiet movements, he took off his coat. His notion of remaining unnoticed was betrayed by the jacket as it tangled in the broom handle, which clattered to the floor. Jimmy cringed in the dimness of the small square foyer at the bottom of the stairs, knowing he would have to face his parents as his coat fell from the hook and joined the broom.

How long had it taken him to get home? His father shouldn't have been there until well after dark. Confused, he glanced outside. It wasn't that late, yet here his father stood, looming inside the door. William Bailor turned and grabbed him. His father twisted Jimmy's palms face up, then dragged the boy into the glow of the lamplight and the gloaming through the windows. Jimmy shrivelled under his father's scrutiny.

"James, it's time we toughen up those hands," William boomed. His barrelled chest was permanently puffed out like a strutting rooster's. "How can I call you my son with the likes of those? I'm ashamed to have you around the docks."

William threw Jimmy's hands away and turned to his mother, Loretta. Jimmy swallowed the urge to say he didn't fancy being around the docks. He didn't bother to look around his father for a comforting smile from his mother. She would be busy placating her husband.

"Leave him alone, Will," Loretta said. Her scolding tone underscored a growing rift between the couple. "Our son is just fine like he is. Aren't you, Jimmy?"

"Loretta, I told you to call him James." William hit the table and rattled the cups. "He's too old for that sissy *Jimmy* business."

Jimmy reddened and lowered his head between his shoulders. A shiver, which wasn't necessarily attributed to the remnants of snow that had melted there or to the draft from the porch, grazed his spine.

He hated these more frequent conversations-turned-shouting-spurts. Jimmy hated his father calling him James. He hated his mother calling him Jimmy. He hated that he had to go to school. He hated everything about his life. While he was listing the things he detested, it was just as well to add he hated not having the opportunity to grab a few cookies and escape to his room.

Jimmy slunk into the gloom. He dared not attract his father's attention for fear the man would see the bruise on his cheek—the one that would surely give him a black eye before nightfall. But his father rarely gave him a sideways glance nor the time of day. Jimmy heard the words *a disappointment as a son* every time the man spat out his name or shot him a glance.

What hurt the most was Jimmy knew his father wasn't wrong. The boys who came to walk the girls home after school each day knew his father wasn't wrong. That's why his cheek throbbed. Terry Hardy thought Jimmy had looked at Emma Winsor the wrong way and had to teach him a lesson. It was a quick one. Jimmy had gone down on the first punch. He heard laughter as he buried his head into the arms of his wool coat, bracing for the kick that thankfully didn't come. Jimmy waited for the crowd to leave and take their cruel, taunting sniggering with them. He refused to cry, though the impulse was strong.

His back had stiffened. He was fifteen, and fifteen-year-old boys didn't cry. Fourteen-year-old boys didn't, either. However, Jimmy had proven that theory wrong the year before. He was still living down that ordeal, which had also been at the hands of Terry Hardy.

Jimmy, whatever about being a sissy, was no tale-teller. He didn't say a thing about any of the misfortunes that befell him at school, but admittedly, that was for a different reason. He didn't want his father to toughen him up. Jimmy saw how that went for other boys in the two-room schoolhouse, and he wanted no part of it. Terry was living proof of what it was like to be toughened up. Jimmy brushed his fingers across his cheek and winced.

"Isn't that right, Jimmy?" his mother asked. "Jimmy, are you even listening to me?" Her footfalls on the kitchen canvas grew louder. Jimmy glanced up before hanging his head deeper into his chest as his mother peeked at him in the shadows. He missed the rest of his parents' heated conversation as he stared at the shiny linoleum.

"James is going with me in the morning, and that's that," William said. The table rattled beneath his fist, and Jimmy flinched. "There's not one other young fellow in school his age. Not one," he shouted as he wagged his index finger at the ceiling. "James is not going back. He's going with me. No ifs, ands, or buts about it."

Jimmy cringed. Where would he be going? He had missed that part. There was no use trying to figure it out. He would do whatever he was told in the morning.

He hated his life. It couldn't possibly get worse than this.

2

Spigot Harbour was named for its unique shape. It was notched into the rocky eastern coastline of Newfoundland, a rugged Dominion of the British Empire. A sprawling, shallow river that drained from the sodden marshes at its farthest northern reaches etched the ovate cove. Steep cliffs shouldered the deep channel that coupled the harbour to the wild sea and afforded shelter from harsh winds and winter ice.

Houses and fish stages huddled along the ocean's edge in various hues of weathered grey. Wharves—their timbered decks and stilted pilings—congregated along the shoreline like fingers operating marionette strings attached to creatures beneath the murky depths. Great stands of black spruce and balsam fir, hobbled by trails and dwellings, cloaked the towering bluffs to either side and the vast barrens atop the hill at the rear. The old folks said the land used Spigot Harbour to pour its excess into the Northwest Atlantic.

The three-masted schooner *Annie May* moaned and stretched the lines taut as a downward draft siphoned through the channel, filled the canvas sails, and propelled her out into open water. There wasn't a light in any kitchen as it pulled away from the wharf behind the handful of other boats that had ventured out this late in the year. Snow squalls and high winds had kept them ashore for four days, and Jimmy's father was anxious to get to the fishing grounds.

Being late, as William Bailor put it, had been another of Jimmy's faults, he said to the other five crewmen who were waiting on the wharf.

"We just got here," Dan Acreman said as he gave a sidelong smile to Jimmy in the lamp glow. "Weren't waiting any time."

"That's time we could be on the water," William said as he made a swipe at his son, who had learned to be ready and succeeded to sidestep the whack most mornings.

Despite the piece of butterless toast Jimmy had eaten before daybreak, his guts wound and twisted into a tangled ball, and bile rose in his throat. That was on land, and only at the thoughts of going aboard. He discovered it was better to have something down to come up than to have dry heaves on the way to the fishing grounds. His father told him he would grow out of the seasickness and deemed it another of his son's useless qualities. But after almost a year, Jimmy had thrown up every single day of the first winter fishery, most of the spring, every day of the hot summer, and so far all but two days this fall.

Jimmy wouldn't have believed he would pine for the times when he had to rebuff the mean streak of Terry Hardy. That was easy compared to his father's constant tirades about his "good-for-nothing" son. He heard this phrase all day, and it spilled over into the evening at the supper table. Unlike school, there was no taking the long way home, either. His father continually called for him to hurry up from the moment he stepped on the wharf until he crossed the threshold at home.

Dan nudged Jimmy. Jimmy's wide eyes reflected an air of gratitude as Dan steadied him on the deck.

"Hang in there. You're doing just fine, lad," Dan said as he clapped Jimmy on the shoulder and indicated for him to release the forward tow rope while he went aft. The rest of the crew didn't give Jimmy the time of day, but Dan was different and always had been. When he started, all five of them had stood head and shoulders above Jimmy, but not so much now. He had stretched out over the summer and had more meat on his bones.

Dan often told William to go easy on the boy, but Jimmy's father paid him no heed. The others jumped when the skipper said jump, Jimmy guessed for fear they would lose their berth. Dan was different. He worked hard, but he had a kinder way about him. He often whistled or hummed a tune when they worked. William cursed the rain; Dan said there would be no flies. William cursed the fog; Dan said it wouldn't be too hot. Dan help Jimmy when he was heaving up over the gunnel. He had a kindness and easygoing way about him that Jimmy wasn't used to but liked just the same.

When Jimmy heard shouting, he turned from where he'd been folded over the gunnel in time to see Dan grab his father's oilskins. Jimmy gasped as another heave overtook him. His body protested, forming a painful bubble of rank air in his gullet that couldn't decide if it wanted to come up or go down.

"I'll not go along with this," Dan said as he pushed William away.

"I'm not asking you," William said as he swung a fist at him, catching Dan on the chin.

Dan staggered backward and fell across the nets before scrambling upright once again. He rubbed his jaw and glowered at William.

"You can't do that," he said as he looked for accord from the others.

"I'm not asking, I'm telling," William said. "I don't pay you to mind my business."

"It's not right," Dan said.

When his expectant gaze didn't find fellowship with the crew, he rushed toward William. William sidestepped and hammered a fist to Dan's back in passing, knocking him to the deck.

"You're off the boat, you hear me?" William said as he spat on boards near enough to splatter the downed man. He strode toward the wheelhouse.

When his father was out of sight, Jimmy slunk beneath the mast and helped Dan to his feet. "What's going on?"

Dan shook his head and scowled toward William. He yanked his arm from Jimmy's grasp and went below.

"Any of the rest of you have anything to say?" William shouted as he came back around the wheelhouse and scanned the crew, his corded neck a sign of his temperament. The men shook their heads, grumbled, and busied themselves at the nets or the twine as the skipper turned his back and trod along the gunnel to the bow.

Jimmy felt the bile rise in his throat, bolted for the side, and retched for what he was sure was the hundredth time that day. He sat on the nets to catch his breath and slouched into the mast rigging to stay upright. Whatever had set his father off would soon be directed his way when he was caught sitting. On shaky legs, Jimmy stood to help the men clear the kelp and other bits of ocean debris from the nets they had just taken aboard. The ropes and buoys were neatly wound and stacked as one net followed the other into the pile. His father expected any mending would be done as they made their way home. Though the deck was cluttered, the work would be completed on the water instead of on the land. "I'm not paying you to sit around," was said more than once and kept the crew busy.

Jimmy wanted to find Dan but feared his father's wrath. Instead, he put his head down and, with cold-numbed hands, began to pull out mangled sculpins and kelp from the webbing. The boat slowed beneath him. Jimmy, thinking he had lost track of time, expected they would soon be home. But a glance at the horizon confused him. It wasn't the familiar bluffs of Spigot Harbour, the ones that always gave him hope to see the end of the day. Though the schooner was riding low, and the hull appeared to be full, perhaps his father had decided to set the nets one more time. Perhaps William, who always wanted more, anticipated bad weather and was racing the elements to ensure he brought home the most fish. Maybe that was what Dan hadn't agreed with. After all, it was the time of the year when the ice made its way down the coast and the gear could be destroyed. But his father knew best—and even if he didn't, who was going to go against William Bailor?

The skipper shouted orders for the men to tie the mast as Dan appeared from below. A bruise had formed around the man's eye. He glanced toward the others, then made his way aft and disappeared for a few moments before joining the work of the crew. There were whispers and grunts and cautious glances from Jimmy to his father before the men finished lashing down the sail.

Jimmy got up to ask what was going on and noticed his father barrelling toward him. The man's stride was long and purposeful and so quick that Jimmy failed to react when William grabbed the back of his coat and pulled him from his perch. He shrank beneath the blow that didn't come and scrabbled to get his footing as his father towed him sternward and all but pitched him over the back rail and into the dory.

He tripped in the pound board of the tiny boat, and inertia sent him flying headfirst into the small triangular space at the bow. His head struck the wood, and he grimaced, sucking in a pained breath. Feeling for something solid beneath his hands, he pushed himself to a kneeling position on the pound board and held the gunnel in a vain effort to stabilize himself. The boat jostled, and he turned to see his father land between the rear pounds, where he immediately took up the oars. William untied the dory as he heard Dan shout from the deck, "Don't do this."

"Mind your business," Jimmy's father shouted over his shoulder, "and I'll mind mine, like I told you."

Jimmy's wide eyes flitted from his father to Dan and the others peering at him from the schooner. Dan was gesturing for him to look downward, and Jimmy didn't understand what he meant. Dan kept motioning toward the sea, and Jimmy looked over the side. When the crewman shook his head, Jimmy glanced toward his feet and saw Dan's lunch bag. Dan nodded, but Jimmy couldn't fathom what was happening nor why he would need it. With a few strokes of the oar, his father moved them away from the *Annie May* and toward land.

The splash of the oars and the lap of the sea against the sides of the dory filled the salty air between them. Jimmy wondered if there was anything he could ask that wouldn't anger his father when the dory gave a jolt, knocking him off the seat. William Bailor leaped from the rear and landed knee deep in the freezing water without a flinch.

He pushed the dory farther onto the beach and glared at his son. "Get out," William said between clenched teeth. "Hurry up. Get out." Jimmy couldn't possibly disobey the command, though he had no idea where they were going. He eyed Dan's bag and grabbed it as he scrambled over the side onto the slippery rocks. His father climbed back aboard and was two dory lengths away before Jimmy realized what was happening.

"Wait," Jimmy said, his voice low with disbelief. "Wait." His father's face was pinched, his lips taut, his eyes as hard and emotionless as Jimmy had ever seen them. He studied the boat and the declining image of his father. He began to walk along the shore to keep abreast of the dory. "Wait," he shouted over and over, flailing his arms in protest, searching for a reason his father had done this. He continued shouting as his father climbed aboard the *Annie May* and tied the dory. The others left the aft railing, set the sail, and guided the schooner away from him.

Jimmy watched until the *Annie May* disappeared beneath the horizon. He silently begged for its return as his body sank farther into the beach. When the rising tide breached upon his knees, he got up. Remembering the rucksack he had dropped, he made his way back along the shore. He stumbled and slipped as each step sent beach rocks skittering, his legs as disjointed as his tormented mind.

A stream split the beach when he began to think he had gone too far. There was no sign of the bag. He turned and slowed his pace until he spotted something floating in the gentle lap of the ocean. Running into the water, he retrieved the saturated sack. He pulled the rope off to see the contents. Soggy bread and molasses met his gaze.

Jimmy fell back on the beach and discovered that sixteen-year-old boys cried after all.

3

Either sullen clouds had consumed the last of daylight and drawn the evening in, or her husband and son were late. Loretta Bailor glanced through the window to determine what was to blame just as footfalls sounded in the porch.

"Where's Jimmy?" she asked when William closed the door. Loretta tilted her head and looked behind him, expecting her son. William sidled along by her, threw his lunch bucket on the table, and sat to pull off his rubber boots.

"Where's Jimmy?" she repeated. She strode to the porch, pulled open the door, and peered into the night. Seeing no sign of anyone, she returned to the table, her gaze moving between her husband and the door, confusion flushing her cheeks.

"William, where's Jimmy?" she asked again, pushing down her rising anxiety. She crossed her arms, holding her elbows.

William didn't speak. He picked up his boots and laid them behind the stove to dry as if it were any other evening coming in from the fishing grounds. He didn't meet her gaze. Instead, he took his lunch bucket and brought it to the pantry before returning to the table.

"What's for supper?"

"Where's our son?" Loretta's voice cracked. She glared into his face, willing him to meet her eyes.

"That good-for-nothing ain't no son of mine." William forced the words between clenched teeth. His neck strained, and his arms bulged as he gripped the edge of the table.

Loretta's eyes grew wide, then narrowed to slits. Her teeth clamped shut, and her lips drew back on a throaty roar before she lunged at her husband. She clutched his shirt and clawed his face, her heart pounding as she kicked his shins and punched him. "What have you done? What have you done?" she demanded as tears covered her pinched face.

"He's fine, Loretta," William said as he snared her wrists and guided her body away as if she were no more than a housefly.

"Where is he? Why isn't he here?" Loretta yanked her arms away but couldn't free herself from his clutches.

"You baby him too much," he said as he gripped her chin with his free hand and pulled her face to his. "It's no good for him. This is for the best."

She screamed and fought to free herself. He let her go in a controlled motion as he manoeuvred her to sit at the table. She stared at him, her eyes raged, and her blood pounded in her ears, but she forced herself to stay seated.

"Loretta, listen to me. The boy is babied. I'm the laughingstock of the crew. He can't do anything right."

"You made him go, Will. It's not his fault." Loretta spat as she readied to spring at him again.

"You don't see what I see," William replied. "Loretta, he needs to be a man." He gave a heavy sigh.

"Where is he? What have you done?" Loretta leaped from the chair and seized his shirt. "I swear I'll go for the constable."

"I'm sure he'll be only too happy to oblige," William said as he pulled her hands off him.

"What's that supposed to mean? Where's my son."

"*Your* son is fine." He emphasized the word. "And Abraham Giles looks for every chance to come see you when I'm gone."

"For God's sake, William Bailor. That's enough of that. I married you, didn't I? Now, where's Jimmy?"

"If you must know, I put James ashore up near the summer fishing camp." William fetched a plate and moved toward the pot simmering on the stove. "I'm starving."

Loretta swung at the plate and sent it flying. It smashed into bits on the oven door. "You did *what*?"

"You heard me," he said as he pulled another plate from the sideboard and angled it away from Loretta. He took the cover off the iron pot and ladled stew onto the plate, then turned his back to her.

"You can't be serious. What kind of father does that?" She tore at his shirt. Her eyes widened in terror as she pleaded, "Where is he, Will? This is not funny."

"I told you where he is. I put him ashore before hauling the last of our nets," William said, his back still to Loretta. "He's all right, Loretta. We'll pick him up in a day or two. It will be good for the boy."

"A day or two? Have you gone out of your mind? He'll starve. You go for him right now," Loretta said, barely curtailing her fury. She turned and paced the kitchen with her hands clasped on each cheek.

"There's food in the old cabin. Enough to do him for a week if he looks after it. I did it for the boy's own good." William took his plate and glanced behind him before moving to the table.

"How can you eat?" she demanded.

"I'm hungry. Working all day. Loretta, the boy will be fine," he said. He snatched the fresh loaf from the table and ripped the end bun free. "I don't want to hear any more about it."

His wife plucked her coat from the hanger. "If you won't go, I'll get one of the men to go. Or I'll go myself."

"You can't, and they won't. If they do, they'll have no berth. They know I mean it and won't risk it," William said calmly as he dipped the bread in the hot stew and stogged it into his mouth.

"Dan will." Loretta turned in a huff.

"Dan doesn't have a berth."

"My God, you've gone out of your mind," Loretta said as she stormed out of the house.

She came back a short time later after being turned down at the doors of the crewmen. Madge Hardy's *maybe it's for the best* had vexed her and still rang in her ears. She had only said that, Loretta guessed, because she would probably be glad to get clear of Terry for a night or two.

Poor Jimmy must be scared. She wiped at her eyes with the backs of her hands as she thought of him shivering and hungry in the dark somewhere. Rage and fear bundled in her gut and burst upward through her throat. She swallowed the burning liquid and grimaced.

Though the dark kitchen was empty, she knew better than to believe her husband had changed his mind. Loretta took the lamp from the table, lit it, and stomped into the store, her face disfigured with rage. She whipped a hoe from the wall and marched upstairs to their bedroom.

William turned toward the window when she entered. The lamp on the night table was still lit as he lifted off the bed to remove his pants. Loretta rounded the footboard and brandished the hoe above her head.

"What the devil," he said as he held up an arm to defend himself, but the low ceiling took care of it with a thump. The hoe fell from Loretta's hands and clattered onto the floor. She reached for it at the same time as William.

"I swear I'll cleave you open if you don't go for Jimmy this instant," she shrieked, her face a crimson red.

He yanked the tool from Loretta's clasp, held it out of reach, and fended off her attempts to reclaim it.

"Loretta, what's gotten into you?" William sputtered. "I said the boy is fine." His voice was softer than she'd heard in years. "I'll go get him in the morning."

Loretta collapsed beside him, and her strained emotions erupted in tears. "He's not fine. Please go tonight."

"I won't ask the men to go at this hour. We'll go at first light." He patted her hand. "James—I mean Jimmy—is sitting by the stove in the cabin with the fire going or probably already turned in for the night."

"I hope so."

The bedspring creaked as Loretta stood. She faced William. "I'll never forgive you for this," she said calmly. "Never."

He reached for her hand, but she turned away. "You'll thank me someday," he said to her retreating frame. "I promise."

Loretta left the room in turmoil. She sat in the rocking chair in the kitchen. Taking her rosary beads from the cupboard, she mouthed a litany of prayers until daylight pierced the darkness and William came down the stairs.

4

"The wind is on the land," Daddy always said on days like this. Days no good for fishing, especially late in the year when the back-breaking row to the shoals outside Juniper Tickle would freeze the hairs on your head before it got to your fingers on the oars. The winter fish had been caught, split, salted, and dried a few weeks before, so Daddy wouldn't attempt a day like this, anyway. Nor would he let his sons go out.

The wind knocked on the windowpanes and sought entrance through the cracked putty and loose sashes. In the summer it would be under the floorboards, but a few days before, when the prevailing wind shifted, Daddy and her older brothers, Bart and Tommy, had added the protective layers of kelp. The weather-beaten house appeared to have tilted backwards from where it clung to the edge of the rocky shore and would upright when it was calm. The shelter of the cliffs to the rear sustained the straightened form if the wind was off the land. For today, they waited. In Juniper Tickle you either worked or you waited. The latter was less for Flory, though neither her father nor her brothers would agree.

Florence Alice White, or Flory to her family, pushed her bottom lip out and blew at a strand of brown hair. It had come loose from under the edge of her mother's faded bandana and fallen across Flory's nose. After three increasingly forceful breaths didn't remedy the annoyance, she dipped her head into her shoulder and manoeuvred the irritant behind her ear.

Flory's fists didn't break stride as they pushed into the warm dough. The fire crackled and popped, drawing her attention. She grimaced, realizing she hadn't closed the drafter. Peering at the reddening iron of the firebox, she flicked the dough off her fingers, dusted them with flour from the abraded table, rubbed her hands together to reduce the stickiness, and turned to the stove all in one fluid motion. She fetched a split from the woodbox and pushed it against the drafter grate to close it before tossing the flour-covered split back with the rest of the wood. Plucking a towel from the warmer, she wrapped it around the handle of the steaming kettle and shook it. The stovetop had turned a burnished red. Satisfied it wouldn't boil dry, Flory laid its blackened bottom on the warmer without adding water and threw the towel over the line that clung to the overhead beam by two small tacks. She squatted and eyed the drafter, then returned to her chore once the firebox quieted.

Flory sighed. She folded and punched the dough with a vigour that came from restlessness. The smell of yeast filled the hot kitchen as several wayward strands of hair fell across her nose. These she didn't bother fixing because she heard the dough cracking and knew she was done. Momma used to say it was a sign of good bread. That made her eyes misty. Momma was gone six years now. Surely it wasn't seven.

She had been ten when the midwife came. It was the spring of the year because the lambs had come, and Daddy had said

Momma was going to outdo the sheep. "It's going to be a fine year, Caroline. Six doubles, all ewes, mind you. Four had singles and only one ram among them."

Momma hadn't been her jovial self. "Something's wrong, Bert," she had said, and Flory saw the scared look masking her features. Momma's cheeks were colourless, and her eyes were dark—they didn't hold their usual sparkle. Daddy had tried to ease her worry, but Momma was adamant something was wrong.

Flory's mother grew tired and took to their bed a few days later. Daddy sent Ralph and Bernard, the eldest, to get the midwife. They were gone two days. By the time they got back, the midwife said there was nothing she could do. The babies had been dead for quite a while. She believed there to be two.

"Save her," Daddy had pleaded, his cheeks stained with tears. Flory hadn't seen him cry before, so she cried, too.

"It's beyond my skill," the midwife said.

"The doctor?" Daddy asked, hope and desperation in his voice. "We'll get the doctor."

"That will take a week," the midwife said. "Mr. White, your wife doesn't have a week."

"We'll bring her there," he replied as he paced the kitchen.

"She won't make it to the dory," the midwife said, her hushed whisper alarming.

"We have to try."

"You can be gone, or you can be with her." The midwife shook a crooked finger at her father. "It's a choice you'll have to make."

The stern-faced woman moved Flory from the room while Daddy stayed with Momma. Flory stared at the closed door, too young to understand what was going on and too old to climb into her mother's arms, though the urge was strong. Sometime later the door creaked, and her father beckoned her in.

"Flory," her mother's hoarse whisper sounded in her ears. Momma's hand lifted off the bed and reached for her. Flory ran to her and took hold of the cool palm. Her mother's grip was weak, but Flory's, though small, was strong. Momma's lips drifted upward in an attempt to smile but fell again.

"Flory," her mother said again.

Flory moved closer and laid her head on Momma's bosom.

"I'm here, Momma," she whispered. "I'm here."

"You look after your father," Momma said, her voice trembling and fading. She sipped a shallow breath as if it were hot tea.

"I will, Momma. I will."

Flory lifted her head from her mother's chest and rested it on the pillow beside her. Her mother's flowing brown hair, much like her own, spilled out over the embroidered cotton. She looked so pale and grey that Flory wanted to pinch her cheeks like she had often seen her mother do to get colour in them.

"You be a good girl, Flory," Momma said before a cough rumbled from her chest.

The midwife took Flory from the room once more. She wanted to scream to stay with her mother, but she wouldn't. Momma expected better than that from her big girl. Instead, she sat on the woodbox by the stove and cried. She stared at the door, not knowing what was going to happen, but she knew that, whatever it was, she wouldn't like it.

A teardrop on the back of her hand interrupted Flory's rumination. She hadn't thought of her mother in ages. Momma had died a few days later when the wind was on the land, knocking at the windows and pushing up between the floorboards.

When Daddy and the older boys brought Momma away, the midwife taught Flory how to make bread, cook, and clean, and it had been a steady gait of going since then.

5

Flory rested her forearms on the windowsill and gazed out at the house across the tickle. Bart and his wife, Lizzy, had the only other light in the place. Bart, Ralph, and Bernard had left a few years before to look for work on sealing vessels in St. John's. Their third year out, only Bart had returned. The next year he went, he came back with Lizzy.

There was no word of Ralph or Bernard, but Daddy said if anything had happened to the other two, they would have heard. Didn't the worst news have a way of making it back to loved ones?

None of the White boys were lettered. Momma had taught Flory the alphabet, but neither her brothers nor her father had any interest. To placate their mother, the menfolk had learned to put their names to paper. It had been so long now, Flory doubted she would remember a thing Momma had showed her. She didn't know how Momma knew them. Daddy, who had depended on Momma, now relied on the men from the collector boats to do right by him when it came to an honourable exchange of fish for supplies. He rarely had any money after such interactions. Even if he had, with only the Whites in Juniper Tickle, there was nowhere to spend any cash.

After Lizzy had little Robert, or Bobby as they called him, Bart stayed in the tickle and fished with his father and Tommy. Now Lizzy was a few months from having her second child, and Daddy hoped Juniper Tickle would thrive like he had planned when he settled there with Momma all those years ago.

Lizzy came by with her son most days during the summer while they waited for the men. But now that the cold had set in and she was getting farther along in her pregnancy, Lizzy didn't venture as often. Instead, Flory would fry dough she had saved for toutons and bring them to her sister-in-law. Lizzy hadn't mastered baking yet, so Flory didn't mind. Flory was surprised by Lizzy. She possessed no domestic skills when she arrived, not even the basics. She didn't cook, bake, knit, or sew, and Flory didn't think she would stay the first winter. But Lizzy loved Bart and was eager to learn and make a home. She didn't talk about where she came from or any family; she just settled into life in Juniper Tickle. Lizzy was good with Bobby. Everything else would take care of itself as time allowed.

Flory stretched and rubbed her lower back before returning her elbows to the windowsill. Daddy and Tommy were late. Tommy, barely eighteen, was all about his gut. They joked he had a hollow leg because he ate so much. It was odd for them not to be back for their midday mug up. Flory eyed the three loaves rising in the pans on the table. She had to wait until the last of the bread was out of the oven before she could go see what was keeping them.

She made several trips between the window and the stove before she saw Lizzy leaving the house with Bobby. The tide was going out, so Lizzy could cross the bar, exposed like a giant back-bone at low tide, instead of going the long way around above the high-water mark. Flory donned her mother's coat, stepped out onto the gallery, and closed the door to keep the draft off the dough. Shivering, she pulled the collar to break the wind. She met the two at the embankment and took hold of her nephew's hand along with Lizzy's to help them up the steep path.

"Is Bart with you?" Lizzy asked, her short breaths coming in bursts. She waved her hand in front of her mouth as she stopped.

"What happened to you?" Flory asked as she took in Lizzy's windblown appearance, red face, and damp knees.

"Tripped. Wasn't careful enough. Fell, that's all," Lizzy said as she wiped her fingers across her knees and pulled at the cotton. She sucked air between her pinched lips, drew back her hand, and nipped her fingertip with her mouth. "Ouch."

"Are you all right? Did you hurt yourself?"

Lizzy dismissed her concern with a shrug. "I'm not hurt. Just a splinter."

"I'll get it out when we get inside," Flory said as she examined Lizzy's dirty hands. "Look at the state of you."

"Clumsy," she muttered. "That's all." Lizzy trembled, and her eyes watered.

Flory linked arms with her sister-in-law, pulled her close, and helped her to the step. "You sound like you've strolled around the tickle," she said jovially as she let go of Lizzy.

"Just this little one is not so little," she replied as she glanced down at her expanding girth. Lizzy rubbed her hand across her stomach, then let it come to rest there. She used her head to indicate Bobby. "And that one is fast. Every step is like walking around the tickle," she said as she blew out a sigh and grinned. She paused. "What about the men?"

Flory shook her head. "I was waiting on the baking before I could go see where they'd gone."

Inside, Flory shed her coat and took the cloth from the oven door. "I have to get the bread out before it burns," she said over her shoulder as she peered in at the golden-topped loaves, "and those three in. It's done. I was going to make toutons." She gestured at the bread pan. "I guess I'll wait until the men get back."

Bobby clapped his hands. "*Doutins*."

The two women grinned. One at a time, Flory upset the five hot loaves onto the table and turned the tops up. They crackled as Lizzy buttered them. Flory laid the last three pans in the oven. Then she took the molasses jar from the pantry shelf and offered hot slices. "This should do until I get to fry the dough."

Bobby was content with the warm, buttery treat topped with sticky black molasses. Flory tended to Lizzy's splinter, then said, "I'll go see where they've gone."

"I'll watch the oven," Lizzy offered. "And make tea. It'll be ready when you return." As she pulled Bobby off the table, where he was reaching for another slice, she laughed. "And I'll make sure there's some left when you get back."

Outside, Flory drew in a deep breath and closed her eyes. She would check the beach first—she hadn't noticed if the boat was pulled up on the slip. Not that she expected otherwise, but a cursory glance over the embankment confirmed her father and brothers were not at sea. Before long, when there was no chance of winter fishing and the snow came, the dory would be laid upside down on a flake beside the house until spring.

Flory waved to her nephew as she passed the window and made her way to the back of the house. Her brows furrowed as she glanced toward the slide path and noticed the axe wasn't in the chopping block. Maybe they had gone paring spring var. She stopped in the wood chips and shavings and listened for chopping sounds. The horse grazing in the meadow and the sheep lying in the shelter, exposed to the sun and closer to the trees, paid no heed when she crossed the bridge on the little stream and checked the barn.

"Daddy. Tommy. Bart," she called to the empty rafters. Hay dust shifted around the slice of light coming from the door. The soft bleat from the goats behind the barn was the only response.

Flory squinted and looked skyward at the sun as she returned to the house. She shook her head at the lateness in the day. Opening the back door, she shouted, "It's only me. I'm checking for the game bags." All three flour sacks she had cut and sewn to make lunch bags were where they should be, hanging on nails near the door.

"I'll be back," she shouted again and heard the mumbled acknowledgement from her sister-in-law through the inner porch door. Flory crossed the beach to her brother's house and skirted the outer wall to the back. Chips underfoot were damp and uneven near the woodpile. She slipped, twisting her ankle. With a grimace, she limped along until the pain subsided to a throb. She tested her gait for a tentative step before resuming her search. Her gaze sought a sign in the meadow and along the treeline. Nothing was out of place. She turned, capped her eyes with her palm, and stared out through the tickle.

Flory cocked a brow and blinked several times when she saw a boat. She jammed her fists into her eyes, waited for the spots to disappear, and returned her gaze to the distant point. There was a boat, and a big one. It wasn't steering in through the channel. Spring and summer, yes, but this late in the year, there shouldn't have been a boat. The vessel was side-on to her view, like it had gone ashore, but that was impossible, because there was no place to land out there. She rubbed her eyes once again.

Figures no larger than ants moved around. She recognized

one on the beach as Bart—his posture gave him away. It looked like Daddy on the deck, but she couldn't be sure. Both he and Tommy wore the same brown coats. They must have followed the path out to the point and discovered the boat. Perhaps Bart had seen it and gone for Daddy and Tommy. It could only be seen from this side of the tickle. Flory cupped her hands around her mouth and called their names, but the wind, which was on the land, didn't carry her voice far enough for them to hear. She made her way back along the bar to let Lizzy know.

"Looks to have two, maybe three masts, near as I can tell."

"I wonder who they are and why they're here," Lizzy said. A flash of fear washed over her eyes.

"We'll know soon enough. Tommy will be hungry and will want to come home," Flory said. She laughed. "He can't help himself. Now that I know where they are, who wants toutons?" She hung her coat and circled the table to poke her nephew.

Bobby clapped and shouted through his giggles, "Me, me."

Lizzy set the table with cups and saucers and eyed the door. "If you don't mind, I'll stay here until they come back."

Flory nodded and squeezed her hand. Lizzy hid her eyes as she dipped her head. Red-cheeked, she gave Flory a flaccid smile.

"There are lots of years ahead to learn how to make bread," Flory said as she grabbed the dough pan to distract her sister-in-law's unease. "Today you can fry the toutons."

"I'm sure I can do that. I'll even take out the three loaves in the oven before they burn."

"If they're burnt, they're yours," Flory said with a nod. She looked toward the ceiling and raised her finger. "Or the strangers can eat it."

They both laughed, and so did Bobby.

6

Jimmy shivered and turned on his side, reaching to pull the quilt across his shoulder. Another snooze was just what he needed before his father shouted from the bottom of the stairs for him to get up. He patted along his arm and around his waist before confusion set in. The mattress beneath him wasn't right. He wriggled, and rocks skittered. His eyes shot open, and he sat upright before his brain caught up with his surroundings.

He was on the beach. Hunger stabbed his gut from the sudden movement, and a dry mouth lamented for water. His damp clothes caused him to shudder, and he tightened his jaw to keep his teeth from chattering. Fog held the sun at bay and heightened the unnerving feel of the morning gloom and his discomfort.

The rising tide banished Jimmy's attempts to light a fire. Without a blackened blemish, driftwood bobbed, taunting and unscathed, just out of reach on the calm sea. He scrabbled backward from the water's edge, unable to get footing in the beach rocks, which slipped and tumbled over each another to escape him.

Exhaustion from crying over his predicament must have put him to sleep long after darkness fell. His last thoughts were of noises in the woods and in the water and of getting ready to run. To where? He didn't know, but run was the only plan he had. He had put his back to the huge trunk of a dead tree that was rooted in the beach. There he cried and waited.

Jimmy's father would come. He had to. There was no doubt about it. Jimmy tried to dismiss the fact he was stranded on a beach.

The boy felt for his rubbers, thankful he had woken before they were set adrift. He had been perceptive enough to hang the boots upside down on the spine of the gnarly spruce that had long ago succumbed to its fate amid tides and time. But that was where good sense had failed him, because the tree had slowly disappeared beneath the glimmering surface of the rising ocean in the morning sunlight. He scrambled upright and stretched to save his boots from vanishing altogether before he stuffed his damp, woollen-socked feet into them.

Jimmy dislodged the lunch sack from where it hung on a knot near his head. The bread had been spoiled, as had the tea and sugar, but two tins of apricots and three tins of peaches clanked together when he moved it. Dan must have fleeced the galley and his father's lunch pail. Mother had packed the fruit for his father like she did most every morning.

Take them anyway, Loretta had said. *You never know when you'll be late and might need them.* Jimmy doubted her sincerity. He often wondered if her buttery words to his father were genuine or served as a ruse to keep him happy. Father didn't seem to mind. Did she have any idea what Father had planned? He didn't think it possible, but he also hadn't thought it possible Father would leave him stranded on a beach overnight, in the middle of nowhere, with no supplies.

If this had been a fishing morning, they would have set their nets by the time the sun was this high. A distant storm rumbled. Lightning tore through the clouds out over the ocean. A narrow band of grey approached, and he had no oil clothes or sou'wester to protect him.

Jimmy crawled beneath the spruce, which were thick and green at the edge of the beach. There he waited as a rush of the rain crept closer with big splats heralding its arrival before the drone of the downpour. Thunderclaps and lightning ravaged the skies and darkened the day as he huddled against the tree trunk. Soon the ominous noise passed over, and the rain turned to drizzle and then faded, leaving the air as damp and heavy as his spirit. Jimmy stayed beneath the tree long after the sun returned. He found comfort with his arms tightly wrapped around his knees and the trunk at his back.

Then hunger took over. By the time night fell for the second time, the realm of the impossible had stretched considerably. His prospect of survival, in his inexperienced estimation, had become dire.

Day three began underneath the limbs of the big spruce a few steps from where he had spent the night before. He had broken smaller branches from the nearby brush with which to cover himself. It did little more than make the night bearable. Chilled to the bone, Jimmy wished for something hot. The dilemma remained—he still hadn't mastered lighting a fire.

Maybe his father was waiting for smoke to rise before fetching him. It would be a sign he could do something right after all. Jimmy had four matches left. The storm had soaked the wood, and he had been wasteful. But he hoped today would be more promising, and he resolved to be stronger and take care of the little he had left.

He crawled out from under the boughs into a world of white. His heart sank like a rock pitched into the pond. Not the flat ones that slitted along the surface for ten to fourteen hops before meandering to the bottom. No, the stone he imagined was oddly shaped, thrown without grace, which broke the surface, splashed violently, and then went straight down.

This would be the end of him.

He would freeze or starve to death. Which one would take him first? He looked at the tins of fruit, grateful he had kept them. Admittedly that had not been intentional. Yesterday morning he had beaten the tin of peaches into submission on a large rock only to lose its contents onto the beach. He swallowed two peaches in one gulp, scraped rocks and debris off what he could salvage, and left the rest for the tide to take. Before nightfall, he had turned to the can of apricots but wasn't able to open them. If he had, and they had gone onto the rocks, there would be nothing left for the tide.

Though hunger was a painful temptress, he decided to wait before opening any other tins. Jimmy needed rescuing, and the fire was the only way to get it. He blew into his fingers until he could feel them again. Now he needed something dry. The evening before, he had pulled a fistful of old man's beard from the spruce and shoved it into his pocket for this purpose.

Years spent overhearing tales from two men who gathered at the store had garnered him that little bit of information. George Dolan told Raymond Blythe about the time he had gotten lost. Raymond said he wandered out of the woods three days after going astray. Mr. George countered he had been gone for five. He had rubbed two sticks together over old man's beard, the dry moss that draped from the tree, to make fire. He chewed frankum gum from the same spruce when he grew hungry.

Jimmy saw him chewing tobacco one time after that and asked if it was the spruce gum he had talked about. Mr. George laughed and said, *Boy, you have a lot to learn.* He asked Jimmy to follow him along a trail. As they walked, Mr. George sized up the trees before finding what he wanted. *See here, young fellow,* he said as he pointed at the trunk. *Where that limb's been broken off, there'll be frankum there in the fall.*

Jimmy, the curious sort, remembered what Mr. George told him later that year. On his way home from school one day, he ran along the trail in search of the frankum. To his dismay, the tree had been chopped down. He didn't know if Mr. George had cut it down so Jimmy wouldn't find out he was fibbing. Perhaps there was no such thing as frankum. But he always gave Mr. George's account credence because, after all, he' had been lost for five days.

Jimmy stumbled along the beach to the little stream that split the beach. He was parched. The scad of snow was melting, and the beach glistened in the morning sun. Barely taking his eyes off the ocean for fear of missing the boat, he hadn't taken the time to look around. His time had been spent in the smallest of settings, where the river was to his right, the woods to his back, the ocean to his front, and a place to relieve himself past the half-buried tree trunk. The boy's father would have no trouble locating him. The man was as good with the compass as ever fished.

As Jimmy turned from the ocean, something in the woods caught his eye. His heart raced. He drew a thumb and finger across his eyes before a second glance confirmed that something glistened where it had no business doing so. Jimmy kept his eye trained to the spot for fear he'd lose it and moved toward it.

As he was speculating what it could be, his footing gave way and he fell face first into the river. Jimmy scrambled to gain a foothold while his hands grasped for the bottom. He gripped a rock but slipped before he could bring himself upright. Tumbling over, he groaned inwardly as his head went under. He pushed up on his hands and knees and crawled to the opposite shore.

Jimmy shivered as he emptied his boots. He could barely feel his hands. What had he done? His father wouldn't have fallen in the river—nor would Mr. George. Jimmy sprawled backward onto the beach.

"*I give up*," he shouted before he closed his eyes. "I give up." His dejected sigh felt like his final utterance. The slap of the waves and the giggle of water on the rocks near his feet were the only response.

This was how he would be found, his body frozen, stretched out. He would be hard to get aboard a boat to take home. They would probably have to break his arms. Jimmy Bailor would be the talk of Spigot Harbour for years to come. Nothing different than now, he supposed. Would anyone have any pity for him? His mother, for sure. She would cry for him.

A gentle breeze wafted over his face. He gazed into the sun. It hurt his eyes, and he turned away. Something glinted not far from him. Suddenly, he needed to see what had led to his demise. Jimmy rolled over and pushed himself up. He swayed as cold and heat fought for control over him, and he hoped the warmth would emerge victorious as he stumbled toward the shimmer in the trees. His legs were heavy and barely answered his call to move. Several strides in, he felt the heft of his clothing. He discarded his coat and kept going.

The layer of snow had been light and melted from this exposed portion of the beach first. A few feet farther on, a small indent—it couldn't really be considered a trail—drew his attention. If the snow had still been there, he wouldn't have noticed it. Then his eyes focused. He had to look away and back again in case his mind was tricking him. But there on the hill, in the trees, was a small cabin. How had he not seen it before?

Jimmy's spirits lifted as he staggered toward his rescue. He fell to one knee and gathered every bit of strength he could muster to stand. Reaching for a tree limb, he was dismayed his hand wouldn't close around it. He willed it to move, but there was no response. Grunting and straining, he managed to upright himself. Pushing forward, he made three steps before the small incline did him in. He collapsed.

Jimmy sighed as heat seeped into his arms and legs. He would just lie here until he was all warmed. Then he would make it to the cabin. But something was telling him this wasn't right.

Raymond Blythe had said something about being fooled by the heat when he was lost. *It wasn't the truth*, he said as he sucked on his pipestem. *The warmth can lure you to your death*, he had warned. Jimmy didn't fancy the idea of dying at that moment—not without seeing the inside of the tilt that was so close. Living was hard enough, but what if dying was worse?

With knees and elbows, he wormed his way to the front of the structure. A loop of fishing twine hung over two pegs, one on the frame and one on the cabin's crude door. Jimmy reached and poked at the line with his numb hand, and it fell clear. The door creaked, and he pushed inward, shoulder first. The place was dilapidated. He stared at the rafters, which seemed too close for tall men. The floor was fashioned from small, supple sticks with moss stuffed between them, both of which had dried long ago.

Jimmy's clothes had hardened. He had to get them off. Despite the warmth that coursed through him, the numbness in his hands and feet told a different story. He blew on his fingers until they were limber enough to unbutton his shirt. Wriggling out of it, he then made short work of his pants, boots, and socks. Several wool blankets covered sticks laid out in tiers, which Jimmy assumed were meant to be bunks, three on opposite walls. Between them, at the back of the cabin, rocks formed a crude, lichen-covered fireplace. It looked like it hadn't been used in years, if at all.

He pulled the wool blankets around him and moved across the floor like a crab until he was clear of his sodden, frozen clothing. When he reached the fireplace, he noticed the kindling had been set. Spalls had fallen away from the slender pieces of wood where the last person to shelter there had prepared for the next. Mr. George said that was customary. The wood was probably dry and rotted. Worse, it was of no use to him without a match. Unfortunately, Jimmy had left them in his grub bag on the other side of the brook.

Trembling incessantly, he pulled the blankets tighter. He used the wall to brace himself and worked his spine along the rippled wood. When he was at full height, he saw matches and flint, but he was too cold to feel optimistic. He flexed one hand inside the wool until he was certain he could manipulate a match strike. For good measure, he waited a few moments longer.

Droplets from his hair ran down his back and across his face. He shuddered as if death were coming at him from all sides. His breath fogged the air, and even that clung to him. Letting go of the wool, he clutched the matches. Jimmy hoped for a controlled collapse when his legs could no longer bear his weight. The wall lent support on the way down. He clenched and released his fist several times until it felt supple, then struck the match.

Nothing.

He tried again, and on the third strike, the match cracked in two. Disappointed, Jimmy let his chin fall to his chest. To his surprise, the knobby match head had landed on his knee with just enough stick left to grasp. He couldn't be certain if it was there to help him or mock him. Picking it up, he dragged it across the hearth. A small flame lit the air, and his spirits rose with the smell of sulphur. With a trembling hand, he laid the match on the spalls. His breath caught. He forced a cough. The match flickered. His whole body tensed until a curl of smoke rose from the little bits of wood.

Jimmy held his breath behind chattering teeth as flames licked across the kindling. A few armfuls of wood rested beside the fireplace. He reached out for a big piece, then put it back, resolving to be patient and let the fire build like he had seen Mother do. Hefting the smallest chunk of wood, he kept it at the ready for when the fire was in full bloom. He laid the piece across the flame and reached for another.

Heat made his fingers burn. Not like the burn of a spark, but something different that he hadn't felt before, not even when he sat on the woodbox in the morning waiting for toast from the reddened dampers. Mr. George said being frost-burned was the worst pain he had ever experienced. Jimmy looked at his fingers. They were whiter than he had ever seen them and blistering in a few spots. He would hold off on putting them near the fire until they were a nice pink colour. Crossing his arms, he jammed his fingers beneath his armpits while the fire grew. He rocked back and forth beside the flames and closed his eyes.

Heat reached him through the blankets, and he considered loosening them to let it in. When he opened his eyes, they stung with smoke. It steamed out from beneath the highest rock in the firebox. Before Jimmy could react, a tuft of twigs fell onto the fire, sending sparks outward. He shuffled away and brushed them clear of his blankets and skin. Fetching his boot, he ground out the embers around him.

Before he could dout them, another pile fell, and another, and feathers rained down around him. Flames seeped out from beneath the jumbled mass before gorging on the empty nest in a burst of heat that drove him back. Cold air on his back reminded him to close the door. Towing his wet clothing closer to the fire, Jimmy, wrapped tightly, slumped against the wall, grateful for the few things that had worked out. He busied himself adding chunks of wood to the fire, at first more liberally than he needed. He realized he should have wrung his clothes out so they could dry faster, but he was so glad to be alive, he basked near the blazing fire like a seal sunning itself on pack ice.

When the cabin grew warmer, he decided to look around. He found a box beneath the bunk. Inside it were two tins each of meat, crab, and lobster, as well as a bag of tea, a knife, a cup, and a rusty kettle. One time while retching over the gunnel of the *Annie May*, he heard Dan mention a summer cabin. *We stock the tilt in the spring each year just in case we get stuck out here for a few days*, Dan had said as he pointed toward the shore. *There's enough to keep the men from going hungry but not enough to keep them from wanting to go home.* Jimmy hadn't even looked up—he had been too miserable from emptying his stomach's contents.

William must have expected Jimmy to know about this place. Jimmy's heart lifted. His father would come and look for him in a day or so. He hadn't yet touched any of the cabin's food supply, a fact that might lead his father to believe Jimmy had been conserving. He wanted his father to be proud he had spared the food, even if it was a lie.

Using the knife, he opened a can of lobster, warmed it on a rock, and ate it. He wouldn't reach for a second one, though hunger dared him. Laying another log across the embers, he curled up in the blankets and slept. He sighed and, for the first time, began to feel the warmth of hope.

7

"It's been two days," Bart said when he entered the kitchen. "No sign of anyone coming for her."

"Let's take the stuff off her," Tommy said. "Surely she's salvage, now."

"Hold on to your whiskers, sons," Daddy said. "The rightful owner could come."

Flory listened to the hubbub in the kitchen. The same conversation had been going on for two days—morning, noon, and evening. Then, if that weren't enough, she even dreamed about it.

"She's tied up good," Bart said. "She ain't going nowhere. But the fish will soon smell. We won't be able to live in the spring with the flies."

"No good now, anyway," Tommy said. "No sense letting a good boat go to waste."

"All right, all right." Daddy rose and donned his coat and cap. "We'll clean out the hold and cover it before the ice gets in her, cracks her open, and spoils the oakum. She'll get soggy and won't be any good to anyone."

Tommy left to get his coat and boots and followed Daddy and Bart. Flory had just finished mixing the dough when Lizzy came in with her son.

"I'm glad they're gone. I was tired of listening to Bart go on about that ship," Lizzy said. "You'd swear they owned her by the way Bart was making plans."

"Tommy, too," Flory said as she covered the pan with a faded tablecloth her mother had used for the same purpose. There was a yeasty odour in the air. "Tea?"

Lizzy nodded and rubbed her stomach. "This one is rolling around today," she said as she sucked in a breath and bent into a cramp.

"Won't be long now," Flory said as she poured two cups from the teapot and pushed the sugar toward her sister-in-law.

"Do you suppose anyone will come?" Lizzy stared through the windowpane, her face awash with worry. "I can't tell if it's good weather or bad weather."

"Daddy just looks at the glass. The needle tells him what he needs to know." Flory pointed to the barometer on the wall. "Daddy didn't like the idea of something that could tell the weather when Ralph had first brought it home. But now he swears by it. It only took about five years." She lifted the cup to her lips and smiled against its rim.

"Is that how long Ralph and Bernard have been gone?" Lizzy asked.

"About that, I think. They left shortly after Momma died and only came back a couple or three times. At least Bart came back for good."

Lizzy glanced at Flory. "Bart says Tommy's talking about leaving."

"Yeah, I'm surprised he's still here." Flory got up and pulled back the curtain. "I think they're coming already." She opened the door and then shut it quickly, remembering what the cold draft could do to the rising bread.

The trio came in. Bart had three cans of fruit. "One for each of you," he said as he laid them on the table. "Apricots or peaches, Bobby? Last time I had either of these, I was in St. John's."

The boy pointed his chubby finger back and forth between the tins before choosing the apricots and handed a similar tin to his mother.

"Peaches for me," Flory said. She grinned, and her eyes sparkled as she looked at the picture on the label. "I'll keep these for something special."

"There was only a few other things on her," Daddy said. "No sense letting the butter and tea go to waste, either."

Bart told Lizzy they had thrown the fish over the side, as it had begun to rot. The tide would take it all away in a day or two. The few barrels were sealed, and by the weight it was probably bait fish that might last the winter if it were salted, or it could already be spoiled. They didn't look to find out one way or the other.

"One of you has lost the axe," Daddy said as he finished his tea. "It's just as well to tell me."

"Haven't used it for a few days," Tommy said as he ate a slice of toast.

"It's not over at our place," Bart said. "I already checked."

Daddy's eyes rose and fell along the length of each son before settling on their faces. "I suppose ours will turn up sometime." He knitted his brow as he drummed the table with his fingers. "We'll have to take the one off the boat," he said. "We can't go the winter without an axe."

Tommy volunteered to fetch it.

Lizzy complained of feeling tired and asked Bart to take her home. Bobby joined his grandfather and uncle chopping wood that afternoon while Flory finished baking the bread and cleaning up after the crowd. As she swept the floor, she thought how exciting Lizzy's life must have been in the big city of St. John's. Lizzy didn't like to talk about it, but Flory imagined there was more to do than cooking, cleaning, and having babies. Bart told stories of so many people living there. She couldn't imagine where they would all fit, who got the eggs and milked the goats or cows, who made the bread and cooked the meals, and how it all worked together. Lizzy shivered each time she thought of it. Such imaginings hurt her head sometimes and she had to stop thinking about it. Perhaps it was for the best she only had two men to go behind with the birch broom and the dishcloth and no chance of babies.

Voices startled Flory from her reverie. Too many voices. She ran to the window and looked across the tickle but couldn't see anything out of place. The sounds were coming from out back. Rushing to the porch, she opened the door. Her heart raced as she looked at the gathering. Several strangers surrounded her father and Tommy. Bobby was sitting in the wood chips, and he was crying.

Vexation engulfed her. Flory plucked her coat from the nail and stuffed her arms into it as she strode through the six men who were ignoring the frightened child. She lifted Bobby, who threw his arms around her and buried his head in her neck.

"They're not here," Daddy said. "You're welcome to look around."

"That's impossible," one of the taller fellows said. "Sherman, check the house. Wilbur, Harvey, you look in the stable, cellar, wellhouse, and outhouse."

"Who are you?" Flory asked as Sherman passed her, heading for the back door. "What's going on?"

"They're looking for the men from the boat," Tommy explained.

"But they're not here," Flory replied.

"That's what we've been saying."

"You there," the first man shouted.

Flory followed his gaze to Bart, who was crossing the meadow toward them. Her brother raised a hand in greeting and jogged toward the group.

"What's going on?"

Tommy repeated what he had told Flory, and Bart's reaction was the same. "They're not here." He extended his hand to the stranger.

"I'm Bart White. I live over yonder."

"Constable Abraham Giles," the man said as he took Bart's hand.

A cup broke in the house. Flory dashed inside with Bart on her heels.

"Hey, there's no need of that," Bart said.

"Sorry," Sherman said. "I hit the table while looking under the bench."

"What are you expecting to find under the bench?" Flory demanded.

"I'm doing what I'm told. Like I said, I didn't mean no harm."

Bart took Bobby from Flory when they went back outside. Daddy and the constable were having words. Both men were nose to nose, both flushed, and both wanted to be heard.

"Why can't we look over there?" Constable Giles asked as he stepped back from Daddy.

"The woman of the house, she's . . . you know," Daddy said.

"About to have a baby," Flory offered, and the constable's cheeks reddened.

"Sherman, check that house," Constable Giles said.

"Now, hold on," Bart said as he stepped in front of Sherman. "I'll not have my wife upset."

"Get out of the way," the constable said.

"You've no reason to go over there," Bart said. "There is nobody here but us. There has been nobody here but us."

"We'd like to see for ourselves," Giles said as he grasped Bart's arm.

Bobby wailed as Bart tried to wrestle free. Another man detained Tommy. Daddy picked up the axe, and one of the others grabbed him.

"See here," Daddy protested. "We want no trouble."

"Well, it's trouble you got," Giles said as he seized the axe. "What have we here?" He rubbed his thumb over the initials etched in the handle. "W. B. Could that be William Bailor?"

"It's from the boat," Daddy said. "Ours is gone missing."

"Well, how could yours be gone missing?" Giles asked. "Like you said, it's only you here. It didn't walk away." He nodded at the men coming from the barn. "Check that house."

"Don't you hurt my wife," Bart said. He laid Bobby in Flory's arms and took a few steps before a shot rang out. He stopped and swung around. Constable Giles had fired into the air and was now pointing his gun at Bart.

"The first one was a warning. There'll be no more of those."

Bart turned and shouted, "Lizzy, there are men coming. They won't hurt you. Let them go in." He turned back to the constable. "I swear, if you hurt her— "

"Calm down," Giles said. "We're not here to molest anyone." He looked toward the two men making their way across the meadow. "Boys, take it easy," he shouted.

Lizzy emerged from the house before the constable's men

reached her door. She waited with her head down, her face hidden by her hair, as they passed her. They reappeared moments later. Both men removed their hats and spoke to Lizzy with an air of apology before returning to the group. Lizzy immediately went inside and closed the door.

"We found nothing," Harvey said.

"Nothing in the stable, either," Wilbur said, shaking his head.

"Like we've been telling you," Daddy said, "there's nobody here."

"You're telling me that the *Annie May* just appeared here a few mornings ago and that there was nobody on board?" Constable Giles tilted an eyebrow and grimaced. "How did you get the axe?"

"I've already told you. The story's not going to change, because it's the truth." Daddy explained what they had done with the fish and why. "That boat is salvage," he said.

"That boat is only salvage because you did something to the men on board with the axe that's conveniently gone missing," Giles pressed. "That's not salvage in the eyes of the law. That's murder."

"I won't lie," Daddy said. "I don't know where our own axe is or what happened to it."

"I don't, either," Tommy said as he shrugged clear of the man holding him.

"Nor me," Bart said.

"Nor me," Flory added, though no one was expecting her to answer. "It's all right, Bobby. No need to be frightened."

"I'm bringing him to his mother," Bart said, indicating Bobby. He looked at the constable. "I assume you won't shoot me."

Giles gave a gesture of dismissal and a nod. “Don’t be long,” he said.

“How did you find the boat?” Daddy asked the constable when Bart returned.

“We’ve been combing the shore for a number of days now since the *Annie May* didn’t return to home port. We saw the dead fish this morning, and that led us here.”

“Where was she out of?” Bart asked.

“Spigot Harbour,” Sherman said. “We’re all from around them parts. A lot of boats out looking.”

“How many men aboard?” Daddy asked.

“Six,” Giles said. “Father and son and four other good men.”

“I hope they’re found,” Daddy said as he shook his head. “An awful thing to happen.”

“Don’t touch anything,” Giles said. “We’ll go back and report what we’ve found and return with a crew to take the vessel home.”

8

“So that’s it?” Loretta Bailor said as she stood face to face with Abraham Giles. “And you believed them? A bunch of strangers who profited from their disappearance?”

Constable Giles didn’t move. He wanted to reach out to her, to comfort her like he had all those years ago, before she married William. He often wondered what had made her choose William over him.

“My little Jimmy, just gone,” Loretta said as she collapsed into the chair. “I can’t believe Jimmy’s gone. He’s all I had,” she said between sobs. “William Bailor, I hope you rot in hell,” she screamed at the ceiling. “Rot in hell!”

“Loretta, you don’t mean that,” Giles said as he crouched beside the chair. He couldn’t bear to call her Mrs. Bailor, though it was more appropriate. Those words just wouldn’t roll off his tongue. He had wished for years that she would be Mrs. Giles.

“Every single word of it,” she spat. “Every word.” She buried her face in her palms.

Giles’s hand hovered just above her shoulder, then he pulled it back. She was a new widow. He would need to be patient.

"Is there anything you're leaving out? Anything at all?" he asked softly. "You can tell me, Loretta."

She glared at him. "What could I be leaving out?"

"I don't know. Could be the least little thing," he replied. Whatever feelings he had for Loretta, they couldn't supersede the law.

"I've told you everything. Will left Jimmy stranded somewhere. I begged him to go for him. It was too windy that first day, so he went late on the second day. I was livid when he refused. Will said it was too late in the day, but I wouldn't hear tell of it. He left and said they would spend the night at the summer place if the weather got bad or the night too dark. When they didn't show up the next evening, I got worried. That's when I called you."

Giles nodded. Loretta's story hadn't changed.

"Near as I can figure, they picked up Jimmy and something happened in the night. What that was, I don't know," he said. "There was no sign of trouble on the boat. No sign of trouble on the land."

"They had days to hide trouble, Abe. Days," Loretta said, digging her fingers into her scalp as she stalked across the kitchen. She was quiet for a moment before she turned back to him.

"They killed my boy. They can't get away with that," she said slowly between gritted teeth. She punctuated every word with a thrust of her index finger at the constable's chest.

Gingerly, he took her shoulders. "Loretta, there's nothing to suggest they did anything." Giles shook his head as he spoke. He had said the same thing to others who had come demanding action at the jailhouse. "It's a small place. Three men and two women. They couldn't have overpowered the crew."

"They did something," she howled at the ceiling and pulled away from him. "It's my son, Abe." Loretta's eyes were pleading as she turned to him. "You hear me? I want justice for him. You should want that, too."

"Of course I want that." The constable's mind raced for a way to appease her. "I'll wire St. John's."

"Whatever it takes."

Loretta reached for his hand and squeezed it. Warmth rushed along his arm and flushed his cheeks. His heart raced, and he quelled the sudden urge to smile.

"Whatever it takes," Loretta cried. "They must pay."

Giles nodded as he ran his fingers through his hair and massaged the back of his neck. He grimaced. There was no easy way to say it.

"Loretta, I hate to bring this up at a time like this, but what about the boat?"

He didn't resist when she leaned into his shoulder. He had to be a gentleman, though he wanted to hold her close and provide comfort.

"That boat. I despise everything about it. That can rot wherever it is. Set fire to it if you want."

"That means those men can do with it what they wish. It's salvage."

"What?" Loretta replied. She straightened and pulled away from Abe. "How is that possible?"

"It's the way of things. It's not against the law."

"No, no, no." Hysteria flared in the woman's eyes. Her words came quick and expectant. "That can't happen. They killed my boy. You have to do something, Abe. I'm depending on you for this."

Constable Giles couldn't think straight. He wasn't a man of words. He was a man of facts. He was dutiful to the law. "Loretta, there's nothing."

"Bring Dan," she blurted. "Dan will take the *Annie May* home. He'll do that for me."

A flash of anger boiled beneath his skin. It had always irked him that Dan Acreman was aboard the *Annie May* right under William Bailor's nose. Thus, Dan had more opportunities for dealings with Loretta. If William Bailor had known that Dan and Loretta were seeing each other even before Abe and Loretta's time, he wouldn't have stood for Dan being part of his crew.

It was no secret that William had a vicious temper. Even Abe steered clear of him. Not that he was a coward. At least that's what he told himself. In truth, he didn't want to get in a racket with the man and be shown up in front of Loretta. Either way, he would lose face with her, and he wouldn't risk that.

Dan was either crazy or stupid to have put himself in that situation. Perhaps he was both. Dan always seemed to come out on top. But not this time. Dan Acreman would not outdo Abraham Giles—he didn't have the power of the law behind him.

"I'll drop in on the way home," he said as he stifled a sigh. "I'm sure Dan will go."

"Abe, you must arrest those murderers. Those wicked men killed my boy," Loretta commanded as her eyes held his. "They can't go unpunished."

"You're upset. I understand," Giles said. She hadn't mentioned her husband, and that lit a spark in him. Perhaps all wasn't well between the Bailors.

"*Upset?*" Loretta threw her hands into the air, her eyes raging and cheeks flushed. "Stop it. Stop it. Yes, I'm upset. But they can't go unpunished. Do this for me, Abe." She said again, softly this time, "For me."

"I'll see what the other constables have to say when they arrive," Giles said as he took her hand. "I'll do my best."

Loretta embraced him, drawing him close. "Do better than that, Abe. Arrest them all. I'm depending on you."

"They'll be arrested," he said as the heat from her body ignited old wants. "I'll make sure of that." Dan might bring home the boat, but he would bring home justice. Loretta wanted that more than anything else. Besides, other families were demanding and pressuring him as well. The widows and orphans of Spigot Harbour were counting on him to uphold the law for the sake of their families, and he wouldn't let them down.

Loretta pulled away and apologized while straightening her dress. "I'm so distraught. I don't know what I'll do without Jimmy." She gave him a shy look before she sniffled into her handkerchief. "Thank you, Abe. I'll be forever grateful."

Her words hung in the air as he left the house.

Three days later, Juniper Tickle was overrun with men, including Giles and two constables from St. John's. They searched the grounds, the woods, and the shore for signs of the crew of the *Annie May*.

Once inspected, Dan Acreman determined the boat's rudder had been damaged. It was too late in the year and too cold to do anything about it. Nothing further could be done with it until spring. Dan suggested it remain pulled up on the beach and secured on the point leading into Juniper Tickle. The men agreed and went to work securing the vessel.

With the constable's approval, the lawmen took Robert, Bart, and Tommy White into custody. The Whites were charged with the murders of the crewmen. Constable Giles went home to Spigot Harbour, while the others escorted the prisoners to the penitentiary in St. John's to await trial. They would telegraph Giles at a later date to attend court and testify to his findings.

For now, he would do what he could to support the widow, Loretta Bailor, as she grieved. Abe was certain he had carried out his duties to the best of his abilities. Thanks to his efforts, bad men would be punished for their wrongdoings.

9

The table squeaked on shaky legs as Flory worked out her frustration on the dough.

"You can't keep this up, Flory," Lizzy said as she laid her hand on Flory's arm. "You just can't."

"I'll be fine. So will you, and so will Bobby," Flory said as she gave the dough one final punch. She spread the cloth over the pan and tucked it underneath. "We have things figured out."

"We have nothing figured out," her sister-in-law said. "Baking bread every third or fourth day isn't figuring things out." Lizzy eyes watered. "Damn tears," she muttered as she dabbed her cheeks with the hem of her skirt. "I don't know what's wrong with me."

"Sit," Flory ordered.

"I can't sit and leave all this to you. Bad enough we had to move in here—"

"That was for company," Flory interrupted.

"Yeah, sure. For the wood that *you* have to chop and cleave and everything else you do. We won't make it the winter."

"What's to stop us? Daddy and Tommy have most of it done. I just have to bring it in out of the weather."

But the truth was she didn't know how she would keep the household going. The junks of wood stacked in the porch and those piled in the yard might get them through a few months, if they were careful, but she would have to haul out the rest from the woods when the path froze and snow gave the sled good traction. They had all gone last winter, including she and Lizzy. She knew where to find the cut-out. The trees were felled, just not pared. Though she hadn't tackled the horse before, Flory was there when her father had done it. She would figure it out.

"I'm going with you," Lizzy said. She pushed off the chair and tried, without success, to hide a grimace.

"How about you collect the eggs? A couple are still laying," Flory said as she helped Lizzy into her coat. "I'll take Bobby."

"I keep telling you, you don't have to do everything yourself. I'll get the eggs, and then I'll bring in wood, too. Even a stick at a time." Lizzy smiled. "I want to do my part."

"How about you break it to them hens that if they stop laying they'll be in the pot for supper?" Flory gave a curt nod.

Lizzy giggled. "I'll make sure they're aware of their circumstance."

"How about you fry the eggs when you get back, and then we'll talk about what else you can do to be useful," Flory suggested as she feigned a push at Lizzy. "Shout if you need me."

Lizzy waddled toward the henhouse, a small building with one side attached to the end of the stable. "Did you feed Dandy?" she called over her shoulder.

"Yes," Flory shouted back. "When I milked the goat this morning. Pay attention and don't let that rooster out."

"I can get potatoes from the cellar."

"Don't you dare climb down there," Flory called out. "I mean it, Lizzy. Don't."

Lizzy laughed and gave a dismissive wave as she plodded across the bridge.

Flory handed Bobby two smaller sticks and collected an armload herself. She guided him to the rear door, where he helped her add to the second tier against the back wall. Daddy only brought in what they needed, but Flory couldn't afford to be caught without wood if there was a storm. Daddy and Tommy had already stacked several rows in the shed that she would use for a crisis. It was hard to contemplate what could be more dire than the reason for the men's absence. Flory shook her head to banish the thought. She would take one moment at a time, because even a day's forecast seemed unconquerable. This moment's undertaking was wood—she had to take what was already chopped and split from the outside to the inside. She could worry about the many other responsibilities when this one was finished.

Maybe these things were before her to keep her worries and fears simpler. She couldn't think about Daddy or her brothers and continue to function. Flory and Lizzy had cried the first three days the men were gone. A promise from Constable Giles that somebody would come and take care of them had been the only thing that appeased Daddy and her brothers.

Bart had been dragged away after being struck in the head with a stick, and Tommy was left bleeding and barely able to stand from a wound he suffered at the hands of a constable. Daddy threw men clear of him when he saw how his boys were being treated. Several men were forced to jump on him and hold him down. Lizzy was screaming at the men to let her husband go while Bobby screeched. And Flory had bolted into the house to fetch the shotgun from the pantry before running back out into the affray.

Daddy stopped fighting when he saw her, and so did Tommy. Bart was lying lifeless—so she feared—on the ground, blood streaming down his face.

"Don't you touch her," Daddy said. "We'll go peacefully."

Several men lifted Bart to his feet and escorted all three White men away from Juniper Tickle. Flory collapsed on the step with Lizzy beside her and Bobby between them. They all cried in unison. They had no idea where their family would be taken, when they would be back, nor what they would do without them. Soon, Bobby complained he was cold and hungry, and they went inside.

Flory filled the stove and Lizzy made tea. They agreed to stay in one dwelling, both for company and to save on wood, kerosene, and food. The cellar was stocked with potatoes, turnips, onions, beets, and the few carrots they had managed to grow. The flour barrel was full and the pantry provisioned mere weeks before when the last collector boat left. It would return for fish in late spring in exchange for household goods. Hay and oats were in the barn for the winter.

Daddy still had salt fish drying on the flake that day. Flory packed it atop the rest in the pound in the cellar that evening while staring into the hard-packed earth. She screamed and pulled the axe from the chopping block on the way back and skirted the house, headed for the *Annie May*. Regardless of the consequences, she would take out her frustration on the side of that ship. How could anyone think her father or her brothers were murderers? She knew they weren't. Others would, too, if they knew how peaceable the Whites were.

"Flory. Flory, stop. You know I can't catch you," Lizzy shouted as she followed her sister-in-law along the path. "Flory, please stop."

Flory wheeled around and faced Lizzy, who was hurrying toward her. "You can't fix this. Not like this," Lizzy called.

Even at this distance, Flory could hear Lizzy's breath coming in shallow gasps.

"Flory, I can't stay here alone if somebody comes for you. Don't do this."

Flory closed her eyes. When she opened them again, Lizzy was standing in front of her.

"It won't help. Believe me, I know." Lizzy's eyes were wide. "Come back with me," she said as she reached for Flory's hand.

Flory sighed. She and Lizzy walked in silence, arm and arm, toward home. Her anger abated with each step. Bobby stayed on the gallery like his mother had instructed.

"You're a fierce woman, Florence Alice White," Lizzy said with a grin. "First the gun and now the axe. I wouldn't want to be the one who crosses you." She tugged at Flory's arm and grinned. "We'll make the best of it, together."

"Those men from the *Annie May* will show up, and Daddy will come back. Bart and Tommy, too," Flory said with more assurance in her voice than she felt in her heart.

"Indeed they will."

"They'll all see how unfair this situation is."

"Fairness is determined by the rich," Lizzy said matter-of-factly. "What happened here will not be unfair for any but the Whites. Don't entertain the thought or you'll drive yourself mad."

Flory nodded. "Maybe you're right. It seems to be the way of things."

"Perhaps someday I'll tell you about it. Just not today." Lizzy's voice was soft and low as she said this. Flory wasn't sure she had heard her right.

Lizzy tickled Bobby as he ran inside. As Flory shut the door, she concluded there was more pluck to Lizzy White than met the eye. They would get along just fine in Juniper Tickle by themselves if determination held any sway.

However, they couldn't eat determination or pluck.

10

"How did you and Bart meet? You didn't tell me yet."

Startled, Lizzy turned toward Flory, and her arm struck the cup and saucer. Hot tea and porcelain alike rained down off the table and onto the floor. Lizzy pushed back from the table, trying to avoid the scalding water, as Flory moved to the stove and snatched the cloth from the oven door.

"I'll get the broom," Lizzy muttered as she tried to manoeuvre her legs between the bench and the table. "I'm sorry. I'm so clumsy lately."

"Stay where you are," Flory said as she laid a hand on Lizzy's arm. "I won't be but a minute and I'll get it cleaned up."

Lizzy stared at the mess and smiled before cloaking her emotions with a frown.

Bart. Meeting him had been complicated.

The first time she saw him, he had been on a stoop in a dark alley in downtown St. John's. She had heard singing—if you could call it that—before she saw his dark outline in the dusk. Lizzy had stepped into the shadows, a place to which she was accustomed, making herself invisible. The man was leaning against the jamb in the wedge of light streaming from the open door. Somebody inside was shouting at him to keep it down, but that only encouraged him to exaggerate even more the off-key chorus of a shanty Lizzy had heard more times than she could count. But admittedly, not like what she was hearing now. A whimsical lilt belied a musical voice. He was a singer.

Lizzy moved along the clapboard, aware that any dampness she touched would have come from more than one sealer who had relieved himself in this alley. She wrinkled her nose at the thought but pushed toward the voice, anyway. He would be easy pickings was her last thought before a hand snaked out and clutched her wrist. He sat—or, more accurately fell, because it wasn't a controlled motion—and pulled her down on top of him.

"What have we here?" the man slurred as she lashed out at him.

He was surprisingly agile for a fellow who was drunk. In the light and the commotion, she realized he was only a young man, probably a few years older than her seventeen, if he was even that. Still humming, he was trying to corral her arms when the familiar tune caught her ear. Lizzy relaxed for just a moment, throwing him off. She stuck a hand into his pocket, nicked the few coins he possessed, then wriggled her way clear.

"Come back here, boy," he said as he pushed off the step and staggered backward into the door frame. He patted his pockets. "That little shyster just robbed me." His incredulous eyes followed the thief out the alley.

Two days later, she sauntered toward Water Street when a hand reached out, grabbed her, and hauled her into the same alley. Before she could look up, a body had pinned her against the dank clapboard and hands moved along her hips. She squealed and writhed beneath him.

"Let me go," she growled through clenched teeth. But as limp as she let herself go, she couldn't get clear.

"Not until I get my money," the man said.

She looked at him and realized who it was. His hands roamed to her rear pant pockets as he pressed against her, trapping her against the wall.

"I don't have it," she snarled. "Let me go."

"Or what? You going to call the constable?" he asked as he pushed into her rear pockets, causing his head to dip and his lips to draw close to her ear.

Fear, and sensations she wasn't accustomed to, swelled within her. She squirmed and kicked at him, cursing herself for not being more careful. As she turned, her cap snagged on a loose nail in the rough clapboard. Her hair tumbled loose. The man yelped and sprang away from her.

"You're a girl!"

His eyes widened, and she quashed a smile as she kicked his bony shin.

"Yeah. Are you in a habit of beating up girls?" she spat. The pain in her toes after connecting with his shin bone made her grimace. Her body trembled as she realized what he could do to her in that instant. She searched his face, uncertain what she would find.

Instead, he held his palms above his shoulders, fingers splayed. "Pardon me, ma'am. I didn't know," he said, his voice high and strained, his face ashen. "I didn't know." He shook his head and backed out of the alley, stumbling over his own feet as he turned onto the street.

Lizzy bundled her hair into a knot and adjusted her cap. She patted around the brim to make sure there were no loose strands. Her mind raced. It was bad enough being an orphan boy on the streets of St. John's, but an orphan girl carried a host of new problems that—so far—she had managed to avoid.

In reality, she wasn't an orphan as long as her mother still lay on this side of dying, in poverty and squalor, in a rooming house reserved for the unsavoury of the city. But what her mother, at thirty-three years old, was expecting of Lizzy to raise her out of poverty in the few months she had left was what Lizzy hoped to avoid the most.

Like mother, like daughter, Elizabeth, Sarah Faraday croaked from her maggoty bedsheets. The dying woman lay on a rickety cot, in a room with thin, tarpaper walls and beer-stained plank floors where other girls entertained men to pay for all their suppers, like her mother had done before them. *Don't think you are better than you are. It's coming for you.* The dire warning was followed by a chesty cough that took her mother's breath and left her retching and gasping long after Lizzy left. Some her age who grew up around the docks and in the same rooming houses had heeded the advice, but Lizzy would resist for as long as she could.

She took a deep breath, straightened her back, and stepped out of the alley, expecting to find the man. He wasn't there. Her breath whistled between her front teeth, and as she closed her eyes, her shoulders dropped. She relaxed her stiffened muscles as she merged with the crowd moving toward the sealing ships. There were pockets to be picked. As long as she was careful, kept her head down, and looked enough like a young boy to be ignored, she would manage to keep herself fed.

Commands and shouts drifted about the din. A flurry of activity and a pressing crowd signalled the ship was readying to depart as she made her way onto the apron connecting the multitude of docks lying finger-like in the harbour. Lizzy wheeled around when somebody tapped her shoulder.

"Are you following me?" the man asked as he patted his pockets.

"I was going to ask you the same thing."

Sarcasm laced her words as she gazed up at him. He was illuminated by the sun behind him, but she recognized the voice before he came into focus.

The man grinned and tipped his hat to her. "Nothing here today."

He indicated his clothing before his gaze flickered across the dock and returned to her. They stared at each other, not in malice but reflecting an edge of wariness mixed with curiosity that was unfamiliar to either.

"Bart," someone called.

"Coming, Ralph." The man gave Lizzy one final look before sprinting off through the crowd, leaving her wondering what had happened.

In the evening, due to her own carelessness leading to missed opportunities, she was left seeking food at the convent and competing with other young marauders behind the restaurants. However, the docks were busier than ever this time of the year, so naturally she found herself there every day. Lizzy was drawn by more than hunger—by a fascination she couldn't explain nor contain.

"Paper! Paper! Constabulary promising to crack down on petty theft," a boy shouted from a wooden crate containing an overflowing satchel of newspapers that was heavier than him. The noise and drone of the docks didn't deter him from making a few cents. "Read all about it here!" He waved the paper just above the heads in the crowd, handed it off to a man who extended a nickel his way, pocketed the money, and waved another paper in one seamless motion.

Lizzy clambered onto a barrel and watched a stream of men come down the gangway of the docked sealing vessel. She took a deep breath to steady herself. There he was. Her heart thudded against her chest when the man caught her eye and winked. She blushed and bowed her head just as a beefy hand clamped onto her arm.

"Caught you," a loud voice snarled.

Startled, Lizzy turned and the barrel wobbled. She jumped clear, but her arm jerked backward and wrenched in its socket—she was still tethered by the man's grip. Clutching her shoulder with her free hand, she clamped her mouth shut when she faced the constable. She resisted her more feral instincts, which wouldn't help her in that moment. The lawman had a solid hold on her and outweighed her by more than a dozen stone. Her mind raced for a way out of this mess, and fear anchored in her belly as she thought of what being revealed would mean.

"What's going on here?" the man called Bart asked as he rushed to her side. "What are you doing with my brother?"

"Your brother?" The constable eyed them both. "This isn't your brother. This is one of the gang of boys that's been thieving."

"You're wrong," Bart replied. "He's here waiting for me to fetch my belongings. We're heading home to Juniper Tickle in the morning." By now, interest was growing in the commotion.

In the distance, someone shouted, "Help! A lad just made off with my pocketbook. Help!"

The constable looked from Lizzy and the man to the general direction from which the cry had come.

"I'd better not catch you around here tomorrow," he said as he let go of Lizzy. "You either." He wagged a finger in Bart's face.

The constable blew his whistle and pushed his way through the crowd.

"Come on. We'd better get out of here."

Lizzy followed him by virtue of his hand on her arm tugging her in the opposite direction of the policeman. She didn't resist until they moved from Water Street to Gower Street.

"Who are you and why did you do that?" She folded her arms and glared at him.

"I'm Bart White." He smirked at her. "Who might you be?"

"I'm Lizzy," she muttered, then clamped her hand over her mouth and gave her head a shake.

"Well, Lizzy, how would you like a bath?" He grinned, put his hand in his front pocket, and pulled out a roll of bills.

"I'm afraid you have it all wrong, mister." Lizzy stared at the money and had to force her mouth closed.

"Bart. It's Bart."

"Bart," she stuttered. She gulped to clear the knot in her throat. "I'm afraid you have it all wrong. I'm not that kind of girl." She rocked on the balls of her feet, ready to flee.

"What kind of girl might that be?" His eyes twinkled with an innocence she wasn't sure was real.

"You know. The kind who takes baths with men they don't know," Lizzy mumbled as her bravado failed her. She stiffened her back, lowered her head, and glowered at him from beneath furrowed brows.

"Hold on," Bart said. He raised his palms to her. "I'm not suggesting anything. I merely asked if you'd like a bath and a place to stay for the night."

"With you?" she asked, her words sounding breathless and incredulous at the same time. Her heart raced. She cleared her throat and added an air of gruffness as she repeated, "With you?"

"No. Nothing like that." Bart laughed. It was a deep musical sound that made her want more. "I noticed you have the same clothes on since the last few times I saw you. Really, you stink." He backed away as she struck out at him. "Look, I have a sister a bit younger than you. Sometimes she likes to soak in the tub in the kitchen and we all make ourselves scarce. That's all."

He sounded genuine.

"I got money," he blurted. He gestured to his pocket as if she had forgotten he'd poked it there. "I'm going back to Juniper Tickle tomorrow. Once I get cleaned up, I'm buying a dress for my sister, sugar, and raisins, and then I have no need for the rest of it. My mother, God rest her, wouldn't allow me to leave you here like this."

Lizzy hesitated. A bath. She couldn't remember the last time she'd had one, nor the last time she had shed the clothes she was wearing.

"Nothing funny? Promise?" she asked, hardly believing she had.

"Nothing funny," Bart said as he reached for her arm. "I reek, too."

They walked to Springdale Street to pay for a room and bath for Lizzy in a boarding house not far from where she had robbed him. The lady there looked them up and down, hesitated, and moved to close the door.

"I assume my money is good here," Bart said as he took out the bills.

"Indeed, sir," the woman said as she stepped aside to allow Lizzy entrance.

"I want to pay for a bath as well."

"Of course," the matron said.

Bart leaned in and spoke softly to Lizzy. "If you don't mind, I'll be around later and collect you for supper."

Her nod came as more of a reflex then an intention of keeping time with him. "You're not staying here?" Confusion clouded her thoughts.

"No," he said. "I'm up the street where you found me before."

Lizzy nodded as he paid the matron and left. She was led to a room upstairs and presented with a key. She stood inside, mouth agape, for much longer than intended. There was nothing grand about the place by anyone's standards, she guessed. Lizzy pinched herself. A bed of her own, even for one night, without having to sleep with one eye open was one thing, but a bath as well! She stepped forward and ran her hand along the bed, the dresser, the lamp, and the cast iron tub.

Lizzy stayed in the massive, claw-footed tub long after the water went cold. She believed she had *uncoiled*, her body straighter and taller now, once she stepped out. Next she washed her clothes, wrung them, and draped them around the small room to dry. Even hunger couldn't make her answer the knock later that evening.

A female voice called through the wooden door. "Delivery from Mr. White."

"Leave it," Lizzy said. Tempering her harsh tone, she finished softly with, "please."

Curiosity took over. She remembered her mother telling her that it killed the cat, though she couldn't recall how. Surely the cat didn't die in a boarding house after taking a bath with a package waiting outside the door. Shrouded by a quilt, she put her ear to the door. She grasped the knob, drew a deep breath, and poked her head out to give the hallway a sweeping look. A package, wrapped in brown paper and tied with a red ribbon, rested against the wall.

Lizzy snatched it, slammed the door, and turned the key. She slumped against the door with a firm grip on the parcel, closed her eyes, and took several deep breaths. On the bed she carefully untied the ribbon and pushed aside the paper to reveal a simple blue plaid dress. She gasped and held it up, then hugged it. Her imagination took over, and she waltzed around the tiny room with the cotton held against her. Lizzy's first and only dress, along with this room and a bed, had her picturing all kinds of possibilities she had no business imagining.

Reality crept back in. What was she thinking? She threw the dress onto the spread as if it were poison and guessing in certain ways it was. Besides, she had no shoes or underthings befitting the dress. She would leave in the morning with the garment neatly wrapped in the paper and take it back to the store to get the price of it. That was the sensible thing to do. It was probably worth more than she could pilfer in a week, maybe even two weeks.

Though she tried, Lizzy's imagination wouldn't let her conceive the practical thing for long. It must have been the soap or the bathwater that made her take leave of her senses. She hauled the dress over her head and stuffed her arms through the sleeves before her senses returned.

In the washstand mirror stood a woman. The image startled Lizzy. She caught her breath and watched her hands run along the cotton. The reflection pinched the cloth and caused her to look down when she felt the sting on her hip. Slowly she combed her fingers through her damp hair and stared.

It must be her, Elizabeth Annabella, a name worthy of the wide-eyed figure staring back her.

With the ribbon, she tied her curls away from her face and let them hang loosely around her shoulders. Patting her underclothes on the radiator, she found them still damp but good enough to put on. She scrubbed the dirt off the shoes. Though no amount of spit and shine could fix the flapping sole, the ripped eyelets, and the busted laces, she put them on anyway.

A knock and a female voice sounded through the door. "There's a gentleman caller for you downstairs."

Lizzy hesitated for just an instant before deciding she would go. For tonight, she would enjoy the company of Bart White. She would be a woman, though she hardly knew what that meant beyond what she had seen of her mother and the girls at the rooming house. Surely the women who ambled arm in arm with their beaus weren't subjected to the same treatment. But she had no way of knowing, so she would simply face the moment. Giddiness overflowed. She would take a chance. She would leave regrets to examine the next day.

But Lizzy had nothing to worry about. Bart was fine company to keep. He pulled out her chair, smiled widely at her, and during dinner he told her about his family in Juniper Tickle. If he saw her stuff extra bread in a napkin, he didn't say. He threw his coat over her shoulders, realizing she had neither one, and walked her back to the boarding house just after dark.

"Goodbye, Lizzy," he said. "Will I see you next year?"

"Maybe," she replied, dipping her head to avoid his gaze. She fixed her dress to cover the exposed toe of her boot.

He leaned forward and kissed her cheek as she straightened. She didn't turn away. The soft flutter of his lips on her skin was as surprising to her as it seemed to be to him. He pulled back quickly, turned away, and then he was gone.

Lizzy watched him board a schooner the next morning. He scanned the crowd from the top of the gangway. She hoped he was looking for her. She watched, concealed in a warehouse alley, wearing the blue dress she believed would change her life. Her mother's warning that she minded thoughts above her station were chased away by the soft cotton and the lingering fragrance from the bath the night before.

It would be almost a year before she would see him again from that very spot. It was an eventful one for her that still made her mad. When she knew Bart had come, she returned to the chimney stack in the alley at the warehouse on the wharf. There she fetched the dress and a pair of shoes she had found in a goodwill bin in front of one of the churches. They pinched her feet, but she only needed to wear them for a short time. She would suffer through it. The rest of the stuff would remain hidden until things worked out, or perhaps until she died.

By the time Bart left for Juniper Tickle, he had asked Lizzy to go with him as his wife. She had said yes, convincing herself it was for the best. Layers of bedraggled clothing hid the curves and bumps that nature levied on young women. Despite attempts to conceal her blossoming from the gangly scrawniness they had become accustomed to, the boys from the gangs were noticing. She couldn't very well be seen as a woman about St. John's. Not after what happened. It was time to get out of the city before she ended up like her mother, or worse, jailed.

"Paper! Paper! Reward offered for the return of the Topsail Star!" The boy's voice followed Lizzy, who climbed the gangway as Mrs. Bart White. "Read all about it!"

11

Northerly winds pummelled the cabin, sought crevices and openings between sticks and boards, and pushed at the door to fill the space with their numbing cold. They ferried the snow across the ocean and wrapped it in tiny balls to whip at Jimmy Bailor's face every time he left the tilt. It dwarfed the heat from the meagre fire that refused to dance with the damp wood Jimmy had found along the shore.

As he stretched his hands toward the pitiful flame, Jimmy sipped air through puckered lips to keep from crying. A whistling sound made him smile. How often had he tried to do that for Mr. George and was rewarded with a simple, heavy sigh? He moved his tongue and blew again. There it was, another whistle. Probably not something Mr. George would have celebrated, he supposed, but Jimmy would, anyway.

Surely he was going mad. The day after he fell in the river, he had burned most of the wood, expecting his father at any time. His clothes were clean and dry. Jimmy had eaten two cans of fish and rescued the peaches and apricots from the other side of the river before consuming one of them. He felt like a man.

Five days in the wilderness, like Mr. George, and he was doing fine. His father should be proud.

The day after that, the winds picked up and grew bitterly cold. He was out of wood, and the scant pieces he managed to bring in barely burned. Cold seeped through to his skin. Jimmy tied the blankets around himself and folded them over his hands, head, and neck when he went out. The woollen blankets kept him warm and dry the few times he left the confines of the cabin.

The fire struggled to boil the kettle today. He was running out of tea. Jimmy had two tins of crab left and a tin of apricots. His mind wrestled with the notion that his father wasn't coming. He wasn't sure what that meant for him. But food was scarce, and he had no means of getting more. He had no skills, and nothing came to mind.

Jimmy thought of Terry Hardy. Terry would have had no problem under these circumstances. What made them so different? Would Terry stay here and wait for death? Absolutely not. Of that Jimmy was certain. Terry would fight. He would come out on top like he did in the schoolyard. Red-faced, cold, nose running, but ready to take on whoever or whatever stood between him and what he wanted. Even if Terry had stayed there, by the time he was found in the spring, when the camp got fitted for the year, he would have pelts or caribou meat for sale, enough to make him the talk of Spigot Harbour. Terry would fare all right.

A stick popped in the fire. To Jimmy's astonishment, the water had boiled. He pulled it away and threw in the last of the tea. Staring at the steam, he watched it rise to be yanked and twirled away by the spindle of draft from the chimney.

His father wasn't coming.

He combed his fingers through his hair and squeezed his head. Jimmy was no Terry Hardy. He sat on the floor and pulled his knees to his chest. His mother hadn't sent anyone, either. He gasped and let go of his knees, holding his gut as if he had been punched. Why hadn't Mother sent somebody?

His breath was shallow and quick. Nobody was coming. He rocked back and forth and watched the tea grow cold. The fire turned to smoke and embers, and he shivered as darkness fell on the cabin. His body was done. His soul was done.

"Okay, death. Come on, have at me," Jimmy whispered to the chopped beams.

Wind picked up and set the door to knocking in its frame. The embers reddened and reflected in shadows on his hands. There was no more wood. This was the last day in the life of Jimmy Bailor, and what a poor one it was.

Jimmy would do one last thing before he went—to prove there was one thing useful about him. He would throw out the cold tea and put the kettle back in the box to be replenished at a time he would know nothing about. Pulling the small crate from under the bunk, he hoisted it and turned it around in his hands. He took out the cup and the last tin of crab. Before he could stop himself, he laid the box on the embers. They protested but did what embers do. As the flame climbed one side of the box, Jimmy pushed the kettle closer.

Shadows rolled and twirled around the room. Jimmy moved closer and pulled a blanket up to stop the draft. He would get in the bunk soon, and there he would remain. But he would have the tea first. The cabin would be used again sometime. He wouldn't be here forever. Jimmy imagined Dan Acreman and his father in the bunks above him and the rest of the men in the others. Did they play cards here to pass the time, or did they just sleep?

The bunks. Jimmy hadn't thought of the bunks. He jumped up as a wild impulse possessed him—he began pulling on anything he could get his fingers around on the three bunks nearest him. They were just sticks somebody had cut a few years ago. He kicked and pulled until the bottom bunk was tinder. When he moved to the second one, the frenzy inside him eased and he stopped the destruction.

A thought knocked inside his skull like a woodpecker. Jimmy had to think differently. He couldn't burn everything tonight. Death could be delayed.

He leaned a stick on the fireplace ledge and jumped on the centre until the stick cracked. When the wood lay strewn in several pieces, he piled it near the fire. He sat, legs crossed, and pondered his circumstance.

There would be a tomorrow for him. He would be clever about using it. First he would learn to make a fire with the flint and the knife. He had seen his father do it. He had seen Dan do it. Only two matches remained, and he would be down to one after he started a new fire in the morning. If it took him all day to learn, it would be something worth doing.

When Jimmy woke the next morning, things didn't seem as dire. He started the fire and brought the kettle to the river for water. Pulling the bunks apart, he cleared one wall. He was surprised to uncover items tucked in where the eaves met the wall. A small hatchet was the first find, then a ball of line with a hook attached. The next few spaces were filled with dried moss, and in the corner he felt a small metal object. When he pulled it out, he saw it was a compass. Jimmy hadn't learned to read the compass, so he didn't think it would be of any use to him. Finally, he found another knife in the eaves over the bunks on the other side of the room. He gathered a fistful of moss while he was searching.

Sitting in front of the fire, he drank the hot, bitter tea. He dislodged a loose rock from the fireplace and laid it on the floor by his knees. Piling on moss, he went to work striking the flint and knife. When his arms grew tired, he rested. By noon he had managed to ignite the dried peat with satisfactory ease. He made shavings from the bunk wood but wasn't as successful, though that didn't distract him from the plan forming in his mind. This would be his last night at the cabin.

Jimmy kept the fire going all day. He cut one blanket into several narrow strips and left a couple of them wide enough to cover his hands. Wrapping another sheet around his back, he pinched it at his shoulders. He punched a hole in the wool and drew a strip through it. After several tries to make a crude coat, Jimmy was satisfied with what he had done. Layering on two more blankets, he laid the first one flat and removed the strips before creating matching holes. He shifted the middle one so he could craft a hood. Folding the final blanket, he strung it around his waist.

That morning, he had stuffed the lunch sack with the remaining moss from the eaves. After laying out the items he had to carry beside it, he crawled onto the bunk and smiled. He was looking forward to the coming day.

His breath fogged the air around him as he opened his eyes. He wouldn't make the fire, but he made shavings and left them on the rocks for whoever was to come. By spring, somebody would know he had been here. Maybe they would look for him, or maybe he would have made it home.

Jimmy dressed, threw the hefty bag over his shoulder, gripped the hatchet with his mitted hand, and stepped outside. He put the string on the pegs to keep the door closed.

The overcast sky painted a gloomy grey hue over everything his eyes took in. Doubts swarmed. His paltry resolve weakened. A whimper escaped him, and he drew a shaking hand to his forehead. Jimmy bent over and rested his hands on his knees. He tensed to stop the threatening gulps. As he looked at the distant whitecaps on the ocean, he straightened, drew in a ragged breath, and stepped onto the beach.

He hadn't decided whether he would cross the river where he had chased his father what seemed like years ago and keep going along the coast, or whether he would go the other way. Jimmy decided he would let the wind decide—he would want it at his back. He looked skyward as the cold breeze clipped his cheeks and turned his back at the insistence of a gust to go the way he had followed his father.

This felt right. He crossed the river where ice had crusted along its edges and it crunched beneath the rubber soles of his boots. His foot slipped, but he was paying attention. Jimmy vowed he would continue to take heed of his surroundings.

He spent the morning following the high-water mark, in and out of coves and inlets, only to come to a cliff that barred his passage. Now he was tired and hungry. Each time he came out of a cove, he saw the not-so-distant beach where he had come from. The cliff only reinforced what he knew. He would have to travel over land to make headway.

Jimmy spent the afternoon butting the wind, looking for a good location to enter the woods. Back at the river, he realized where he had left from was indeed the best place to start. He would try again in the morning. Re-entering the cabin for another night, he lit the shavings, ate the last tin of crab, and lay on the bunk until morning.

The next day came cold, but the ocean was calm and the sun shone. This time he closed the cabin door with a feeling of certainty he wouldn't be back. No thoughts to the contrary were allowed in. By the time the sun was high, Jimmy was looking out over the ocean from the top of a hill. He gave up on blazing his way through the dense tree growth near the riverbank and opted for more barren ground that was easier to traverse.

Over the next three days, he learned some lessons the hard way. To start, the bogs weren't frozen and wouldn't hold his weight. He spent a night under a tree with a small fire going to dry out a boot and sock to teach him that one.

Also, he needed to learn how to master the compass or mark his trail. Jimmy realized this after he returned to the same spot where he had already made a fire. He couldn't tell if the fire he had left was a day old, two days, or five.

But he caught two trout in the river. He found frankum gum like Mr. George had described. Chewing that moved his hunger from overwhelming to tolerable. The blankets kept him warm. There were dry twigs under big trees, and he could make a fire from old man's beard.

Day ran into night. His legs pained, his stomach pained, and his head pained. He tried to keep to open ground, but the terrain was unpredictable, and Jimmy was neither woodsman nor explorer. A snowstorm kept him in the same spot for a day.

He slept for most of it and shivered for the rest of it as he tried to keep a fire going. Red berries on a tree were a welcome find, and he ate them. He found more on the marsh and ate them and filled his pockets. At this point, if they were poisonous, he believed he would welcome death. But he kept going.

His spirits lifted when he found a trail. His pace quickened until the trail led under brush. Rabbits, probably. He didn't know of any other kind of animals and didn't want to imagine those more ferocious. Though his spirits were lower than they had ever been, he stumbled onward, resting every few steps. His ears perked at the sounds of water. He pushed on until he came out to the shoreline.

There, in front of him on the beach and as out of place as he, and as large as life, was the *Annie May*. Jimmy Bailor fell to his knees and clutched his face. He had finally lost his mind.

12

Over the past week, Flory had to chide or stop Lizzy from doing more than she should. Lizzy was less than a month away from having her baby. Flory didn't even want to think about those complexities. But Lizzy insisted on helping keep the place going until the men returned.

On her way home from the henhouse, Lizzy stopped and shouted, "Flory."

"What's wrong? Is the baby coming?" Flory asked as she poked her head around the door frame.

Lizzy beckoned, then she gestured toward the beach. Flory ran to her. Her sister-in-law's face was white.

"I saw someone," she murmured, blinking rapidly She pulled Flory's arm and pointed toward the tickle. "There."

"I don't see anyone," Flory said as she scrutinized the area from the side of the house outward to the woods. "Are you sure?"

"I don't know what I saw, but I saw something or somebody moving," Lizzy said. Flory made eye contact with her when Lizzy's voice rose in bewilderment. "Perhaps someone really is coming to check on us."

"I doubt that. You go in the house. I'll go around."

"Be careful, Flory. We don't know who it is."

"Make sure Bobby stays inside."

Flory circled the house, staying close to the side wall. She scanned back and forth, near and far, but saw nothing stirring. Lizzy must have been seeing things. When Flory reached the front step, she climbed with her back to the house. She urged her eyes to move slowly from the beach to the trail.

The tide was high. Waves breached loudly. That sometimes happened this time of the year when stormy seas outside forced their way in through the channel and broke on the shore. It was why Daddy used the glass. He had learned the glass was more reliable than what he saw from the beach or the hill overlooking the sheltered tickle. That was also why Flory didn't think anyone was there. She checked the glass every morning for that purpose—a boat hadn't come today, because the sea wouldn't allow it.

As she turned to go in and let Lizzy know, she noticed something out of place. She squinted at an oddity between the shoreline and the trail coming from the point. Stepping down to the ground again, she hesitantly made her way there to investigate. As she rounded a bend where the higher grass had hidden what lay beyond, she stopped.

"What is it?" Lizzy called from the step.

Flory turned and saw her sister-in-law on the gallery with the shotgun resting across her belly. "I thought I told you to stay in the house," she shouted.

"You did," Lizzy said simply.

Flory shook her head and turned back to the trail. Crouching low, she crept forward. She halted when she saw something lying on the path. Edging onward, she prepared herself to run. Her heart raced.

Was it an animal? It was covered in bog and matted with hay, sticks, leaves, and all sorts of debris she couldn't name. She kept moving toward it, when two eyes opened and stared blankly at her. They closed again, and she rushed ahead. Though the gaunt and dirty features blended with the ground beneath, she was sure it was a person lying there.

Flory pulled away the covering. It was a blanket, she surmised, though she couldn't be sure. But underneath it was a second blanket, and beneath that was another she recognized as grey wool.

"Can you walk?" she asked as she nudged the arm splayed across the ground. "You'll need to help me."

The response came in the form of a grunt and leg movements. Flory felt the muscle tense beneath her palm as what she assumed was a man tried to get his hands under him. A shadow crossed them both and gave Flory a start, until she saw Lizzy standing nearby pointing the gun their way.

"Put that away and go back to the house. Whoever it is, he is no harm to us in his condition."

Another grunt came in response.

Lizzy stood her ground. "I'll make sure," she said.

"That gun is going to your place when we get back. It's been nothing but trouble," Flory said under her breath as she pulled the man upward. He got to his knees and tried several times to stand before Flory pulled with him. When he got his two feet grounded, even stooped over he was as tall as Flory. Lizzy went to the other side despite Flory's warning not to hurt herself. Flory took the gun from her and shouldered the weight of the man as he limped toward the house.

"This stinks," Lizzy said as she pulled on the knot at his neck. She worked it loose until the cape fell with a thud. They left it on the ground. Lizzy peeled the wool off his hands and threw it aside. There was still one piece around his waist that she made quick work to loosen. By the time he got to the step, all he had left were his shirt, trousers, coat, and boots.

"That's not much better," Lizzy said as she wrinkled her nose and stared at Flory. The man's head hung low as he attempted to lift his foot upon the step.

"Get him water," Flory said as she laid the gun on the gallery and grasped the man's waistband. Lizzy nodded, headed inside, and brought a cup of water moments later. The man sipped it and urged. His throat moved in quick swallowing motions before he sighed and drank again.

"Easy," Flory said. "There'll be more inside." She tugged on his waistband as she pushed his weight with her shoulder and lifted him onto the first step, then the second and third. Lizzy held his collar to keep him from toppling backward.

Flory was breathless and sweaty by the time she got him to the door. "He'll revive in the heat," she said. "We'll make him some sweet tea. That should rouse him."

Once inside, the women deposited the man on the daybed in a tangle of limbs. Flory gagged and held her nose as the warm air hit him. He groaned and tried to sit up, but Lizzy pushed him back. "Wait for a bit. We'll make tea." He nodded and settled. The sloped end of the daybed kept his head and shoulders elevated.

"Put molasses in that," Flory said. Lizzy nodded and retrieved the molasses from the pantry.

"Me too," Bobby said when he saw the molasses.

"I'll make you toast," Lizzy said as she scruffed the child's hair. He nodded and climbed on the bench behind the table.

Flory pulled a chair close to the man. She took the cup from

Lizzy and blew on the tea, then raised the spoon to his lips. He sipped it and then coughed. Flory waited and gave him more. After the first few attempts, it got easier. When she was done, the even sighs from the stranger signalled he was snoozing.

Flory pushed back the chair. "I'm going across to your place for the tub. We can't leave him like this."

"We can't leave *us* like this," Lizzy said as she wrinkled her nose and smiled. The sentiment didn't reach her eyes. Lizzy was worried. But, Flory admitted, she was, too.

13

Flory didn't like guns. She didn't know why. Daddy had shot rabbits and saltwater birds with it as far back as she could remember. Sometimes the mutton in the spring was a sign the gun had been used. But the only time it had been held in protection of family had been at the hands of her and, now, Lizzy. She toted the gun to Bart's house and stood it behind the door as she collected the aluminum tub.

As she crossed the meadow, Flory contemplated what one could interpret as a first sign of trouble. While the man recovered, if she saw anything like anger or aggression, she would deal with it with the gun if she had to. She ran through ideas of tying him up in the barn with Dandy, or in the shed with the wood, or in the cellar. No, not the cellar, because he might get loose and ruin the vegetables. But if he got clear in the barn, he could hurt the animals or let them loose. It would have to be the shed. She didn't know how long she would keep him tied, but at least until spring if nobody came before then. Before she got home, Flory scolded herself for letting her thoughts run wild.

The tub was big. It was used as a washtub on times, though

only for the bedding. When Flory was younger, the boys would fill it in the kitchen and leave it for her to bathe. Daddy got a special bar of soap each fall just for her, and she made it last the whole year. She hadn't unwrapped this year's bar yet, and she wouldn't this evening, either. This man would use the Sunlight soap to clean off what was caked on him. She dragged the tub back home and into her father's room.

The more water they could boil, the better. Lizzy filled the kettles—two now after going back for Bart's—and kept the fire hot. Flory made a dozen trips to the wellhouse to fill the tank on the stove first, then the tub.

"Do you think he could be one of the men from the *Annie May*?" Lizzy whispered as she emptied the boiling kettle for the third time.

Flory eyed the stranger on the bench. "Hard to say, but he had to come from somewhere."

"If it was the *Annie May*, how would we get word to his people? Or to the constables? He'd be proof that the men weren't murdered."

"Better not get our hopes up," Flory said. "Let's see who he is first."

"It only makes sense that he came off that boat," Lizzy said. "It has to be. It just has to."

"Don't get worked up." Flory reached for Lizzy's hand and squeezed it. Lizzy nodded and smiled, though torment still shadowed her eyes.

Flory poured boiling water into the tub and began bailing the steaming reservoir into it as well. The water was better than tepid when the next kettles went in.

"Do you suppose he might have murdered that crew?" Lizzy asked.

"We don't know that they were murdered," Flory replied. "He doesn't look like he's in any condition to murder anyone."

"But he might have been."

"If it will make you feel better, I'll hide the knives."

Lizzy nodded toward the warmer. "I already did," she said. "Couldn't help it."

"Okay, enough of this talk. We have to get this poor fellow into the tub." Flory poured the last kettle in and brought the soap from the pantry. She nudged the stranger, who jerked and then groaned. She helped him sit. Flory spooned more tea into him until he reached for the cup. With trembling hands, he drew it to his lips and drank it down. "Careful," she warned. "Looks like you haven't eaten in a while."

He shook his head.

"What's your name?"

"Jimmy," he said. The strain forced a cough.

"Where did you come from?"

"Lost," he managed to get out.

"Well, Jimmy," Flory said, and he nodded. "We have a tub of water to clean you up and get the life back in you."

Jimmy stared at her, his eyes wide and his body tense.

"You'll be doing your own cleaning," she added. "The tub is behind there."

Flory held his arm and helped him stand. She guided Jimmy to the room. "You're not going to give out on me, are you?" she asked.

Jimmy trembled but shook his head and leaned a hand on the wall to stay upright.

"I'll help you get that shirt off, but the rest you have to do yourself. We'll take them outside and wash them next fine day. You will fit into my brother's clothes. I'll bring you something."

The man mumbled something that could have been appreciation, and she nodded. She unbuttoned his shirt and pulled it off his arms. Flory sucked in a breath. He was the thinnest person she had ever seen.

"You've been out there awhile?" She touched a bruise on his side and noticed the scratches on his face and neck that had bled and dried and were crusted with dirt.

Flory balled the rotted shirt around her hand and held it out in front of her as she left the room, taking as few breaths as she could manage. "Take your time."

She threw the shirt out the back door, then dipped cold water from the bucket and poured it over her hands. Lizzy had changed the daybed cover by the time Flory returned to her. A few rustling sounds came from Daddy's room, and it was a long time before the water splashed.

"Poor fellow," Flory said. "He's near starved to death. We won't have to worry about him making away with us."

"I never did fry those eggs," Lizzy said. "I'll do it now." She laid the iron frying pan on the damper and threw in a dab of butter.

"He'll be hungry when he comes out." Flory searched the box in Tommy's room and took the pants and shirt folded there. She held them up as she came out. "These should fit. Tommy might be a bit shorter, but these will have to do."

Her heart raced as she pushed open the door. Jimmy's back was to her. His spine nearly punctured the skin where he leaned forward with his arms wrapped around his knees.

"I've got clothes for you. When you get yourself cleaned up, we'll have eggs fried."

Jimmy didn't turn at the sound of her voice, but she saw tiny ripples around him. He was trembling.

"Is the water that cold?"

He shook his head.

"I can add another kettleful."

The stranger shook his head again.

"I'll leave you to it, then," Flory said as she laid the clothes on the end of Daddy's bed and collected the pants and socks. "I'll lay the boots to dry. There's a towel in the box at the end of the bed. Call out or rattle the tub if you need help."

She lugged water between the well and the house until she filled the stove's reservoir and the kettles, then left the full bucket on the bench in the porch.

"Any sound yet?"

Lizzy shook her head. "I suppose he's all right."

Flory went to the door and cleared her throat. Then she backed away when she heard a splash. She sat with Lizzy and Bobby. The boy giggled and reached for the molasses.

"That's three slices for the little fellow," Lizzy said. "He loves the sweet things."

"He's a growing boy," Flory said. "He has a hollow leg like Uncle Tommy." She tickled the boy's calf, and he giggled.

They ate in silence, with nothing but the wood crackling in the firebox. A thump and a splash from the room set Flory into motion.

"Did you fall?" she called through the door.

"No," came a croak from inside.

"Okay," she said.

Flory shrugged her shoulders and glanced at Lizzy. Her sister-in-law raised her eyebrows. Flory poured tea, then put her hand up for Lizzy to stay seated as she returned to the stove with the teapot. She pushed the frying pan onto the damper, where eggs sizzled and popped.

Daddy's door opened, and Jimmy came out. His bare feet shuffled as he moved. The shirt was buttoned in two holes and out of line with the seam. He clutched the pants at the waist as he moved and stood by the stove. Flory had to look twice, taken aback by his youth. His face was gaunt, his dark eyes sunken. It was clean but for the growth of fine hair around his jaw that she hadn't noticed before. Scratches, a few with a trace of fresh blood and others with pink scabs, criss-crossed his forehead and cheeks. His wavy brown hair was matted and clung to his scalp. Jimmy was the poorliest looking thing Flory had ever seen. But there was a familiarity about him that she couldn't quite place. His thin frame swayed as he shifted his feet to stay upright.

"Come sit," Lizzy said. "Before you fall down." She gestured to the chair.

Everything about him was slow. By the time he reached the table and sat, Flory had eggs on a plate before him and tea poured.

"Am I dead?" he asked when he was on his second egg. His voice came as a whisper. He cleared his throat and tried to repeat his question.

"You were in a fair way for dying, but you're in Juniper Tickle," Lizzy said. She gave him a long stare. "Don't talk. You're safe here."

Jimmy held her eyes before looking to Flory, who nodded and smiled. Flory fetched his clothes, which sat in stiff clumps by the back door. She dipped them in the tub to block the smell, lathered them with Sunlight soap, and rinsed them several times before wringing them. Outside, she hung them over the clothesline.

"I'll give them a good wash tomorrow," she said as she began bailing the tub. Jimmy tried to get up when he saw her. "Stay where you are," she said.

"Toast?" Lizzy asked.

He nodded and made to stand up, but Lizzy said, "I'll get it." Jimmy shook his head, but she was already on her way to the stove with a slice for the damper.

Flory's trips in and out made the house cool, and Jimmy trembled. Lizzy pulled a chair close to the stove. "Sit here," she ordered, leaving little room for debate.

"I don't want to be trouble," he said, his voice low and coarse as he looked at his hands.

"The trouble is over now. Come here and sit. What trouble could that be?"

Jimmy did as she told him. He chewed the buttered toast and finished his tea just as Flory took the tub from the room. She made eye contact with Lizzy and signalled she would bring the tub back to their place. Her sister-in-law gave her a quick nod and went to the table with Bobby. He was staring at Jimmy but was otherwise quiet.

"Are you full, baby?" Lizzy asked.

"Yes, Momma," Bobby said. He rubbed his eyes.

Flory returned and hung her coat in the porch. "That's done," she said.

"I'm going to lie down with him for a bit," Lizzy said. She locked eyes with Flory.

"Everything all right?"

Lizzy nodded. "Let's go for a rest," she said as she took Bobby's hand. They moved away from the bench to the room behind Jimmy and closed the door.

Jimmy's head was bobbing in the heat.

"Tired?" Flory asked.

He looked at her and stifled a yawn.

"Why don't you lay on the daybed?"

The young man laid his cup on the warmer and used the chair to push himself up. Limping to the bench, he sat and shook his head when Flory asked if he had hurt himself in the tub. He lay on his side, and within moments his chest rose and fell in a restless sleep. Flory took a quilt from Daddy's bed and draped it over him, and then she sat for the first time that day.

14

Flory awoke, confused by her surroundings. An arm across her shoulder gave her a start. Then she realized it was Bobby—she had slept with Lizzy and her nephew. Still wearing the clothes she'd had on the day before, she eased out from under his arm.

The big junk she had put in the firebox before going to bed would have gone out, but the house would still be tolerable. She was used to Daddy having the fire in when she got up, but that comfort was over. Last night she had stared into the darkness long after she had put out the lamp. She hoped Jimmy would be strong enough to answer questions today. Flory wasn't afraid of him during the night, but all the same, she was uneasy that somebody they didn't know was asleep under their roof.

Creeping from the room, she closed the door and tiptoed into the kitchen while the stranger snoozed on the daybed. She took the knife from the warmer and chuckled to herself as she looked over her shoulder. It wasn't the best choice for a hiding place. Retrieving three splits from the woodbox, Flory made shavings. She opened the drafter and gave the embers in the firebox a poke. They glowed, then ignited. She would spare a match.

The shavings caught, and the fire slowly built. Flory closed the drafter and pulled the kettle to the damper before grabbing her coat, yesterday's food scraps, and the milk bucket before heading to the stable. She tossed the bread crusts and eggshells in the hens' coop and then made her way to the stable door.

"How's Bess this morning," Flory said as she tied the goat to make room for herself and the stool. The high-pitched bleat accompanied the tap of Bess's hooves as she stood still for milking.

"You miss Daddy, too, don't you, girl?" Flory cooed. She doubted Daddy talked to her, but she guessed the goat would miss his presence as much as she did. Moving to the other side, she told Bess all about the young man who had shown up the day before. Flory did her best thinking when she talked to Bess.

"I'll tell you more when I know more," she said as she moved the pail from underneath the goat, laid the stool on the stand above the stall, and petted the animal. "I'll let you and your buddies—oh, and you too, Dandy—out later if the weather is good."

The horse neighed and stomped. Flory smiled as she ran her hand along his back and checked his water and hay. The rope barring the end of the stall had a little bell that jingled when the horse stepped back. Flory smoothed her hand across Dandy's nose. "Poor boy. I know it's hard being in." She laid her forehead against Dandy and kissed the horse on the nose before she left.

Back at the house, she poured the milk into the pan on the stove and waited for it to boil. Once it was scalded, she would lay it in the wellhouse to cool. Checking the pantry, she was happy to see two loaves of bread. She would wait until tomorrow to mix more. There was lots of time.

As the tea steeped, Flory sat at the table and gazed out over the tickle. She pictured Daddy, Tommy, and Bart and whispered their names into the solitude of the morning.

The door creaked as Lizzy joined her. "Looks like it's going to be a good day."

Flory eyed the sinking hand of the barometer. "Maybe not all day, or so the glass says. Not that it matters, I suppose."

"I wish you wouldn't worry so," Lizzy said as she nudged Flory with her hip to move in farther on the bench to make room.

Flory paused with the cup against her lip and said, "I forgot to check for eggs. Again." She grinned against the warm rim. "I hope you told those hens what would happen to them if they stopped laying."

"I did indeed," Lizzy said as she squeezed Flory's shoulder and chuckled. "It was made clear."

"Still okay?" Flory asked. She frowned until Lizzy nodded.

"No sign of baby. He or she is taking their time."

Jimmy pulled back the quilt and sat up. His face showed bewilderment. "It wasn't a dream," he whispered. He looked from Flory to Lizzy and smiled sheepishly. "And I'm not dead." He tried to stand, staggered backward, and landed hard on the daybed.

"Take it easy," Flory said as she moved around the table. "You've been through a lot."

"Come sit with us," Lizzy said softly. "I'll get you tea."

"You both sit," Flory said as she went to the pantry and brought out the milk and bread. She made a second trip to top up the molasses glass and fetch the breadknife.

"Can you talk?" Lizzy asked. She leaned toward Jimmy and smiled.

Jimmy cleared his throat. "I think so," he said. He took a swallow of tea and tried again. "Yes."

"You're not as hoarse as yesterday," Flory said. She laid a slice of toast in front of him.

"We've honey at our house," Lizzy said. "I'll go over later and fetch it. Bart had it for his sore throat."

Jimmy ate slowly. He covered the rumble in his stomach with his hand. His cheeks reddened. "I haven't eaten in days."

"Where did you come from?" Lizzy asked.

"I don't know," he said as he looked from one to the other. "I've been wandering and lost track of days. More than a week, for sure."

"That's a long time." Flory stared at him. "Were you on that boat when it came ashore here?"

"No." His answer came quickly. "Was there a wreck?"

"Yes and no," Lizzy said as she lowered her head and frowned. "The boat isn't wrecked, but nobody was aboard when she came ashore."

Jimmy's tea went down the wrong way, and he coughed. He doubled over and hugged his stomach.

"Take it easy," Lizzy said as she reached a tentative hand toward him and then withdrew.

The young man swayed and rubbed his palm over his midsection before straightening in the chair. "Nobody?"

"No," Flory and Lizzy said in unison.

"How long ago?"

"A week or more," Flory said.

The colour drained from Jimmy's face. He pushed away from the table and went outside onto the gallery. Leaning over the rail, he vomited. He groaned and retched until he was done. Flory laid her hand on his shoulder when the heaving stopped, then guided him back to the kitchen. He trembled beneath her touch.

"So, you weren't on her when she came ashore on the point," Lizzy said. "You can tell us if you were."

Jimmy shook his head and mouthed the word *No*.

Lizzy bent her head and wept softly. She sat up and drew her fingers across her eyes to wipe away the tears.

"Did you know them?" Jimmy rasped as he stared at her.

"No, nothing like that. My husband and Flory's father and brother were taken away. The law thinks they did something to the men. I hoped you could prove differently." Lizzy lowered her head into her palms.

"I'm sorry," Jimmy said. "I know nothing about it." His voice trailed away to a whisper.

Flory watched Jimmy as Lizzy explained what happened. She didn't believe he was on the boat. He seemed sincere. She didn't think he was lying.

"I'll make a slice of dry toast," she said. "And no milk in your tea. That should perk you up."

"There's ginger wine at the house, too," Lizzy said. "That might help the stomach."

Flory volunteered to go and in no time had hot honey and ginger water for Jimmy. He sipped it and picked at the food. Soon he was dozing at the table, and Flory told him to lie down. He went to the daybed and slept fitfully most of the day.

Flory filled the washtub and scrubbed Jimmy's clothes. She changed the water twice to get them as clean as she could. Then she hung them outside to let the fresh air take care of the rest. They were stiff when she brought them in to hang on the line above the stove.

By evening, Jimmy's pallor was improving. He was quiet as he sat with the women through a meal of pork and mashed vegetables.

"You're going in Daddy's room tonight," Flory said. "You can stretch out in there."

Jimmy protested, but Flory insisted, as did Lizzy, so he agreed.

Flory went to bed restless and slept less than soundly. There was something about Jimmy that bothered her. Lizzy didn't sense it, but Flory did.

"You're making too much out of it," Lizzy whispered in the dark. "He's just a boy." Lizzy yawned and turned. The bedsprings creaked.

"You're not making enough out of it," Flory admonished her. "Something's not right." She contemplated what wasn't right, but nothing came to her. Maybe it was his reaction to the news. "And I believe he's older than me."

She waited for Lizzy to say that Flory was just a girl, but the soft sounds of her sister-in-law dozing were the only response.

15

Jimmy heard the kettle scrape along the stovetop. In that moment he thought he was home. Then he opened his eyes to the dimness of a room that was strange to him for the second morning in a row. He blew out a long, loud breath through pursed lips and threw his legs over the side of the bed.

With feet planted on the cold floor, he squeezed his temples between his palms and worked his fingers through his hair until the tips touched. He slumped forward and rested his brow into the heels of his hands. Jimmy stayed there, fingers splayed across his forehead, thumbs resting on his ears, breathing deeply, and willing his racing heart to calm.

He would go to the boat today if he had enough strength. His father had come for him, but something terrible had happened. Jimmy was relieved knowing he hadn't been abandoned. In the coming days, he would make his way home to his mother. Perhaps Flory or Lizzy would lend him the money. He would get his mother to send it to them when he got home. Perhaps the boat captain, once he knew who Jimmy was, would give him passage with a promise of payment when he got to Spigot Harbour.

After a few more days in Juniper Tickle, he would be well enough that a few hours of seasickness wouldn't kill him. Then he could convalesce under the care of his mother. She would cook fine roasts. He would have bacon in the morning like she made him when he wasn't fishing and he had dared not eat. Jimmy would have all the apricots and peaches he wanted.

Mr. George and Raymond Blythe would come to the store and marvel at how he had survived long past the point they would have given up. Terry Hardy wouldn't lay another hand on him for fear that Jimmy had a new unexplained strength that Terry couldn't overcome. Maybe Terry would try to hit him, and Jimmy would come back with a wallop that would take Terry off his feet. Emma Winsor would let him look at her the wrong way, and he would instantly know what that meant.

Jimmy rubbed his hands together and pushed off the bed. His departure couldn't come soon enough, and he would suffer the short-lived sickness even if the boat came today. He pushed his legs into his own pants. They were cleaner than he remembered them ever to be, as was the shirt. They smelled of lemon and sea air.

Flory and Lizzy and the little boy met him in the kitchen. They offered him tea and toast after greeting him with a smile. Once they were all gathered around the table, Jimmy asked questions.

"Is there anyone in Juniper Tickle who can take me home?"

Lizzy and Flory looked at each other and laughed. He looked from one to the other, trying to figure out what was funny. The bigger his eyes got, the more they snorted. He was vexed. Heat rose in his cheeks and his nostrils flared.

Flory asked, "Are you serious?"

Jimmy didn't know how to respond. Flory waited for an answer, so he nodded.

"We're it," Flory said.

"What do you mean, you're it?" Jimmy asked as his brows furrowed.

"We are Juniper Tickle," Lizzy added. "Us." She pointed to Flory and the boy, then herself. "Well, now you, too. I suppose."

"I thought there were more houses farther along the harbour." Jimmy glanced toward the window.

The two young women locked eyes and grinned. They both shook their heads.

"You are putting me on," he said. He smiled awkwardly, his eyes searching the distant shore. "Well, I want to go home on the next boat. When will it be here?" he asked as he dipped toast in his tea and took a bite.

"Maybe April," Flory said, looking at Lizzy.

"Has been as late as May," Lizzy put in.

Jimmy coughed as the food went down the wrong way. "Now you have to be fooling with me." He gritted his teeth. "I can't stay here until April or May."

"The constable told Daddy he'd send somebody to check on us," Flory said, her look sincere.

"Did he say when?"

"We doubt he'll send anyone," Lizzy said matter-of-factly.

"We'd just as soon be left alone," Flory said, her tone suggesting it was perfectly reasonable.

"Two women, by themselves, brings all sorts of complications," Lizzy said as she looked at her sister-in-law.

Flory raised a questioning brow and smiled at her. The sentiment didn't reach her eyes.

"Wouldn't men take care of you? Cut wood? I don't know, do whatever men do?" Jimmy asked.

"Exactly," Lizzy replied. "All sorts of complications."

Jimmy pretended he knew what that meant, so he merely

nodded and took a swig of tea. By the way she fidgeted in her seat, he didn't believe Flory knew, either.

"So, you had planned to spend the whole winter here by yourselves?"

"No, we had no plans, but that's what happened after that bloody boat came ashore," Flory replied. Anger and frustration lit up her face. "I can't even think about William Bailor or talk about him and his crew without getting beside myself."

Jimmy gulped. "Why did they think the crew were murdered?" He couldn't absorb the information. *Murder* came with a lot of entanglements he couldn't fathom.

"I don't know. They left here satisfied that the men had been lost and the boat drifted in, like we said. A few days later they came back and took Daddy and the boys. Claimed they'd killed the crew."

"We don't know if they'll ever return," Lizzy said, her face white as a pall of fury enveloped her. "Now I'm mad."

"I'm sorry," Jimmy said. "I shouldn't have brought it up."

Flory shook her head. "It's not your fault. You had nothing to do with it."

Jimmy thought about that. She couldn't know that she was wrong—it was his fault. His father had left home to come for Jimmy. If he hadn't done that, he wouldn't have been lost. So, not only were his father and the crew all dead, the women were stranded here and their men had been sent to jail.

The understanding hit him like a punch in the gut. Jimmy pushed back the chair and stood up. He had to get out of there. Snatching his coat from the nail behind the stove, he jammed his arms into the sleeves before pushing his feet into the boots drying by the stove. All the while, his mind raced with guilt. This calamity was the worst of all. It wasn't fish, or being late, or being too weak to contribute, or being a good-for-nothing. No, this time lives and livelihoods were lost. These women were all alone, and God knew what else his mother was going through. He had certainly done it this time.

Why did he have to survive? Maybe everyone, including his present company, would be better off if he hadn't. Jimmy brought death and misfortune wherever he went. It was as simple as that.

He bolted from the house and strode away in search of the trail to his father's boat. Bits of ice tore at his skin. He hadn't noticed them at first, intent on getting away. Arctic winds drifted horizontally as cold pellets bounced on his clothes and on the ground around him, making the land seem like it was alive.

Jimmy was numb, but he couldn't blame the cold. As he stomped toward his destination, notions churned loudly and mercilessly in his ears, things his father would have pointed out. Like what kind of person was he? This morning, he couldn't wait to get out of there. Thoughts of the two women and the child and their distress hadn't crossed his mind. It was all about him. He had made assumptions about their well-being without asking.

Was this the lesson his father had tried to get in his head? He would think on it, because Father had died because of it. No, he had died *because* of Jimmy. What had he done?

The *Annie May* loomed ahead of him and blocked nature's assault. The ground was wet but not white in her shadow. It must have taken a lot of men to move the boat in this far on the beach. A thick rope sagging with icicles stretched from her bow and twisted around a large tree a few feet into the woods. The deck faced him as she lay on her side.

A dozen or so barrels were stacked in front of the tree. Jimmy surmised they were empty, since they had been the last time he saw his father. However, his curious nature made him look. He stepped over a stump and the ice pellets struck him now that he was no longer sheltered. The first barrel was sealed and heavy. Something was in it. Guts and gore had dried on the rim, so he expected to find herring for bait.

Jimmy dipped beneath the line, his head sheltered behind an upturned shoulder. All the barrels were full. Despite his heroic notion that his father had died in an attempt to rescue him, the reality was his father was a fisherman and he did what fishermen do. Jimmy sighed. He would have been the last stop for the *Annie May* before going home.

There was no way to tell when the boat had washed up. It could have been two days ago, or it could have been seven. By the look of the barrels, Jimmy was certain the *Annie May* had been there for a while.

He whirled around when he thought he heard his name. The last thing he saw before his head hit the stump was Flory running toward him.

When he opened his eyes, he was looking up at Flory White. His head was paining. Flory pulled at his collar, trying to get him up.

"I need you," she said. "Do you hear me?"

"What? Yes. Yes," Jimmy said. "You need me."

"I don't have time for this. Get up. Lizzy's in labour."

"What?" Jimmy's eyes bulged.

"Lizzy's having her baby," Flory said between clenched teeth.

"I don't know anything about babies," he replied. He scrabbled to his feet with her help.

"I don't want you to know anything. Haven't you been listening?"

"What?" Jimmy asked, confused.

Flory gripped his hand and tugged him toward the house. "Come on. We have to hurry," she said.

Jimmy's breath came in gasps before they had made it halfway. He pulled clear of Flory and waved for her to go on. "I'll . . . be . . . right . . . behind . . . you."

She reached for him again, but he avoided her grasp this time. Doubled over with his hands on his knees, he knew he couldn't keep up with her. Flory eyed him for a second before turning to run. She had no coat on—she must have been freezing. Jimmy straightened and pushed on.

Lizzy wasn't in the kitchen when he entered. "She's in the room," Flory said. "I need you to take Bobby and go across the tickle to Bart's place and stay there."

"What? Take the little fellow? I don't know what to do with him."

"He's a child, Jimmy. He won't bite." Flory squatted in front of Bobby. "You go with Jimmy and be a good boy." She patted the top of his head as she stood. Bobby nodded.

Jimmy stared at Flory and didn't speak. Questions wouldn't form. He was stunned.

"How hard did you hit your head?" she asked as she moved behind him and ran her fingers along his scalp. "No blood but a bit of a knot. You'll be fine."

Flory grabbed the matches and four shavings from the box. She took Jimmy's hand and turned his palm up, closing his fingers over the matches. Then she lifted his arm, laid the shavings against his side, and pressed his arm in to secure them. "Jimmy, go." She stood behind him and pushed him toward the door, opened it, and shoved him out. "Come back for Bobby when the fire is going. There's still wood there from when Bart brought it in."

"Jimmy," she said, waiting for him to look at her. "I'm depending on you. I can't do this myself."

"I'll make in the fire and come back and get the boy," he said flatly.

"Thank you," Flory said as she closed the door.

Jimmy wasn't sure why she wanted him to go to Bart's place, but he would do as she asked. The house was smaller than Flory's. He made quick work of the fire before checking for food, but there was none. No kettle, either. The boy might get hungry, so he would have to bring something back. He would work out the rest as the day went on. The woodbox had enough in it to last the day. When he filled the stove and got the fire roaring, he returned to the house across the tickle.

Flory came out when she heard him in the kitchen. "There's no kettle," he said. She pointed to the one on the back of the stove. "What about water?" he added.

"There's a bucket in their back porch. You may need to go to the wellhouse." Flory gestured toward Bobby. "Leave him here and take the kettle and get the water."

Jimmy nodded and headed out. When he returned, he checked the bucket in the porch and ran to the well to replenish Flory's. He took a bun off the bread, tucked it under one arm and Bobby under the other, and battled the wind across the way to Bart's house.

To his recollection, he had not been left in charge of another person before. Not somebody so young, for sure. Worries played on his mind—some of them as grave as simply keeping the child alive.

16

Lizzy had two regrets, though only one really mattered. She couldn't help but hearken to the first one and Albert Williams. Back then she should have stood up to him, but in a way he was the reason she was in Juniper Tickle. Ultimately, the reason she was dying. Maybe she deserved to die—that was how it was for people like her. Those who tried to climb from the gutter, where they belonged. She found reassurance in the glimpse of something better with Bart. He was a good man.

But Albert Williams, he was something else. Though it was too late for such foolish thoughts, she wished she had been braver. Maybe both her regrets had everything to do with her lack of courage.

Back then, before Albert, she had turned away from the docks and set out from St. John's along the railroad bed. The blue plaid dress she had worn for the first time just the day before swayed around her old leather boots. The scent of lemon, which was still on her from the bath, inspired a confidence she would find something better. Or maybe it was the feel of Bart's warm lips on her cheek. Whatever it was, that was the day she believed she could be more. For the first time, she felt lighter. Perhaps it was hope—Lizzy had heard there was such a thing.

The house by the river was imposing yet promising. Three storeys, but not like the city's three-storey dwellings, which were narrow and connected from one street to the next. This one spread out in every direction with windows all around speaking of wealth rather than necessity. The gardens had flowers in colours she had not seen in her seventeen years in the city. She closed her mouth, which had hung open since she had first laid eyes on the place. A carriage glistened in the afternoon sun. Two horses grazed near the stables while a tall, straight man closed the pasture gate.

Lizzy wasn't sure how she should proceed. She regarded her dress and practised a crouch that would hide her boots without looking absurdly out of place as she presented herself. Should she go to the front door? Was there a side entrance? She dug her nails into her palms to quiet whatever was jumping around in her belly. The sound of a leathery chafing and approaching hooves drumming the dirt demanded her attention. She stepped out of the way as the driver manoeuvred a cart around her and onto a secondary path through the trees along the side of the house.

She followed. As she drew near, her gait faltered as she witnessed a flurry of activity. Several people, young women in light blue uniforms and men in dark coats and trousers, rushed toward the wagon. There was urgency in the conversation, though Lizzy couldn't tell what they were saying.

"You there," somebody called. Her eyes followed the source. A man beckoned to her. "Are you the new maid?" Lizzy looked behind her and back to the man. She nodded slowly.

"Come on, then. There's no time to waste."

Lizzy stepped into a line of workers taking boxes and bags from the buggy to a huge kitchen.

They were getting ready for a party, she learned. The owner was hosting a soiree to gain support for his candidacy for prime minister of Newfoundland. She was to be the chambermaid. The last one had left unexpectedly. For today, she just needed to pitch in, as would be required of her at any time above her regular duties. Lizzy would sleep with the other girls in the attic, where there were five beds, three already occupied by Nancy, Mary, and Susan. Mrs. Williams would show her what she had to do the next day once the party duties were carried out.

Nancy hurried her into an oversized dress. She tut-tutted at Lizzy's boots before finding a pair of shoes in a box at the bottom of a wardrobe. Next, she raced her down the servants' stairwell at the rear of the house to the bustling kitchen. Her only instructions were to keep her head down and her mouth closed. Lizzy could do that.

Though pockets were tempting among the suited and gowned throngs that evening, she resisted the urge. The din and camera flashes when Mrs. Morris, adorned with a necklace designed by R. H. Trapnell Jewellers, made a grand entrance didn't draw her from the kitchen. What she did to survive before this was out of necessity, and that would stay in the past from now on. Lizzy had a job, a dress, a bed, food, and now a pair of shoes. She didn't need to steal any longer.

Hope really did exist.

"That's too much water," Mrs. Williams said the next morning. "Wipe it up. Quickly. Quickly." She clapped her hands to emphasize the speed she expected as Lizzy cleaned. "Where did you learn your barbaric domestic skills?"

Lizzy assumed this was an observation rather than a question and squeezed the rag tighter after dipping it in the bucket.

"I want these floors shiny when I return."

Lizzy nodded at the command.

Later that afternoon, the talk in the kitchen centred on the St. John's newspaper, the *Telegram*, and the picture of Mrs. Morris wearing what the papers were calling the Topsail Star. It was the most exquisite jewel in the Dominion, according to the reporter and to Nancy. Lizzy's roommate traced her finger along the newsprint with a look of envy she couldn't contain.

Heels clicking on the tile scattered the girls. Nancy shoved the folded paper at Lizzy before exiting through the stairwell.

"Well, who do we have here?" Albert Williams asked as he approached, a smile building with each step as his gaze scanned the vacant area. "You are a pretty young thing." He pressed his index finger beneath Lizzy's chin, applying pressure to raise her head. She didn't comply but stared at the paper she was holding instead.

Albert, the son of Mrs. Williams, was a scrawny, excessively freckled young man who wasn't well-liked by the others—again, according to Nancy. *He's the reason Henrietta had to leave*, she had said in a conspiratorial whisper.

Stay clear of him, Mary reiterated.

Don't let him catch you alone, Susan warned. *You'll regret it.*

"Where did you get that?" Albert asked, frowning. He gripped the paper from Lizzy's hand. She held it for just a moment before releasing it.

"It was on the table."

"It was on the table, *sir*," Albert corrected her.

"It was on the table," Lizzy repeated with a defiant smile.

He waited for her to finish the sentence, but she stared at the wall just above his ear and cloaked her face with boredom.

"Are you deaf?" He pushed his face toward her.

Lizzy stood her ground. "I am not," she said sweetly. "Your mother said I should keep my mouth shut and only answer questions if I'm asked. I've done that."

Turning to leave, she reached for the bucket. Albert grabbed her arm, and the contents of the bucket splashed. He jumped back, but not before soapy water drenched one of his shoes.

"You did that on purpose," he spat, his eyes filled with rage. "Clean it up."

Lizzy took the sodden washcloth and slapped it on the floor. Albert jumped away as droplets scattered across his shoes and trousers.

"I did *that* on purpose," she said flatly as she swiped the cloth, wrung it in the bucket, and dried up the mess.

Lizzy felt his eyes on her back as she marched from the kitchen with the bucket by her side. She gasped as she narrowly avoided colliding with Nancy.

"He won't like that," she said as she glanced nervously toward the door. "Not at all."

"I don't care," Lizzy said as she stepped around Nancy and ascended the stairs. "I have floors to do."

"You *will* care. He'll make things hard."

"I'm okay with hard."

Nancy shook her head. "You will care," she said again. "Be careful."

Albert harassed her at every opportunity. He knocked over her bucket, dragged muddy boots across her clean floors, and even took to tormenting the other girls in an attempt to turn them against her. It was childish behaviour, which Lizzy dismissed. Even when he put something in the coal that smoked out the parlour, she didn't respond. With humility and apologies, she took the admonishment from Mrs. Williams for her stupidity. She had food every day and a place to sleep—she would endure whatever he could come up with.

However, the night of another big political shindig, she realized her mistake. It was too late. Before the party was over, she was wandering in the dark with her meagre belongings tucked under her arm, back to what she knew—poverty, hunger, and picking pockets to survive. That was until Bart returned.

Now, pain seized her. She pinched her face through spasms that threatened to strangle her. This life, which continued to take her down no matter what she did, made her scream in defiance all the more.

"I'll try something," Flory said. "I've seen Daddy turn the lambs and the kids before."

"I'm neither a ewe nor a nanny goat," Lizzy growled through clenched teeth.

"Birthing is birthing," Flory said as she mopped the sweat from Lizzy's forehead. "It's been all night. You can't keep this up. It wasn't like this on Bobby. I don't know what else to do."

Lizzy clutched her sister-in-law's apron and dragged her closer as another wave of pain shuddered through her. Her body was too tired to react with a push. She grunted until the tremor passed, allowing her moments to say what she needed to say.

"Tell Bart I'm—"

The words stopped as her body clenched.

"—sorry."

"Tell him yourself in the spring," Flory said as she pulled out of Lizzy's grip. She probed Lizzy's belly. Her fingers explored the hard lump pushing out through Lizzy's side, and she forced the heel of her hand upward beneath it. Lizzy sank deeper into the straw mattress and cried out as another pain tore through her. Flory pushed again and again. Lizzy screamed and flailed her hands at Flory, but they fell by her sides.

"Tell Bart it was me," Lizzy whispered through exhaustion and pain, fighting for control. "It was me."

"It was you, what?" Flory asked as she pulled Lizzy forward on her next pain.

"I can't," Lizzy said, her confession forgotten in the midst of paralyzing spasms. "I can't."

"Don't you die on me, Lizzy White. You hear me?" Flory commanded as she turned her head away and wiped at her eyes. "Don't you dare die. I'm only beginning to like you."

The corners of Lizzy's lips turned upward. She was going to die younger than her mother. How was that for fate? Pain was constant now as Flory pressed her belly.

"You have to help me," Flory said as she laid her forehead against Lizzy's. "You have to help me."

Flory's face was inches from her own. She looked so much like Bart. Poor Bart. What had she done? It should be her in prison, not him. Flory stood, and Lizzy shoved her head into the pillow.

Bobby's cries came from the other side of the door. Flory sprang toward the noise.

"Take him out of here," she said, her voice low and firm with authority. "It's not fit."

Bobby's wails disappeared with the sudden winter draft and the closing door. Lizzy drew a deep breath at the sound. She wouldn't see her precious boy again. Maybe it was for the best. She hoped he would never know what she had done to his father.

Flory was pushing on her again, sitting her up, laying her down. Lizzy's mind left her and brought her to the house on Waterford Bridge Road. Would she have died there like this, or would the maids have known how to help her? She suspected the latter, but it wasn't to be.

Her body wrenched, and she heard a cry. She wasn't sure if it was her own. Everything faded, and then the face of Albert Williams appeared in the blackness.

You will do what I ask or you'll regret it, he said.

"No!" Lizzy cried out.

Flory shushed her from somewhere in the distance.

"It's a girl, Lizzy," her sister-in-law cried. "A baby girl. You did it."

The words came as if through a haze. Lizzy trembled and reached for Flory. "Caroline . . . after . . . your mom."

Flory's face streamed with tears as she kissed Lizzy's forehead.

"Take care . . . of . . ." Lizzy swallowed air as she tried to finish what she needed to say.

"Elizabeth White, you hold on for baby Caroline, and Bobby, and Bart. Don't you dare leave me here by myself."

Heat and cold all jumbled together in something that was far from warm. Pain returned and skewered Lizzy.

"Don't . . . forget . . ." The rest of her thoughts were lost to the abyss that claimed her.

"Lizzy? Lizzy! *Lizzy!*"

17

Wind howled while snow and rain pelted against the clapboard. Jimmy thought it must have nudged the house farther from the safety of Flory's with every gust. Over there the light winked a taunting beacon since nightfall.

His own lamplight cast through the windowpane barely penetrated the pitch. Jimmy held the lantern above his head and pressed his nose to the glass. Steam fogged his view, and everything went dark across the tickle. He furiously wiped the pane with his forearm to bring the light back, but all remained dark. Closing his eyes, he rested his forehead on the sash and heaved a sigh that shook him to the tips of his toes.

Bobby had finally gone to sleep after Jimmy lay with him and held his hand. He pitied the child and commiserated. Jimmy didn't bother to cry for the sake of the youngster, though the urge was strong. He lingered until Bobby's hiccoughing sobs subsided before going to the window to keep vigil.

After bringing the child home earlier, he regretted it the moment he heard screams from the bedroom. He wasn't privy to the length of time it took a woman to have a baby and thought that perhaps they had forgotten about him and Bobby. When the child heard his mother, Bobby had howled, and Flory came out. When Jimmy saw her, he gasped at her bedraggled appearance and the exhaustion she wore so openly. If that was how hard it was to assist a birth, he hated to think what Lizzy must look like.

Looking after a little boy was foreign to Jimmy, and he feared he might do something wrong. Peering through the glass one more time, he moved to wait on the bench atop the woodbox. He kept the fire going until his head began to droop, then cupped his hand on the glass and blew, but he was absorbed by the night.

Jimmy had hoped Flory would come and take the child back to his mother before she douted her own lamp. Then he hated himself for wishing it. He was sure she would come because she would have no faith in his ability to care for the boy. When she didn't show up, he suspected she didn't know him enough to judge. Maybe no one, including him, looked incompetent at first glance. So, he waited until the darkness mesmerized him. He left his post and lay down with Bobby again.

In the morning, soft fingers pinched and explored his face. Jimmy's eyes shot open. After his initial start, he smiled at the little eyes looking into his own.

"Bobby," he said, more as a reminder than anything.

The little boy grinned.

"Hungry," Bobby said as he patted his belly. Then he looked around. His lip quivered and he began to wail. "Momma," he repeated until he was hoarse and the sobs became hiccoughs.

Jimmy's attempts at comforting pats and shushes weren't working. He jumped out of bed and pulled the boy with him. It was cold, so he hauled the quilt to them and covered the child.

"We'll go see her," he said.

Standing Bobby on the bed, he grabbed their clothes on the

chair. He glanced through the window as he pulled a shirt on the boy and noticed smoke coming from Flory's chimney. His insides unfurled as a sense of relief came over him. The ground was covered in snow. Not much, by the looks of it, as tufts of dead grass stained the white pall.

Jimmy and Bobby crossed the distance from one house to the other in short order. The child was bundled inside the quilt under one arm, and Jimmy used the other for balance on the slick meadow. Flory called to him from the back door. He changed course and met her on the step.

Flory took her nephew and squeezed him without saying a word. Her eyes were red and puffy, and she had a distant look about her. She handed Jimmy a metal bucket and stepped back into the house, closing the door behind her.

Jimmy looked from the bucket to the house and waited a few moments before following her. He wasn't sure what to expect. Certainly, he had no idea what she wanted him to do with the bucket. He peered into the kitchen. Flory sat by the table undressing Bobby. She was softly chattering to the little boy as she removed his coat. The young woman wasn't as jovial as Jimmy had seen her the morning before.

When she saw Jimmy, she turned, her eyes wide and questioning. He gestured to the bucket and shrugged his shoulders.

"I don't know what this is for."

"For the milk," Flory said in a tone that suggested it should have been obvious.

"Where is it?" Jimmy asked, blushing.

"In the stable. Where else would it be?" She looked at him oddly, one brow raised.

"I don't know. Mother kept it in the pantry. I'll go get it."

"Jimmy," Flory said. "You have to milk the goat."

"I have to what?" His eyes were enormous, and his brows disappeared beneath his hair. "Milk a goat? I've never milked anything before."

"You can't be serious," Flory said. "You can't be serious. Where did you come from that you've never milked a goat before?"

She turned and quickly aligned the lapel and buttoned Bobby's shirt. Hoisting him off the table, she scooted him toward Jimmy. With that, she took the bucket out of Jimmy's hand and stepped around him.

"Make the child tea and toast."

Flory hauled a coat from the nail and it caught, ripping the fabric. She lifted it higher to get it loose, then glared at Jimmy. Her red face and glassy eyes pinned him in a fury unlike anything his father could spawn.

"Whatever you do, that boy must not go into that room. I'm counting on you for that. No matter what." She spun around and stormed out of the house.

Bobby whimpered, and Jimmy went to him. "You sit in there, and I'll make you toast."

Jimmy's voice was soft as he coaxed Bobby onto the bench. The boy complied but continued to whine as Jimmy crossed to the pantry in search of bread. There was none. He had taken the second loaf when he arrived with Bobby the evening before. Jimmy had been hungry and anxious after the little fellow went to sleep, and finding nothing else to eat, he had eaten the last of the loaf.

Tipping the milk jug toward him, he saw it was empty as well. He searched the small pantry for something for the boy. Bags of beans, peas, oats, and flour were stacked on the floor. Tea, and a few packages of hard bread and crocks of unlabelled jams, filled the shelves. A glass with molasses was the only other item that took his interest.

Then he saw something familiar that had been poked behind the bags. There was a single can of peaches like the ones his mother had packed for him in what seemed like a different lifetime. He laid his hand on the label, closed his eyes, and thought of her.

Seeing nothing that could bring immediate satisfaction for the child, Jimmy took the can of peaches and the molasses. Surely Bobby would eat the fruit. Tea was already made, so he poured a cup for himself and one for the boy, using a ladleful of water from the porch to cool it down. Bobby balked at the tea, so Jimmy spooned in the blackstrap liquid to sweeten the brew. He added a little to his own so the child could see it was good.

They were both sharing peaches when Flory came back with eggs and a bucket of milk. She didn't look their way as she laid the articles down and shed her coat. Absently, she ran a gentle finger over the ripped seam. The loud bang of metal on the cast iron stove drew a second gaze as Flory poured the bucket's contents into a pan. Beads of milk hopped and sizzled on the damper. Tiny tendrils of smoke curled toward the ceiling and disappeared in the beams.

Flory pulled the frying pan to the damper and cracked three eggs. The rest she carried into the pantry. She went to the porch and filled the firebox before standing with her back to them and tending to the eggs.

"Can I do something?" Jimmy asked hesitantly.

"Can you bake bread?"

"No," he said sheepishly.

"We're all going to perish," Flory said. Her statement of resignation held no emotion that he could hear.

18

Flory was more tired than she had ever been. Overwhelmed by the ordeal of the day before and all that there was yet to do, she allowed self-pity in. It wrapped her in a warm cloak and radiated so that the world could see that she, Florence Alice White, was to be left alone.

But who was there now who would see her? A three-year-old boy and a man who might as well have been another three-year-old boy judging by the aid he could provide.

Then, smothering, the gloom slowly tightened around her, as if being wound by the capstan of all she had in her care. Tend the animals, keep the fire going, keep food on the table, look after the new baby, look after Bobby—the list doubled, and doubled again, and took control. What if her father didn't come back in the spring? What would she do with Lizzy? Her legs grew weak. Her misery became a harbinger of death. Everything that she was responsible for would die. Daddy would come back and all would be gone, and she would have broken the promise to her dying mother.

"We're all going to perish," she whispered as every bad thought of what could be folded over one another to form a thick, unconquerable, and consuming bleakness. Her stomach knotted and forced sour acid into the back of her throat. Flory's heart thundered against her chest, and her head ached. Her shoulders fell as the weight of her world descended and came to roost on her. She shuddered.

The memory of her mother pushed its way through. She remembered trying to write the alphabet while Momma scalded the milk, just like she was doing. Momma encouraged her from a distance. She was patient and had faith in Flory's ability.

When the seeds of tranquility germinated in her heart, a spark flared. It ignited in the cumbersome darkness and pulsed in her ears. Her mother was present, standing beside her. Flory closed her eyes and reached for her. *Don't give up, young lady*, Momma murmured. *Don't give up*.

Flory dabbed at the traitorous tears with the sleeve of her dress. Forcing herself to straighten up, she lifted her shoulders and swallowed the bile. She took a deep breath and then another. An egg yolk sizzled and a pinch of hot butter splattered on her cheek. She placed her fingertips on the tiny sting, a reminder to concentrate on one thing at a time.

For now, it was the eggs.

She turned to get a plate, when one appeared at her elbow. Flory glanced over her shoulder, and Jimmy was there, red-faced with fear and concern in his eyes.

"I'll help," he said as a plea rather than a commitment. "It might be a you-point-and-I'll-do situation, but I will do the doing."

Flory wanted to ask what that meant. But her emotions were not yet reined in, and tears were at the ready, so she nodded, afraid to speak. After plating the eggs, she pulled the frying pan off the damper, laid the milk pan in the pantry, and busied herself putting wood in the firebox with her back to the table.

She took more time than necessary before turning around. Jimmy had set a place for her. He came to the stove and brought the teapot to the table. Laughter suddenly bubbled to the surface, and she had to clamp her jaw to keep it back. She was losing her mind.

"Tell me what needs to be done," he said. "Just tell me."

She held up her hand for him to stop.

"Let me say this first," Jimmy said, asking permission with his eyes.

Flory nodded and took a sip of tea, still holding back the dam of tears and the rising hysteria.

The young man cleared his throat and made an effort to speak—then another, and another.

"Jimmy, just say it. Whatever it is," Flory said, trying hard to stay composed.

"I'm not handy," he blurted out. "I don't know how to do things." Jimmy's faced turned a brilliant shade of red.

"I don't know how to do things, either."

"No," he said. He closed his eyes. "I am really not handy at all. I fool things up. I get in the way. I do things wrong."

"Jimmy," Flory said, seeing the petulant child in his face. She didn't have time for this. It was hard enough to deal with her own self-pity. But she would not resort to being unkind. "Jimmy, we all do that."

"But I'm good at it," he said, his eyes wide, begging for understanding.

She laughed inwardly. With a straight face, she said, "See? You're handy at something."

"I want to do my share," Jimmy said, dismissing her attempt at levity. "I want to do more than my share. You both saved me."

Flory felt his earnestness. "Okay, you're in charge of water from now on. You can't fool up water."

"This is where not being handy comes into it," Jimmy said. "What does it mean to be in charge of water?"

"That's easy," Flory said. "Keep the reservoir on the stove full, keep the kettles full, and always have a bucket of water in the porch."

"That's it?"

"That's it."

"I can do that. You won't have to carry any water as long as I'm here."

"Today I need you to do extra," Flory added.

"Name it," he said confidently.

"I mean with water." Flory's eyes misted over, and she swallowed hard. "I have to clean the bedclothes. I'll need the tub brought back from the other house, and I'll need it filled."

Jimmy stared at the door. He hadn't asked her about Lizzy.

"I don't want Bobby in here when I'm doing the work," she said. "You probably wouldn't want to be here, either."

"Is she all right?" Jimmy asked. "The baby?"

Flory shook her head. "The baby seems fine. Lizzy lost a lot of . . . you know," she said, and mouthed the word *blood* so the child wouldn't overhear. "So much that I'm afraid for her."

"I'll get the water boiling," Jimmy said. "I'll take Bobby . . ." He looked to Flory for an answer.

"It's cold," she said. "Leave him here until the water's all done." She thought about it for a moment as Jimmy got up from the table. "Maybe I'll wash the stuff when he has a nap."

Jimmy murmured in agreement as he pulled on his coat and boots and went to the porch. The bucket sloshed in his hand as the door opened.

Flory picked the empty peach tin from the table and rolled it over in her hand, tracing an outline on the label with her finger. She sighed. She had looked forward to eating the peaches and was saving them for when Daddy came home. Thoughts of Daddy brought a smile to her face.

"And by the way, since we're being honest," she mumbled, "you owe me a tin of peaches."

She laid the can on the table and chuckled. *What a silly notion*, she thought. *You wouldn't know but the tin had control of Daddy coming home.*

Flory was startled when Jimmy poked his head around the door and said, "You'll get it," referring to the peaches.

"I thought you'd gone. Forget it. I can't miss what I never had."

"I promise you, you'll get them," he called before a draft of cold air and the door closing signalled he had finally left.

Flory took her nephew by the hand. "Do you want to see your little sister?" Bobby's eyes lit up and he nodded. "Be very quiet, though, because Mommy's asleep."

Bobby put his finger to his lips and smiled.

19

Thunder rumbled in the distance while rain and sometimes freezing rain pummelled the roof for the third day. The house was damp where the heat from the wood stove couldn't penetrate. Jimmy lingered in the porch, studying the downpour, waiting for a break in it so he could sprint to the wellhouse.

"Come in," Flory said.

"I want to fill the water bucket," Jimmy said as he held it up to her. "That's all that's left."

Flory caught his shoulder and guided him away from the door. She offered her hand and eyed the bucket. Jimmy laid the handle across her fingers. Pulling open the door, she laid the bucket on the step.

"At this rate," she said as she squealed and flicked at the drops of water not yet absorbed by her dress, "it will be full in no time."

Jimmy smiled.

"It's all right to make things easier on yourself," she continued as he followed her to the kitchen. "But I'd rather this than snow. We'd be in for a long winter."

Flory talked while he shrugged off his coat and boots, filled the firebox, checked the kettles, and looked for something else to do. Bobby had pulled the splits out of the box near the stove again. Once the box was empty, he would put them back. Jimmy sat cross-legged by the child.

"Want to learn how to count?" Jimmy asked.

The boy beamed up at him and nodded. Jimmy began to form the words and waited for Bobby to repeat them. He went as far as ten before pulling the splits from the box one by one to start over. After several attempts the little fellow lost interest, and Jimmy returned to sit on the daybed.

Flory was covering the bread pan when she paused to stare at Jimmy. "You're good with him," she said. "Patient and kind."

Jimmy blushed.

She made a pot of tea, and he joined her at the table. "It's another day for sleeping," Flory said over the rim of her cup. "That's what the men say, anyway." Her eyes drifted to the window. "Wish they were here to sleep." She turned her eyes to Jimmy. "What do you do on days like this?"

"Read, mostly."

"You read?"

"Yeah," Jimmy replied, a little confused. "You don't?" He was sorry for asking once he saw her crimson cheeks.

Flory lowered her head. "No. Momma wanted us to learn, but Daddy said there was no need."

"I'm sorry," Jimmy said. "I meant no harm." He reached to pat her arm but pulled back before making contact.

"Not your fault," she said as she stood up to busy herself moving pans and kettles around on the stove.

"I have a habit of saying the wrong things," he said.

"It's not you." Flory pulled her dress's sleeve across her eyes. "I miss everyone, that's all."

Jimmy opened his mouth and closed it again. He took a swig of tea. "Tell me how that glass thing works," he said.

Flory went to the barometer and ran her hand across it. "That hand there is way down, a few days now. When it goes up, the weather will be changing for the better."

"So, yesterday you knew there would be bad weather again today." Jimmy gave his head a shake. "And weather it did."

"Daddy didn't think much of it at first but swears by it now. Well, swore by it."

"Does it work winter and summer?" Jimmy asked.

"It does. Daddy knew when to leave the animals in and when they could go out for the day."

Flory sat once again and picked up her teacup. Sounds of rain, the kettle boiling, wood cracking in the firebox, and Bobby's murmurs hung in the air.

"You know, Momma had a couple of books that are in the box under Daddy's bed. I don't think he threw them out."

"Want me to check?" Jimmy asked.

"Only if you want to read."

"Do you have a pencil? And paper?"

"Yes, in the sideboard in the pantry. There's a drawer Momma kept stuff in," Flory said as she rose.

Jimmy followed her.

"I forgot about them," she admitted.

"And the books," Jimmy said. "Can we look for those?"

They found three. "Your mother picked fine ones," Jimmy said. "I've read two of them."

He turned over the musty copy of *The Count of Monte Cristo* by Alexandre Dumas in his hand. "Not this one, though." He read the insert aloud as Flory stared at him. "This one looks good."

"It sounds quite good," she agreed.

Jimmy sat on the daybed and opened the book. "I have a habit of reading out loud," he said. "Would that bother you?"

"Really, Jimmy?" Flory rolled her eyes. "You don't have to do that."

"What about if I want to? If it bothers you I'll stop."

Lizzy's hoarse *yes* from the bedroom was all the encouragement he needed. Jimmy started reading the book aloud and Bobby curled up against him while Flory busied herself about the kitchen. Soon she sat beside him and gathered her nephew in her arms. A while later, she passed the boy to Jimmy and stood up again. "The bread is going over."

"I'll get the water bucket," Jimmy volunteered. "I'm parched, anyway."

Lizzy called out. Flory returned moments later.

"Lizzy wants you to stop."

Jimmy's cheeks burned.

"She needs to nap and doesn't want to miss anything," Flory added quickly with a grin.

Jimmy laughed. "I thought I'd been mortally wounded." He laid the book on the bench. "We'll take it up again later," he called to the open door. The responding mumble was all the affirmation he needed.

The sullen skies continued to batter them with rain, and the glass showed no sign it would let up any time soon. Once Flory had transferred the dough to rise in the baking pans, Jimmy brought the pencil and paper to the table. His mind raced as he tried to find a way to ask her.

"Just say it, Jimmy," Flory said as she laughed. "Your face is as brooding as the weather."

He patted the seat next to him. "I'd like to help you learn how to write."

"I appreciate the offer, but what need will I have of it?"

"Maybe none, but you will only have wasted your time." He looked at the window. "Or . . . if you're afraid . . ."

"Afraid," she snorted. "I'm not afraid."

"Let me finish," he said. "Maybe I used the wrong words. If you're unsure, we can just look at each other until the weather gets better or Lizzy wakes up."

Flory snapped the dishcloth at him, and he pulled away with a grin. "So, it's fear," he declared.

"Momma showed me the alphabet," she countered.

"Well, that makes things easier," Jimmy said as he patted the chair again, his eyes questioning and expectant. "Unless you're afraid," he teased again. He liked the ease he found in this place. Flory and Lizzy were so different from his mother. He could get used to it.

Flory harrumphed and settled on the chair. "Flory White does not back down from anything," she said.

He laughed and she hushed him, motioning toward Lizzy's door.

"Of that I have no doubt," he whispered.

20

“We have to do something,” Flory said. The fish stacked in the cellar was no longer waist high, and though they probably wouldn’t run out, she was, plain and simply, sick of salted cod.

“Don’t kill the hens,” Lizzy whispered. “I told them we wouldn’t.” Her mouth turned upward in a smile before falling limp again.

“I doubt they’ll remember that promise,” Flory replied as she tucked the quilt around Lizzy. “You’re too thin. We need something for soup.”

“Not the hens,” her sister-in-law said. “They won’t forgive me. I won’t eat them.”

“Don’t worry. They’re safe enough for now.” Flory turned to leave the room, taking the mug with her. “Unless they stop laying,” she said in jest as she toed the rock in front of the door to keep it open. She made a chopping motion at her neck.

Lizzy rolled her eyes.

Flory laughed. “Want the baby for a spell?” she asked before she went to the kitchen. The baby was swaddled in a box on the table. Bobby peered over the side at his sleeping sister.

"You want to go lie down with Mommy and Caroline?"

Jimmy motioned toward the door and raised a questioning brow as he glanced at the book. Flory gave a slight shake of her head. When she returned to the table, she said, "Lizzy's still pretty weak. We need more than fish and brewis to pick her up."

At her request, Jimmy went to fetch a piece of salt pork from the cellar. She would fry it and add it to boiled beans. "They'll do for a few days, but we need meat."

"What about rabbits?" Jimmy asked as he chewed a crust of bread.

"I forgot about rabbits," Flory said as she poured a bowl of white beans into the pot. She topped them with rashers and boiling water and laid the pot in the oven. "Daddy used to set snares just after the first snow. Do you know how?"

"Me, no," Jimmy said. "I remember following a path out on the point, that's all."

Every day, Flory gleaned something new about Jimmy that didn't fit with the world she lived in. Her brothers had followed Daddy after rabbits for as long as she could remember. She went a few times when she was younger, too. Maybe a time or two after Momma died. Later, as the boys grew into men, most of her time was spent looking after the house. Chasing rabbits wasn't something she did anymore.

"Daddy kept wire in the shed," she told Jimmy. "Maybe in the eaves."

Jimmy retrieved the slips and laid them on the table. "Now what?" he asked, looking from Flory to the wire.

"We find a rabbit trail and set them."

"I remember one near the boat. What do I do?"

Flory explained the art of rabbiting.

"So, I just hang it on a limb? How high.? Jimmy used his hand to denote distance. He held it at his waist.

"Perhaps this first time I'll go with you," Flory offered. "I don't know what kind of rabbits you think we have around here." She grinned at him as he shrugged his shoulders.

Flory liked that Jimmy didn't get mad. He was jovial and didn't complain. The young man allowed her to show him how to do the simplest things, like pin clothes on the line. He didn't mind nor think it odd. Flory wasn't sure what to make of him, but he didn't question her when she asked him to do something. In return, she wouldn't question him, either.

They dressed Bobby to accompany them and laid the sleeping baby beside her mother before leaving to set the snares. A few inches of snow had fallen two nights before, and a dusting followed that overnight. It covered their tracks to the stable and wellhouse. The sun shone brightly, with not a cloud to be seen. Flory checked the glass before she left. It was calling for a nice day.

They trekked to the point and veered off before reaching the *Annie May*. The sight of the boat stirred emotions Flory refused to entertain.

"In through here," Jimmy said.

"You have no real idea, do you?" Flory asked, ducking under the limbs of the tall firs.

"Well," he said as he looked about, "I came out on the beach near here, so it had to be this way."

"You're turned around," Flory said. She took his arm and turned his body. "The beach is over that way, so you would have come from there."

"That's what I meant," Jimmy said with a sheepish grin. "I was making sure you were paying attention."

"I knew that," she said as she made a playful slap at him. They both laughed and shooed Bobby ahead of them through the trees.

Flory picked up a weathered stick and nudged the snow from the boughs in their path. "Saves a neck full of snow," she said. As they broke out onto a small frozen marsh, Jimmy raised a hand. There, along the treeline, was a rabbit run. He felt as excited as Bobby must have when his aunt made molasses buns. Flory couldn't help but mirror the smile that filled his face.

"Looks like they went in this direction," she said.

"How do you know?" Jimmy asked.

"Daddy showed me."

A sad look crossed Jimmy's face, and Flory guessed he hadn't hunted with his own father. She showed him the prints and how the snow falling away from the tracks indicated direction. With a grin, she made motions as if she were the rabbit, sending Bobby into fits of giggles.

"How do you know the rabbit won't see the snare?" Jimmy inquired.

"We'll make a little fence and guide it under that limb where the snare will be waiting," Flory explained. "Bobby, crawl under that tree and get me a few twigs."

Her nephew did as she asked, and she encouraged Jimmy to help forge a trail to steer the rabbit.

"If he's already gone by, what will make him come back?"

"We won't be catching that one. It will be the one that comes behind it."

Jimmy nodded and screwed up his face. "I think I would have followed the trail until I found the rabbit."

"What would you do with it then? Ask it to come home for supper?" Flory laughed.

"If I was nice about it," Jimmy replied, "maybe it would." He grinned and pushed her into a snow-filled bough. She recovered and tossed a fistful of snow in his direction.

"Let's get out of here," Flory said as she reached for Bobby's hand, "or there'll be neither rabbit come." Her eyes were radiant as she pushed her shoulder into Jimmy's arm and knocked him sideways.

They talked on their way to the house and while they worked their way through the path that Daddy used for wood. They found two more rabbit signs and set the snares like they had done near the *Annie May*.

"Now we wait," Flory said as she dusted the snow from her mittens and contemplated their handiwork.

The next day, they found two empty snares. The wire had been pulled from the third. They set another to replace it and secured this one tighter.

"Do you think we'll catch one today?" Jimmy asked as they walked along the point.

"Why do you suppose we're checking?" Flory replied.

Jimmy stopped and turned to her. "I didn't think of it that way," he said ruefully before breaking into a run along the path.

"Hey, wait for me," she cried out, giggling and chasing after him as he darted into the woods.

She found him, wide-eyed and on his knees, in front of the snare. Jimmy wore a grin he simply couldn't contain. He jumped up and lifted her off her feet.

Flory laughed when he released her. "All this for a rabbit?"

"All this for a rabbit," he said. With that, he fell to his knees once more and went about collecting the animal and resetting the snare. Flory knelt beside him and let him do the work. "I thought you were placating me," he said as he gave her a sideways glance. "I didn't think you believed there'd be a rabbit here."

"That's an odd thing to say, Jimmy. Why would I do that?"

He studied her face. There was a long yet comfortable silence before he spoke. "That's just it," he whispered. "You wouldn't."

Flory watched his features relax. His eyes sparkled. "You wouldn't," he stated matter-of-factly before returning to the snare.

Jimmy fumbled with the wire and hesitated with the animal, but she didn't interfere.

"Tie a length of line around its hind legs and hang it over the hatchet," she instructed when he got up. "That's what Daddy used to do."

Jimmy nodded and took the twine she offered.

"You came prepared," he said.

"You have to be prepared," Flory replied. "Always."

21

Flory believes in me. It was the oddest thing. Something had come over him in the woods. It was a different Jimmy who entered the house with two rabbits swinging from the helve. His mother had coddled him for as long as he could remember. She had never made him feel the way Flory's simple statement had.

No matter how badly he did in school, no matter how many times he fooled up in the store, no matter what other mothers might have said about his spoiled upbringing, Jimmy's mother always explained it away. He would run to her and tell her about the things that made him feel bad so she could comfort him and say the right words to excuse him.

Like the time he had taken Emma Winsor's scribbler and torn out two pages so she would get in trouble for not having her homework done. Jimmy's mother spoke to the teacher and donated pencils to the school. She gave Emma's mother three scribblers for Emma and one for each of her siblings. Jimmy didn't get in trouble like the rest of his classmates would have. He had been downright mean to Emma because he could—and because he could get away with it.

William Bailor, his father, had been trying to change this behaviour—probably the only way he knew how. Jimmy had been too stupid to see that. His father would have had sympathy for Jimmy's seasickness if he had shown interest like the rest of them. Instead, he sat on the nets and did minimal work. He ate peaches and apricots while the crewmen had bread and tea.

Yes, he was seasick, but there were times when he wasn't. He laboured hardest when he was afraid of his father's wrath. Even then it was minimal. It dawned on him that if he were any of the others, he wouldn't like Jimmy, either. But that was the old Jimmy, the entitled one who couldn't get out of his own way, the good-for-nothing son that his father had tried to change.

Why would I do that? Flory had asked him. Jimmy shook his head and closed his eyes when he remembered those simple words and the innocent way in which they were spoken. She believed in him. Flory had no doubt that he had seen a rabbit trail. She had no doubt they would catch a rabbit—she had no doubt in him. In truth, he was the one who had doubted himself.

Perhaps that was what Mr. George and Raymond had tried to relay in their own way when they told him stories. He had listened, and he hadn't dismissed them like *he* had been dismissed. The two old gentlemen were often dismissed by others. But Jimmy gave them his time and didn't judge their words.

He smiled at the thought of the two old men smoking pipes on the bench in the summer. Mother would have put the bench in the storeroom for the winter, and Jimmy suspected they wouldn't be allowed to go into the store. His mother tolerated them because they talked to customers, so she wouldn't have to. When he thought about it, he had seen his father sit with them on blowy days. He didn't remark on it at the time because he was too self-absorbed.

Jimmy Bailor, what a waste of your years.

That waste was over today. He mattered. He contributed, and he did his share. He didn't need reminding of that. He wasn't a child.

"How do I clean these things?" Jimmy asked as he offered them to Flory.

"I'll show you. We have to go out to the chopping block."

Flory poked her head into the bedroom. "Lizzy, rabbit soup for supper." Indiscernible mumbling from inside distracted Flory before she returned.

Outside, she showed Jimmy how to skin and clean the rabbit and left him to take care of the second one. Once he had mangled the rabbit, he wasn't sure what to do with the waste. Gathering it up, he tossed it on the manure pile behind the barn. He would check with Flory when he went inside.

The door to the bedroom was closed. He laid the pan on the table, washed the blood from his hands in the porch, and went for vegetables from the cellar. When he returned, Lizzy was sitting on the daybed. His breath caught. He hadn't seen her since she had delivered the baby weeks ago. She was gaunt and whiter than anyone he had ever seen.

Lizzy gave him a flaccid smile. "I can't look that bad," she muttered, and he strained to hear her.

Jimmy wasn't sure what to say—and he was horrified when he heard the words, *Yes, you do*, come out of his mouth. However, Lizzy's lips twisted upward in a faint smile.

"You're a fright," Flory said from the doorway. She carried Caroline to the table. "But you're up. That's a good sign."

"I'll get you tea and molasses," Jimmy said. When he brought them to Lizzy, she couldn't hold the weight of the cup. Jimmy sat beside her so she could lean on him for support.

Flory cut and fried the rabbit and peeled the vegetables. She made everything look so easy, Jimmy observed. Once the soup simmered, she noticed Lizzy asleep against his chest.

"She drank it all," he said.

"Let's get her settled on the daybed. It'll be good for her to be out among us."

The baby cried. "I'll feed her," Jimmy volunteered.

"Are you sure?"

"Yes. Might as well help with that."

Flory lifted the baby and smelled the diaper. "I don't think you want to deal with this first." She laughed when he blanched. "Don't worry. I'll do it."

She settled Caroline into Jimmy's arms, and he stiffened. "You won't break her," Flory reassured him. She rubbed his shoulder. "Relax. She'll sense you're afraid."

Jimmy's heart raced. He took a deep breath before settling himself with the little girl. Flory busied herself about the kitchen and kept her eye on him. When the infant stopped drinking, she showed him how to burp her.

"Did that noise come from this tiny thing?" he asked, and she laughed.

Bobby climbed on the bench beside him and rested against his shoulder. The boy asked him questions, stuck a finger in his ear, pulled his hair, and smoothed it out. Flory sat by the stove and drank a cup of tea. She mouthed *thank you* when he glanced her way.

Jimmy did his best to stop himself from blushing. She smiled, and that turned him crimson.

Flory took the sleeping baby from him after the second round of burping. He put a coat and mittens on Bobby and took him to the barn to tend to the animals.

The boy was a welcome distraction. Jimmy liked showing him things. Perhaps the child looked up to him, and that balanced his sense of worth, because his secret gnawed at his sense of right and wrong. Juniper Tickle and its inhabitants were growing on him. He wouldn't ruin that by telling them what he really was.

A coward.

22

Winter coveted its hold on Juniper Tickle. It began as a blinding snowstorm in late February that lasted into the night of the third day. Then bitter temperatures accompanied high winds from the north and didn't let up for several days. Everything outside was a constant shifting white: the land, the air, and the sky.

The stove wouldn't heat any of the adjacent rooms, so they closed the doors to protect against the draft. For added warmth they laid clothing to fill the gaps between the bottoms of the doors and the floor. They spent days and nights in the kitchen.

Jimmy went to the barn daily to feed and water the animals, using a rope strung between the clothesline pole and the barn to make his way back and forth. He got himself turned around the first day after a white squall blew in the path he had shovelled to the wellhouse. By the time the heavy blow passed, he couldn't get out of the wellhouse. Flory came to his rescue after he was gone too long for her liking.

"What have you gotten yourself into this time?" she said as she scraped snow from the door.

"I got what I came for." He grinned, holding up the bucket.

"Oh, Jimmy, what would we do without you?" Flory said as she secured the door's latch and followed him back to the house. "I would have left you there, you know," she said impishly. "Only for Lizzy wanted you to finish the book, you'd have suffered the cold a bit longer."

Flory had a way of making things all right. Her words didn't hurt. If it had been his father who had found him, Jimmy wouldn't have lived it down. But with Flory, things were forgotten.

"I am the way I am, just like you are the way you are," she said one day while she was showing him how to milk the goat. "How could you know?"

"But *you* know," he replied.

"It's easier for me because I've seen it done so many times." Flory laid her hand on his shoulder. "Jimmy, whatever came before now doesn't matter. You can't let it get in the way. We need the best of you, here and now, if we are going to see that boat in the spring."

It took him three days to go to the stable for milk without her, but he went alone every day since.

"Bess is starting to dry up," Flory said as she looked over his shoulder. "I think it's all this cold." She had accompanied Jimmy to the stable to feed and water the livestock and, as she had put it, to get the stink of the house off her.

"Isobel and Jack have to go in one pen for a while or there'll be no milk," she said as she pulled hay from the loft. Daddy kept the goats on a cycle, she explained, so there would be milk year-round.

"Do you name them all?" Jimmy asked as he finished with Bess.

Flory laughed and nodded as she stepped into the horse's pound. "Dandy, boy," she said. "You won't get to stretch your legs for a while."

The horse neighed and fidgeted.

"What's wrong, boy?" She patted the horse's neck. "Jimmy, help me take off the blanket." Flory indicated for him to approach the horse from the other side. "It's just Jimmy," she cooed at the animal.

"What's wrong with him?" Jimmy asked as he slid along the wall toward the trough.

"He probably senses your fear. You're not afraid of Jimmy," she added, softening her tone. She met Jimmy's eyes. "Hand him some hay. That might quiet him."

The horse's skittishness transferred to Jimmy. He reached in for hay, and the horse pulled toward him. Jimmy yelped, but Flory kept a firm hand on the horse's mane. "Dandy," she scolded. "It's Jimmy. Behave yourself."

Flory coaxed the animal as Jimmy offered it hay. The horse's eyes were wide. "Let's not bother with the blanket until tomorrow. I'll brush him down then."

She herded Isobel in with Jack in the small pound. The goats bleated and the sheep *baaed* at the change in routine. "You'll all be out tomorrow," Flory reassured them. She collected a fistful of hay and threw it in the manger.

"They're as restless as us from being crammed in here so long."

Jimmy closed the door and followed her lead.

"We'll have to shovel for a bit and break the ice on the stream before letting them all out in the lower meadow. We can give them hay there," Flory said as she watched her footing on the way to the house.

Jimmy turned when the barn noises grew louder. The chickens clucked and flapped, and the horse's stomping mixed with a cacophony of cries from the goats and sheep. Flory laid her hands on his waist as she passed him on the narrow-beaten path.

"Something's wrong?" Jimmy asked.

"Something's wrong." She plodded ahead of him.

Flory's hand capped her eyes as she gazed into the distance. A vast whiteness showed nothing out of place. Drafts of wind picked up snow and swirled it into eddies before dropping it and taking the next flakes for a romp. The landscape had a fluidity that gave it life when a dusting of snow blew across the meadows.

Jimmy ran his gaze from the ice-packed ocean on the horizon to the stable. The animals' distress increased, but he saw nothing out of place. He answered Flory's shrug with one of his own. The pair shuffled toward the stable and across the bridge as they searched for what the animals sensed.

"Might be a fox got the chickens all worked up. That might make the others restless after being in the stable so long."

"What do we do with the fox?" Jimmy asked.

"If Daddy were here, he'd shoot it. We need every one of those chickens to get through the winter."

"Will you shoot it? Have you ever fired a gun?"

"Nope," Flory said. "But I'll do what I must. Scaring it away won't work if it's hungry."

The truth of it wasn't lost on Jimmy. He knew from experience.

Suddenly, Flory, red-faced and frantic, grabbed on to him and yanked him in the opposite direction. She shouted, "*Run!*"

Jimmy turned and lost his balance, but she propelled him forward. Flory was fast, and something told him not to delay her.

Panic assaulted him by the time he laid his foot on the back step. She clambered to rush him through and slam the door.

"What are we going to do? What are we going to do?" she cried. Flory's chest heaved as she pressed her back to the door.

Jimmy folded over and laid his hands on his knees as he tried to catch his breath. Fear gripped him. "What is it?" he wheezed before a thud sounded outside, followed by a snarl. Something scratched and pushed on the door.

"I don't know," Flory said. "It's enormous and white with sharp, bloodied teeth. It came around the barn from the manure pile."

"A polar bear?"

"I don't know. I've never seen one," Flory said as she pulled Jimmy from the porch into the kitchen. She closed the second door behind him. "Until now, I suppose."

Lizzy's ashen face looked up from the daybed. Her sunken eyes met Flory's. She pulled the quilt back and struggled to sit.

"What's wrong?"

"There's a polar bear outside," Jimmy exclaimed.

"A . . . a polar bear?" Lizzy looked from them to the baby in the box beside her and then to Bobby, who stared at them from the table.

"The gun is at your place," Flory said in resignation.

"I'll get it," Jimmy said. He held the knob on the front door and gazed back to them.

"No! Take the babies," Lizzy begged him. Wood splintered behind the house, and a fierce growl split the air. "Go," she pressed. "Leave me. That will give you time."

"Elizabeth White," Flory said. "As much as we need a miracle, it won't be you."

"I'll slow you too much," Lizzy replied flatly. Her words, spoken in a matter-of-fact tone, were not wrong.

"We'll all go," Flory said, her tone just as sharp and leaving no room for debate. "Besides, if that bear caught hold of you, you'd be gobbled in one bite and he'd still be hungry." She helped Lizzy from the bench and into her boots. "We'd stand no chance at all once he got a taste of flesh."

"There's no path," Jimmy noted as he gazed across the tickle. "The snow is deep."

"Then we'll follow your tracks," Flory said breathlessly. "No need to look back. We'll be there."

Flory held his eyes. "Just go."

Jimmy heard Lizzy's protests as he sprinted from the gallery. He loped and plowed through the snow. His heart pounded as wood shattered and Bobby screamed somewhere behind him.

This wasn't a time for Jimmy to second-guess himself. There was only time for him to be the best he could be—anything less would mean death for them all. Thoughts of Flory's words, and him letting Flory go for the gun, and carrying Lizzy and the children, were fleeting distractions. They depended on him. He hopped the ice pans and scaled the embankment on the opposite shore. Scrabbling for footholds, he plunged forward, eyeing the house. A snowdrift blocked the door. His foot went down in a hole and threw him off balance, but he recovered before falling. His mouth throbbed where his teeth had slammed shut on his tongue, and he tasted blood.

Pushing snow with his arms and legs, and with his heartbeat pounding in his ears, Jimmy bypassed the steps, hoping he could reach the window from the ground. He breathed a sigh when he rounded the corner, but his relief was short-lived. After pushing up under the sash, he was dismayed when the window wouldn't budge. He struck it with his elbow, and glass shattered inward. Jimmy went through behind it, headfirst.

When he spent the night there with Bobby, he had moved the gun to the pantry, and he made straight for it. With the gun in hand, he dived through the window again and rolled in the snow to break his fall. As he rounded the corner, his heart exploded into a gallop.

Flory was trying to pull Lizzy onto the sea ice, but her sister-in-law wouldn't budge. Instead, she handed baby Caroline to Flory and lay down on the ground, refusing to move. Flory turned to Bobby, laid the baby in his arms, and pointed him toward Jimmy.

Panic seized Jimmy. The ice pans were ragged and pushed up with the tide. Bobby could easily fall between the chunks and be lost along with his baby sister.

That got him moving.

Jimmy couldn't hear anything over the roar in his ears. His legs wobbled before catching on the ice pan, and he sprinted ahead, holding the gun in front of him.

The bear hadn't spent much time inside the house. It broke through the front door, stood on its hind legs on the steps, and roared as Flory dragged on Lizzy's leg. Lizzy turned over and used her elbows to pull away from her.

"Stay there," Jimmy yelled as he swept up Bobby and Caroline in his arms and sat them on the middle of a flat ice floe. Bobby was bawling right along with his sister. "You're a brave boy," Jimmy said as he sidestepped them and kept going. "Everything will be all right."

"Let me go," Lizzy screamed. "Let it have me."

"Come on, Lizzy," Flory growled through clenched teeth.

"Save the children. Flory, you must save them youngsters."

"You're not getting out of looking after them that easy," Flory yelled back at her. "You hear me?" She braced her foot into the icy ridge and hauled.

Jimmy leaped onto the bank beside Flory and lifted the gun. Flory was calling to him, but he was so focused on what was in front of him he didn't catch what she was telling him. Everything in him was pounding and trembling. He had seen his father and Dan Acreman shoot seals and saltwater ducks. They just pointed and pulled the trigger.

"It's easy," he whispered. "Point and pull."

That's what he did.

Nothing happened.

The bear was still coming.

"Jimmy, I have the cartridges," cried Flory.

The polar bear galloped toward them. Flory leaped up to face it. Stretching her arms wide, she shouted and snarled. She tossed Jimmy a shell from her apron pocket as she continued to bellow at the massive creature. The bear slowed and stood to face its opposition. Lizzy propped herself up on her elbows to edge toward it.

"I don't know where this goes," said Jimmy.

Flory grabbed the gun, inserted the shell, and returned it to him. Turning back to the beast, she made herself as big as she could and shouted again before grabbing Lizzy's ankle.

Too scared to think, Jimmy raised the gun and fired. The force of the recoil landed him on his rear.

He had struck the bear in the throat. It shook itself, sending blood across the white terrain. Then it roared, batted its head with its paws, and charged. Flory took the gun, ejected the cartridge, and loaded it again in one fluid motion. Jimmy was scrambling to his feet when she fired directly into the polar bear's face. She threw the gun at Jimmy as she was sent backward into the snow.

"I lost it," Flory screamed as she fumbled for another cartridge. Jimmy fell to his knees beside her and pressed his hands into the snow. After several terrifying seconds of searching, he snatched the missing cartridge from the snow.

"It's the last one," Flory breathed. "I only took three."

Jimmy nodded and tried to calm his shaking hands. He reloaded, planted his feet, and fired, aiming for the biggest part of the enraged beast. He lay prone in the snow, paralyzed, as he stared up at the enormous creature. The bear staggered toward them on its hind legs, its growls ripping the air. Finally, it slowed and fell mere inches from Lizzy's outstretched hands.

Jimmy's relief was short-lived.

"Jimmy," Flory shouted. "The children."

He dropped the gun and leaped to his feet. Without hesitation, he stepped onto the unsteady ice. His foot twisted as he landed. Despite the pain, he dashed to Bobby. The boy had stayed where Jimmy had told him to stay. The baby, wrapped in Flory's coat, was crying on his lap.

"You did good," Jimmy said quietly as he picked them up and headed toward shore.

Flory pulled Lizzy from the snowbank, hugged her, and then issued her sister-in-law a tearful tongue-lashing for defying her.

"You'll catch your death," she said as she brushed snow from Lizzy's nightgown. Tears flowed freely from both women as they embraced.

"Fresh air is good for the soul," Lizzy said through a fit of coughing. Her face was the colour of snow. She gestured to the fallen bear. "Don't worry, Flory. Only that thing will be dying today."

"You take them in," Jimmy said as he motioned to the children. "I'll carry Lizzy."

"I can walk," Lizzy protested.

Flory let her go and immediately reached out to keep her from falling. "Sure you can," she said as she nodded to Jimmy.

Jimmy scooped Lizzy into his arms. She was surprisingly light. They gave the dead bear a wide berth as they made their way back home. By the time they reached the house, Jimmy's heart rate had almost returned to normal.

"We have to make sure it's the only one," Flory cautioned as she beckoned to Jimmy. She snatched cartridges from the pantry as he retrieved the gun. When they passed the stable, they saw remnants of the skinned rabbits from a few days before had been unearthed.

"Sorry," Jimmy said. "That thing must have caught their scent."

"I'd rather that than the animals," Flory said without breaking stride. "Or worse, imagine if it had gotten in the house when we were here. Good thing for those rabbit skins, I'd say."

They followed the bear's tracks to the ice, all the while searching near and far, gun loaded and ready. When they approached the beach where the bear had come ashore, they stopped to watch the ice-packed sea. Nothing moved on the ice. It groaned as slabs pitched and piled against each other. Flory's eyes darted with frustration and fear as her head turned toward every sound. Jimmy accompanied her along the shoreline in both directions before she concluded the bear had been alone.

Back home, Flory was shocked by the state of the house. She ran to the pantry. "Thankfully it thought us more appealing," she said. She reached out and tousled her nephew's hair before moving her fingertips across Caroline's blanket. "Not you, though, Lizzy. You're too thin." That put a smile on both women's lips.

"We were lucky," Lizzy said.

Jimmy and Flory worked on the structure of the house. They managed to seal the front door with a couple of nails they found in the barn. The hinge could be fixed when Daddy came home. The back door was in tatters, and the door between the kitchen and porch hung loose.

"We can't leave it like this," Flory said. "The storm door is all right, but it's not meant to stop the draft." She had kept it closed over the main door during the night or before a snowfall to provide an extra layer of protection. It wasn't meant to be used for any other purpose.

"Get the door at our place," Lizzy offered. "Bart can fix it in the spring."

Jimmy trailed Flory, and he cleared the snow from the step before they took the door, hinges and all, back to the house. He was happy enough to fix it into the frame with Flory's help, though every cluck, bleat, or neigh from the barn kept them both on edge.

They slept in the kitchen for the next week, Flory and Jimmy taking turns on watch. It took them that long to stop imagining every sound was something ominous. They ate roasted bear and bear soup. The meat revived Lizzy's poor health better than anything else she had eaten. Though she was tired and listless, Lizzy managed to stay awake a full day at the end of the week. Flory's spirits lifted, and so did Jimmy's.

23

“Yes, Jimmy,” Flory said as she trudged along the trail behind him. He held her nephew’s hand on one side and the axe helve, which was resting on his shoulder, on the other. “The wood is already down. We just have to pare the limbs off it and pile it.”

“Do you think we’ll figure out the riggings?” Jimmy asked.

“I’m sure we will.”

They had put Dandy in the yard for two days. The first day, the horse got tired of moving forward without the sled, and they let him loose in the meadow for a run. The second day, they harnessed Dandy so he couldn’t move. When they finally set the animal free, he walked away with Jimmy in tow, tangled in the reins. Flory grinned as she thought of him squealing. She laughed so hard she couldn’t command the horse to *whoa* until Jimmy was legs up in a snow pile near the river. He untangled himself from the rope before Dandy decided to cross the river and head for the trees. Jimmy had the biggest smile when he popped out of the snow a free man. He let Dandy go for a trot on the hillside before bedding him down in the barn.

If that had been Daddy or Bart, they would have been vexed. There would be cursing. But Jimmy, he took everything in stride with good humour. Flory had yet to see him cross.

Today, they decided to give the horse a break. It didn't do much good knowing how to tackle the horse if they had no reason to tackle Dandy.

"Turn that axe sideways," she reminded him. "We don't want you slipping and cleaving yourself open." The axe head shifted to point toward the woods, and Jimmy didn't break a stride.

Flory held the hatchet and carried a lunch sack. Today she wore Tommy's pants. She had tied them around her waist with a rope. It was easier to get around the tangle of felled trees without a skirt catching in the limbs.

She looked skyward. The glass was true again, forecasting good weather. The wood had to be brought out to the yard while the sleds still had snow. Spring was coming fast. Flory thought she had seen a gull the day before, and that had set them in motion with the horse.

When she returned her attention to the trail, Jimmy and Bobby were sprawled on the ground. She gasped. "What happened?" she called as she hurried toward them.

Bobby's loud giggle echoed in the still morning air.

"We're making snow angels," Jimmy said as his hands and legs swung across the snow.

"What? I thought you'd fallen."

"No," Jimmy said as he grinned up at her. "Make an angel with us."

"I'm not getting covered in snow," Flory said. She smirked. "That looks more like a crow than an angel."

Flory eyed Jimmy's big boyish smile beside her nephew's. At a glance they were so much like each other she had to close her eyes and look again. When she opened them, Jimmy had snaked a hand around her ankle and tugged her down.

"Jimmy," she groaned as she hit the snow.

"You worry too much," he said as he flicked snow her way.

Her nephew's red face looked down upon her, and he kissed her forehead. "Angel," he said as he flopped back in the snow.

"All right. Just one, then we have work to do." She scooped a mittenful of snow and walloped Jimmy. After making four angels each, they set out again.

They came to a clearing, where Flory announced they had arrived.

"Everything looks white," Jimmy said. "How do you know where the wood is?"

"The branches sticking up would be what we are paring," Flory said as she swept her hand toward a mound at the side of the path. "We can work our way in."

Jimmy rolled his eyes. "I knew that," he said.

She laughed. "I have no doubt."

Bobby explored the trail where they began their work. They untangled downed trees that had dried out over the year, making them lighter and easier to handle. As they chopped the limbs, Jimmy stacked them for the little fellow to play in to keep the child from wandering away.

"Do you think we have a load for Dandy yet?" Jimmy asked.

Flory sized it up. "That's not a load for me," she said with a grin. "Dandy's loads would be piled almost to my head."

"Really? I never know when you and Lizzy are fooling with me and when you're serious."

"Yes, Jimmy. Really." Flory smiled. Then, after a pause, she added, "Maybe."

"See? You womenfolk are good."

Mid-morning, Flory boiled the kettle for tea. They ate raspberry jam bread with it. When they went back to work, they took turns, one pulling out the tree while the other pared it. They both shed their coats and worked in harmony until Flory declared, "I think that's a horseload, now." Jimmy had already cleared a tree. He locked eyes with her and cocked a questioning brow, so she said, "Maybe one more stick."

Jimmy let the big tree fall across the path toward her. Flory stepped in with the axe and hacked at the lower branches. She ran the blade beneath the trunk, where the metal clanged on the frozen knots as she worked. Her arms grew tired from swinging the axe. A branch snapped underneath, and the stick shifted enough for the blade to strike a glancing blow. Flory lost her footing with the unexpected ease at which inertia took the axe. She reached for the trunk to steady herself, but that movement sent the tree rolling on top of her. The axe fell from her hand, and she yelped as she went under.

Jimmy was there in an instant and pulled the half-pared tree off her. His eyes were wild when they met hers.

"I'm all right," she assured him. "I took a tumble, that's all. It happens."

As she moved her legs under her, she felt a stab of pain. She reached a probing hand to her calf. Her mitten was red when she pulled it away.

"You're cut," Jimmy said as he tossed the tree away from her and dropped on his knees before the injured leg.

She twisted her knee to see what had happened. The axe lay on the ground beneath her, and Tommy's pants were ripped and saturated with blood.

"I wasn't expecting that," she said as she stretched her leg out and reached for Jimmy. "Help me up."

"Up?" Jimmy said. "What do you mean *up*?"

"I have to see how deep this is," Flory said as she tried to move without his help. "And I want to get off the snow."

Jimmy let her go and assembled an armload of discarded limbs. He made a place for her to sit, then lifted her with care, moving her to the seat. She winced, and he apologized.

The ground was red. "It looks worse than it is, I'm sure," she said. "Do you have your knife?"

He patted his shirt, then snatched his coat and took the blade from the pocket. Pulling it open, he handed it to her. Flory cut the pant leg above the injury and peeled away the material. Blood oozed down her leg, soaking her sock and boot.

"What can I do?" Jimmy asked.

"I have to get home and get it cleaned. First, I've got to stop the blood. I need something to tie around my leg."

"You won't get home like this," he said. "I'll carry you."

"You're not going at that. I'll be all right."

"You're not all right." Jimmy glared at Flory. "You're not."

"First things first," she said. She was losing a lot of blood. It looked like the axe had peeled away the skin, and the flap had to be closed.

"I must stop the blood," she repeated. Jimmy pushed his coat toward her, but she shook her head. "It's too bulky to knot."

Jimmy tore at his shirt. Buttons burst clear and flicked into the snow. He pulled it off and handed it to her. Flory tied it tightly around her leg. Blood blossomed on the cotton.

"I need snow around it," she said as she reached for a fistful. Jimmy dug his forearms into the soft drift at the side of the path. He scooped as much as would balance there and dropped it on her leg. Flory patted it in.

When Bobby climbed up behind her and saw all the blood,

he started to cry and wrapped his arms around her neck. Flory began to shiver as Jimmy helped her into her coat.

"Bobby, you sit here on Flory. I'll bring you both for a ride."

The little boy's eyes peered at him over Flory's shoulder, and he nodded. His crying subsided to sniffles as Jimmy sat him on her lap.

She looked at him questioningly.

"I have to get you out of here."

"I can try walking," Flory said as she pushed her hands beneath her and attempted to stand.

"Stay where you are." Jimmy rooted through the boughs and selected the biggest one. He laid several others crossways on the branches, stretching another one in line with the bottom. "I'll sit you here," he said as he pointed to the greenery. He grabbed the limb and said, "I'll be like Dandy. I'll sled you home."

Helping Flory to the centre of the boughs, he placed her nephew in her lap. "Hold on here," he said as he clutched the thickest part of the limb and pointed them for home. Before he pulled away, he took his coat and draped it over the two of them.

"Jimmy, you should put that on," Flory said. "You'll catch your death."

"I'll be fine," he said as he tugged the makeshift sled. Once it started moving, it became easier to tow. Flory wouldn't argue. She had to get home.

"Jimmy," she said. He looked from her to the path and back again. "I need you to get turpentine when we get out. I have to seal the cut."

"I'll get whatever you need." He concentrated on the path, giving them a furtive glance with every other step.

"We can't lose the axe," she cautioned.

"I'll go back for it. Don't worry, Flory. I'll take care of things." His voice was calm despite his grim countenance.

Bobby whimpered as he clung to his aunt.

"I know." Flory directed a smile his way before she sagged into the branches. She rested her hand on her nephew's chest.

The way home was mainly a downhill slope. Jimmy gained speed, and his muscles strained as he controlled the makeshift sled amid many erratic stops and starts. He shouted to Lizzy from the bridge as they passed the stable.

Lizzy came to the door and took her son from them as Jimmy picked up Flory and carried her to the daybed. Before she could say anything, he pulled his coat from atop her and rushed through the door.

Flory explained what had happened as Lizzy boiled the kettle and ripped a pillowcase into strips to soak. Uncovering the wound, Flory watched as the bleeding began anew. Lizzy clicked her tongue and mumbled something about her being in the woods in the first place. Flory let her go on. She knew Lizzy was worried.

Jimmy returned a short time later. He carried a dozen strips of bark peppered with turpentine bubbles. "Is this enough?" he asked, his voice so low they could hardly hear him. He fidgeted while he waited.

"What's wrong?" Flory asked.

"What's wrong? What's *wrong*? How can you ask that?" he asked, his words coming quickly. "You're hurt and it's my fault."

"How did it get to be your fault?" Flory asked as Lizzy dabbed her leg. "You didn't have the axe."

"Exactly," he said. "I should have been doing it." Jimmy turned away from them toward the stove. There he lifted, shook, and moved the kettles several times.

"Hold on," Flory said. "No one is to blame. It was an accident." She watched him busy himself.

"Leave him alone," Lizzy whispered. "He's scared, that's all."

Flory nodded as Bobby sat beside her, clutching her arm. He was scared, too. Maybe when she thought about what could have happened, she would feel the same. She concentrated on Lizzy's ministering, holding the rind while Lizzy burst the bubbles and dripped the turpentine on her torn skin. Flory sucked in a breath as Lizzy pinched the wound and went to work with the needle and thread. Jimmy had disappeared, and she lay back on the daybed as Lizzy sewed. She was suddenly tired.

"Finished," Lizzy said. "Thankfully we've had lots of practice on Bart and Tommy." She grinned as she patted Flory's arm. "Have a nap."

Flory nodded. Her leg pained. She would have to take it easy for a few days. Her mind raced to all the things she had to do. Thoughts swirled in her head as she closed her eyes.

When she awoke, Lizzy was at the stove having a hushed conversation with Jimmy.

"I'm awake," she declared before she yawned.

"Time for you," Lizzy said. "I don't know how anyone can sleep in the middle of the day." She laughed, and so did Flory, remembering Lizzy's recent recovery.

"What can I say? It's my turn, I suppose."

"I have the axe home," Jimmy said. "The stable is done. The eggs are in."

"And the fool isn't long home from the woods," Lizzy said. "He pared out another pile of wood."

"Aww, Jimmy, you shouldn't have done that," Flory said.

"I have to earn my keep," he said. His face reddened as he cast his gaze downward. "I'm glad you're all right, Flory. I was petrified."

"You didn't look scared to me," she said softly. "That was some quick thinking. I allowed I'd have to hop all the way home."

Jimmy caught her eye and blushed again. "I wouldn't have let you do that," he said. "I would have brought you home on my back if the boughs didn't work."

"I wasn't scared," Flory said. She reached out toward him. He came to her, and she clasped his hand. "I knew I'd be just fine with you there."

"You'll be just fine on that daybed for the next week," Lizzy chided. "Don't you dare disobey me." She shook the spoon in her sister-in-law's direction. "Now, stew is done. Time to eat."

Flory groaned.

"You have to put up with my cooking, young lady," Lizzy said with a wide grin. "And best of all, there is nothing you can do about it now."

Jimmy laughed as he looked from one to the other. "You two frighten me."

"Good," the women said in unison.

24

Jimmy's apprehension for the coming spring was different this year. Last year he had dreaded the fishing season. His daily grind was meted out equally by his father and the sea that hated him—both disdained the lifestyle that had been soft on him.

Despite the lack of comforts in Juniper Tickle, and his growing list of faults, Jimmy had learned a lot about life and about himself in a few short months. Failings weren't forever under the right circumstances. Difficulties could be overcome.

He liked being seen as useful. He liked knowing he *was* useful. Outside influences that drew attention to his limitations, in what some would say were menial tasks, worried him. Perhaps if his father had been patient like Flory, Jimmy might have gained competence at fishing instead of always being a liability.

Here, he didn't feel like he was in the way. On the contrary, he contributed. He would even go as far as to say that his being there was vital to survival. Jimmy walked straighter, so confident in that knowledge. He grinned, though his cheeks protested, as if smiling were new to him.

He didn't feel small or inadequate for not knowing something. Instead, he was eager and capable, and Flory was willing to show him for those reasons. Today would be no different.

Jimmy laid potatoes in the middle of the kitchen as they made ready to set gardens.

"That's the last sack," he said as he eyed the three lumpy burlap bags. "Now what?

"We need to cut them," Flory said.

"All of them?"

"Yes." Flory laughed at Jimmy's expression. "I meant to tell you to bring in an empty sack. It'll give us a place to keep them. We have to leave the seed potatoes in the heat for a few days."

Jimmy returned as Flory settled on a chair in front of the potato mound, a knife in her hand.

"What are we cutting?" he asked as he took another knife from the table and pulled in a chair, along with another next to him for Bobby. Lizzy wanted to join them, but Flory had warned her it would be too much.

Flory hurried to the pantry. "Bobby can put the sculps in here for us," she said as she laid a pan near his chair.

"Sculps?" Jimmy asked.

"It's just the part without eyes. We don't want to waste."

"Eyes?"

Flory grinned. "I think you're kidding, but I'll show you, anyway." She rolled a potato in her hand. "These indents are beginning to sprout."

She poked her finger at her nephew's stomach. "It's the potato's belly button," she said as she tickled the boy. "You'd better keep yours covered or you'll sprout." The little boy giggled. "Some of the potatoes have lots of belly buttons," she went on, playfully reaching for Bobby again. He scooted backward on the chair, laughing.

Flory eyed Jimmy. "We have to cut chunks around the belly

buttons." Again she reached for her nephew, who howled with laughter.

She rolled the potato and pointed. "This one has two. The potato is small, so we can cut it in half, making sure there's an eye on each one." Picking a larger potato, she pointed at it. "This one has only one eye at this end. We don't want to waste the whole thing, so we cut the sculp off and keep it for stew."

Flory gave the potato piece to Bobby, who climbed off the chair and dropped it in the pan. She put the other piece into the empty bag. "That's a start," she said.

Jimmy took one and cut it. He asked for her guidance a couple of times when the eyes were close or he wasn't sure. Before long they were working in a comfortable silence, side by side, while Lizzy dozed on the daybed and Caroline in the cradle.

When she got up, Lizzy sliced more than a dozen sculps and fried them. They stopped for tea and ate the light meal before finishing the task in the afternoon. After they filled a sack with seed, Jimmy pulled it to the porch.

"It will be warm enough there since we don't have an inside door to leave open." Flory didn't need to raise her eyebrows as a reminder of the bear, but she did.

A few days later, Jimmy dug furrows in the meadow alongside Flory. They had barrowed the manure and spread it in rows on the field. Jimmy learned not to waste the dung. Spreading it here and there wasn't acceptable. Flory used green twine to keep the rows from going askew and her heel over toe to mark the width. Four foot lengths for the ridge and two for the furrow. She said her father liked it that way. The ridge was the only section they fertilized.

Jimmy took Bobby to lay the seed. Flory forgot to tell him the eyes had to be up, so she went along behind him and fixed the first ridge, and he made sure the rest were correct. She was patient. He liked that about her.

"Don't go too far ahead," she said. "We have to put the clay over them before the crows or gulls see them."

Jimmy took a shovel and followed her lead. He covered two ridges to her one as the day grew hotter. Blackflies congregated, and no amount of swatting would get rid of them.

"Why don't you go in?" Jimmy suggested. "Take Bobby. I'll stay and do a bit more."

"We've got to get it done," Flory said as worry filled her face. "That won't happen with me in the house."

Jimmy's hands had blistered. Hers surely had, too. He knew she wouldn't go unless he did.

The next morning, Jimmy snuck out of bed at dawn and was in the garden before the sun came up. He had covered several ridges when he paused to watch the fog burn off the distant bay. The soft mist peeled back to reveal the thick forest on the shadowed side of the island. The trees waited patiently for their turn to bask. The ones in his view knew nothing of sunrises, only sunsets. They didn't long for nor expect anything else. He couldn't help but think that he had been like those trees in the dark the longest.

"You're on the go early," Flory said as she stood beside him. "What are you looking at?"

"Nothing, really," Jimmy said without taking his gaze from the vista. "And maybe everything."

"Wow," Flory said. She watched the horizon with him. "Can I interest you in porridge?"

"Yes," he said, but he didn't move.

"What do you see?" she asked.

"I can't explain it. There's peace here or something. Acceptance, maybe. I don't know. I like it."

"Well, porridge can't top that," Flory said. "But perhaps it will do."

"It will more than do," he said as he watched the first dregs of sun spill onto her face. It was his turn to bask. He sucked in a breath, confused by something foreign that hit his gut and spread warmly from there. Flory was the finest thing he had ever seen. Emma Winsor was pretty, according to the crowd in school, but he didn't see it. Emma wouldn't hold up in front of Flory. She was his first glimpse at something beautiful.

Flory must have felt his eyes on her, because she turned to look at him. She smiled, and her cheeks grew red.

"What? Is there something on me?" She patted her hair and her face. "What is it?"

"I thought there was a bee," Jimmy said as he reached out and pushed a strand of Flory's hair behind her ear.

"Too early for bees," she said. " And too early for Jimmy to be in the garden. Something's gotten into you. Come on."

Flory grabbed his hand and pulled him toward the house. She let him go and broke into a run. He chased her, and they both reached the step at the same time, laughing and breathless.

Jimmy couldn't shake the notion that this feeling of happiness wouldn't last. He had gained a taste of it here, but he was living a lie. As spring intruded on the land and the sea, it stirred Jimmy's wariness of what was to come. The old Jimmy and the new Jimmy couldn't coexist—and the new Jimmy couldn't come to terms with how he could resolve the issue of simply being Jimmy Bailor.

25

Flory sat on the back step and watched the sun drain into the horizon. Clouds swirled, red and golden, in its wake.

"Red sky at night, sailor's delight," she murmured.

The old wives, or whoever told that tale, clearly were not in her predicament. Maybe they had only conjectured to give a taste of hope because there was neither a sailor nor a delight to be found in Juniper Tickle. Hope was just as scarce.

What would have taken Daddy, Bart, and Tommy the better part of a day to do had run into a week for her and Jimmy. The dark rows of the potato drills deepened in shadow as the last of the light pulled out of the day, leaving no sign of their toil.

Flory rubbed her hands together, letting her fingers caress the hardening skin. At least the sting was gone. To her credit, Lizzy had refused to let Flory dip her blistered hands into the dough pan and had taken on the task herself. Though Lizzy had to lie down the rest of the morning as the dough rose, rise it did, to Lizzy's delight.

Maybe that's how the saying should go—Flory's hands are a fright, to Lizzy's delight.

Flory chuckled. The worry over Lizzy's recovery was in the past. She sighed. Despite her admonitions, Lizzy was pushing herself, and Flory saw changes in her every day. She was able to stay up later, take full care of Caroline—and now bake bread.

There were newer troubles, or maybe older problems that had been given room to blossom. If Daddy came home, the vegetables were in the ground. If Daddy didn't come home, it would be impossible to survive in the tickle despite the potatoes. She couldn't fish. Fish turned into kerosene, flour, salt, sugar, and everything they needed to get through the winter. Without staples, they would have to leave. But they had nowhere to go. Everything depended on Daddy coming home. As dire as their predicament the previous fall had been, as spring came to Juniper Tickle, the outlook was even worse. This was something she wouldn't have thought possible, yet here it was.

Flory shuddered. The transition from a black sky to a starry one had begun but did nothing to lighten her mood. She rested her forehead on her knees and closed her eyes. Footfalls and the door's creak roused her. She leaned on the door jamb as Jimmy came out on the step.

"Lizzy said to come get you," he said softly.

"Is anything wrong?"

"No, nothing like that," Jimmy said as he laid a hand on her shoulder. "She said we need to discuss something, that's all."

Flory followed Jimmy inside.

Lizzy's sallow cheeks looked grim as she raised her eyes to greet her sister-in-law. "Thought we'd help you work through your troubles," she said as she pointed to the teacup steaming on the table. "Don't say you have none, either."

"I can leave you to it," Jimmy said.

"You're as much a part of this as any of us," Lizzy replied as she gestured to the bench for him to sit. She wagged her finger at Flory to silence any protest.

"Okay, what are we going to do?" Lizzy asked them. "I know that's a big question, but we all have to answer to it. It can't be on you alone."

"Jimmy will be leaving on the boat," Flory said.

"Let Jimmy speak for himself," Lizzy interrupted. "We have to figure this out. Jimmy?"

"It doesn't have to be the first boat," he said. "I can wait until—"

"Jimmy, there may only be one boat," Flory said.

Lizzy gave her a look. "How do you figure that? There was one every month or so last year."

"Only if there's fish." Flory looked at them both. "That's the limits we live within."

"Then we'll fish," said Jimmy.

Flory couldn't help but laugh. "Have you ever fished from a dory before?"

"No," he said, his cheeks reddening in the lamplight.

Lizzy patted Jimmy's hand. "Though it's kind of you," she said, "you go on home."

"Your mother and father will have you given up for dead," Flory said. "Maybe you've a sweetheart waiting." She left that sentiment dangling, but to her dismay, Jimmy didn't acknowledge who or what waited for him back home. Flory realized then she knew very little about the Jimmy before Juniper Tickle, the young man who seemed to have led a bit of a charmed life.

"You don't want to be stuck with two crooked women and two children, besides," Lizzy said softly. "You owe us nothing, Jimmy. This is our trouble. You go home when you get the chance."

"I can't just leave you here. I know I haven't been much help—"

"Jimmy," Flory cut in, "we would not have made it through the winter without you. That's the truth."

"Well, I can't just leave you here," he repeated, pushing his fingers along his scalp. He ensnared fistfuls of hair and pulled as he squeezed his eyes shut.

"The thing is, Daddy, Bart, and Tommy always got us ready," Flory said. "We may not have them this year. We just don't know." A wave of sadness moved through her. "They may never be back." Her last words were a whisper acknowledging this as truth. The words, once spoken, had sharp, jagged edges that tore at her throat as they reinforced the notion that she might never see them again.

She crossed her arms and stroked her elbows. One thing at a time was the only way to deal with it, but the uncertainty meant they had to prepare for the worst. The finality was in accepting the loss of her father—her family—and she certainly didn't want to deal with that on top of her daily affairs.

"Your family is probably going through the same thing," Flory said. "Not knowing. You have to go back."

Jimmy stroked the bridge of his nose until he held it in a pinch. He said, "I can't see how I can leave you to do this all by yourselves. What would that make me?" He pushed away from the table and went outside.

"Even if Jimmy stayed, it's not enough," Lizzy said as she clutched her sister-in-law's arm to keep her from following him. "He can't fish by himself. I certainly can't go. You can't go, either, Flory. That would take the life right out of you."

"I don't know how to fish. Not like Daddy," Flory admitted.

She hearkened back to last year, when the men rowed in,

dories full, and to all the work that was still left to do. Gutting and splitting—she couldn't do what was integral to the grade when selling the product. She did the work of making it and drying it, and that was hard enough with Lizzy helping, which she couldn't this year. Catching the fish was only part of it. Brining it just right, then lugging it out to dry, turning it, and barrowing it back to be packed. Lastly, taking it all out again for the merchant boat. Then starting over. This was all back-breaking work. She wasn't afraid of it—she just didn't have the time to do it all.

"What will we do?" Flory asked, not expecting Lizzy to know any more than she did.

"If Jimmy left on the first boat, do you think he'd come back?" Lizzy asked her. "Even if we go, we can't leave here on our own."

"I don't know where we'd go. How would we survive? What about the children?"

Lizzy shook her head. "I don't know."

But a flicker in Lizzy's eye indicated to Flory she might know, and that maybe an uncertain winter in Juniper Tickle wasn't all that bad. Flory wouldn't ask. She had enough to deal with.

Jimmy returned and sat at the table. "I'm not going," he said emphatically. "I'd be dead if it weren't for the both of you. Maybe dead is how I should remain at home."

"Jimmy," Lizzy chided him. "You can't mean that."

"I do," he said. His face was sincere yet sad. "Nobody is looking for me. Dead is the best place for me."

"Nobody was able to look for you over the winter. Do you know how hard it is to get in here?" Flory reasoned.

"It wasn't so hard that a boat couldn't make it by itself."

"That's different. Currents, winds, and tides can do strange things when left alone. We know that from the bear."

"It's when you get people involved, that's when things get complicated," Lizzy added as she patted Jimmy's forearm. "That boat mightn't have ended up here if people were on board to change its bearing."

"And we wouldn't be in this predicament," Flory added.

She took a long sip of tea and looked at them both. Both Jimmy and Lizzy were waiting for her decision. She held the fate of Juniper Tickle in her seventeen-year-old hands. Well, almost eighteen, she supposed, once summer came in.

"Even if you stayed," Flory said as she looked at Jimmy, "there is no guarantee that we could catch and make enough fish to get us through. Even with the know-how for it, we don't know the fishing grounds. Daddy had his shoals that didn't fail him, but I don't know where they are."

"We could find them. Or find new shoals."

Jimmy's excitement for the possible made her smile. "I wish it worked like that." If it had, she would almost be willing to try. Almost. But she had to be realistic—possibility was not something on which to gamble their lives. They couldn't eat likelihood.

"I think we all need to leave on that boat," Flory said. "There may be no other chance."

"What?" Lizzy asked, her eyes wide. "That was the last thing I thought I'd hear from your mouth."

"Me, neither. And it's not easy," said Flory, her face pensive. "But we didn't think we'd be here by ourselves, either. We didn't think Daddy would be accused of murder. Lots of things happened that we didn't expect. But we've got to think about lots of other things now. Leaving is one."

"Flory, they'll be back. I know they will."

"What about if they don't?" Flory asked, waiting for Lizzy to meet her eyes. "I saw Momma die here. You almost met the same fate. What about if one of us falls and breaks a leg or an arm? What if something worse had to happen when I cut my leg? It will be the death of us all."

"Now you're just being silly. We can't live for what-ifs."

"We have to this time," Flory said softly. "What if Daddy doesn't come back? What will happen to Bobby and Caroline?"

"I wish that boat had come ashore somewhere else," Lizzy said. "Looks like William Bailor and his crew will be the demise of Juniper Tickle."

Jimmy stood up and checked the fire. He laid in a junk and closed the damper.

"I wish we never knew a lot of things," Flory said. "But there is one thing I do know—if Daddy, Bart, and Tommy weren't in prison, they'd be here no matter what. They'd have come in on that ice with that bear. They are still in jail. What does that say about their fate?"

"I'll do what you do, Flory," Lizzy said. "If you say leave, we'll leave. Sell all these belongings for passage somewhere. Maybe to wherever Jimmy comes from . . ."

Jimmy left the kitchen and went outside.

"What's got into him?" Lizzy asked.

"He worked hard the last few days at the potatoes. Probably tired is all," Flory said, though she wondered the same thing.

"And he wants to stay," Lizzy said with a grin. "Maybe he's smitten."

Flory blushed. "It's late," she said as she picked up the cups. "Time to get to bed. Daylight will be here soon enough."

Lizzy laughed. "Maybe I have it wrong. Maybe it's somebody else who's smitten."

"Elizabeth White, you give that up now and go to bed," Flory said as she playfully whipped the dishtowel at Lizzy.

Lizzy yawned. "We can talk about the serious stuff in the morning. A good night's sleep might be all we need."

Flory's mind was tossed. Should they go? Should they stay? What if they chose wrong? She slept fitfully, haunted by a nightmare filled with bears.

The next morning donned a cloak of fog. It was so thick that Bart's place vanished within its clutches. Drizzle alternated with rain to add to the dreariness.

"I'll put bread in rise," Flory said.

"How about you lower the hem on Bobby's pants, and I'll mix the dough," Lizzy offered. "You can keep me in line from the daybed."

"I'll take care of the stable," Jimmy said. "Eggs, too."

He returned with the water bucket and five eggs a short time later before going to feed the animals.

Flory and Lizzy chatted, avoiding the conversation about Juniper Tickle for a more jovial morning. Lizzy mixed the dough and covered it when Flory mentioned Jimmy.

"He's gone a long time."

"Probably asleep in the hay," Lizzy said. "It's that kind of day."

"I suppose he's all right."

"Always the worrier. What could happen to him? We'd hear him calling if something was wrong."

"I can't help it," Flory said. "So much going on."

"We weren't going to talk about that," Lizzy said. "I'll take a walk when Caroline is fed. Want to fry an egg for Bobby?"

Flory put porridge in the pot and cracked yesterday's eggs into the pan. "Might as well have something warm," she said as she stirred the oats. Footsteps by the back door drew her attention.

"Jimmy, I thought you'd gone," she said.

"Who's Jimmy?" a familiar voice asked. "And what happened to the front door?"

Flory turned and faced a man who looked shockingly similar to her father. He was thin and gaunt and—older. His eyes didn't hold the twinkle she remembered. They were hard and bitter. She squinted to be sure she wasn't in a dream.

"Daddy," she said, her breath leaving her. He nodded and held out his arms. "Daddy," she cried as she threw herself at him. "You're home!"

26

Jimmy spent the morning heating water at Bart's place. He lit the fire, cleaned the glass from the floor, and hung a quilt over the window to keep out the draft. Debris had drifted in through the storm door since they had removed the porch door, but the mess was confined to a small area and hadn't made it to the kitchen. With the fire going, it was plenty warm for a bath. He swept and cleaned while he filled the tub.

He had told Lizzy what he wanted to do for Flory, and her, too, if she'd like. Flory had been working beside him in the garden for over a week. Digging and planting was hard work. All the while, she kept Bobby busy laying the seed potatoes and didn't waver with her smile. He didn't know another like her.

Lizzy had said to wait for just such a day as this or Flory wouldn't bide by a bath with work to do. He tried in vain to whistle. It just wouldn't come. Jimmy did a lot of thinking. He had to tell them who he was. Then his decision faltered, because they would think he was filling the tub so they wouldn't be mad.

Jimmy shouldn't have left it so long. That he knew, but time made it easier to continue than to shatter the existence he liked more and more. It wasn't a lie. That's how he had convinced himself to let it go on so long. But it wasn't the truth, another part of him argued. The truth was bent so much around the premise of a lie it no longer looked like itself, anyway. Or was he twisting the lie—or the absence of truth—to be something he could live with?

Either way, he would wait a few days.

Coward.

That would allow enough time for Flory to enjoy her bath.

Coward.

She would be nice and warm here. He would fill the stove, and she could stay as long as she wanted. Lizzy had given him her soap. It smelled of wildflowers. He could picture her wrapped in wildflowers. That was Flory.

Back home, his mother had grown accustomed to the bath his father had installed. Running water, too. She would think this to be primitive, while to Flory it would be a luxury.

Jimmy smiled as he poured the last boiling pan of water into the steaming tub. He hoped she would be pleased. She might make a fuss, but he believed she would like it. He wasn't sure why it mattered so much to him to make something a little easier for her. But it did. This was so simple, he didn't know why he hadn't thought of it sooner.

He blocked the firebox with wood. Turning to go fetch Flory, he heard her quick footsteps approaching. Lizzy might have told her, though Jimmy had asked her not to. Or perhaps she was just looking for him since he had been gone so long. That warmed his heart.

An unfamiliar voice said, "What the devil happened here?"

A tall, thin man who looked a lot like Flory stood before him. This was Bart or Tommy, he guessed.

They both stared at each other before Jimmy's brain caught up. A fist struck his jaw, knocking him backwards. He staggered, his calf caught in the rim of the tub, and he went down in the corner as warm, soapy water sloshed out onto the floor.

Bart caught his shirt, pulled him up, and stood him against the wall. "Where's my wife? And who are you?" he demanded. He drew back his fist again.

"Bart," Lizzy called. "Bart, where are you? *Bart?*"

The man loosened his grip on Jimmy's shirt, and he turned toward the voice. Footsteps pounded along the path as Lizzy called out. The man let Jimmy go and ran out the door.

Jimmy was stunned. Where had he come from? He didn't know whether to stay where he was or go to the main house. Closing the door, he retreated until a chair hit the back of his knees. He sat and waited, ever the coward. Some things ran deep. What was it his father used to say? *What comes by nature costs no money*. From which side of the family had he inherited his cowardice?

Someone came for him. He didn't hear the person approach and was startled when the door opened. A silhouette glowed against the fog. Bolting from the chair, Jimmy prepared to defend himself if Bart had returned. Perhaps *defend* was too strong a word. Perhaps he would run. Perhaps he would run to Flory. Then the figure spoke.

"You did this for me?" Flory asked, her face radiant as she stepped into the kitchen. "I wondered where you'd gone." She furrowed her brow as she moved toward Jimmy and touched his jaw. "Did Bart do that? Oh, Jimmy, I'm so sorry."

"I'm fine. Are you?"

"Daddy's home," she said simply.

Jimmy nodded. Flory's eyes were glossy and luminous. Her

smile was the biggest he had ever seen it. It went all the way to her eyes. Even her hair shone. He stopped himself from touching her, an act that was meant to save himself. From what, he didn't know.

"We're going to be just fine," Flory said. She squeezed Jimmy's arm and searched his features, her grin unrestrained. He couldn't say if she had found what she was looking for or not when she let go. Now, he was severed from this new Flory, and he felt a pang of something undeniably sorrowful.

"I can't believe you did this." Flory backed away, unaware of Jimmy's mortal wound. She moved lighter on her feet while his own felt like they were nailed to the floor. "This is sweet, Jimmy. I really appreciate it.

"Come over to the house," she said. "Daddy wants to meet the man who saved his daughter from the bear. By the way, they don't believe a word of it."

Fear took a foothold in his belly. It swelled and pushed upward, blocking words. Jimmy couldn't find his voice. The words wouldn't come.

"About the bear, I mean," Flory said. "Come on, Jimmy."

Taking his hand, she guided him out of the kitchen and all but danced across the bar ahead of him. He lagged and gave her a strangled smile when she nudged him onward. As they rounded the house, two men met him—Bart, who had Lizzy leaning on his shoulder, and her father.

"Robert White, Bert to most," the older man said as he offered his hand. Though his voice held an air of friendliness, there was a wariness about him that did nothing to put Jimmy at ease. "I heard you did good by the womenfolk."

Jimmy stammered an assent and shook the offered hand. It was a strong grip despite the man's withered appearance. Flory's father picked up a splintered piece of clapboard and eyed the claw- and bite marks. Astonishment filled his eyes as he looked at Flory. "There really *was* a bear?"

"You're Jimmy?" Bart asked. "Sorry about that back there. No hard feelings." He reached out. Jimmy took his hand—another sturdy grip—while he shook his head, confirming Bart's sentiment.

"Did you say Jimmy?" a man behind him asked, giving Jimmy a start.

He turned to see a younger version of Bart alongside Constable Abraham Giles.

"Jimmy Bailor, as I live and breathe." Constable Giles moved forward and clapped him on the back. "Jimmy Bailor, you were given up for dead last fall. You've been here all this time, son."

Jimmy froze when he heard Flory gasp. He dared not look her way. If there was a way to go back to before Juniper Tickle, he wished he could find it quickly.

Coward.

"Jimmy Bailor?" she echoed. "Any relation to William Bailor?"

"Why, yes, William Bailor was his father," Constable Giles answered for him. "Son, you have a lot of explaining to do."

Jimmy nodded, closed his eyes, and turned to meet Flory's gaze.

"How could you?" she spat.

He wouldn't let himself forget the look of betrayal that had shattered her happiest day—he had put it there. Tears welled in Flory's eyes.

"How could you, Jimmy? That is just cruel. I never dreamed it of you."

"Let me explain. Please?"

"If I never hear another word that comes out of your mouth, and I do mean *never*, I'll be happy. Goodbye, Jimmy Bailor. I hope I never see the sky over you again."

Flory ran into the house, followed by Lizzy.

"Where's your father?" Constable Giles asked him.

"I don't know," Jimmy said flatly. His eyes followed the women.

"Take him out of here or you'll have to arrest me again," Robert said, his face reddening and hands clenched into fists.

"I wish I had hit you harder," Bart said as he moved closer.

Constable Giles stood between him and the Whites. "I'll get to the bottom of it," he said. "Jimmy, do you know where your father is?"

Jimmy's back stiffened. "No, sir. He didn't come back for me, and I made my way here." He stared at the clouds over the constable's shoulder.

"Jimmy, did you harm them women in any way?"

"No, sir." Jimmy's eyes flew to the constable, unsure what he was being asked. "I did not."

Giles nodded.

Robert grabbed Jimmy's arm. "If I find out different, I'll find you, and I'll kill you." The frenzy in the man's eyes left no doubt he meant it.

Constable Giles pulled him away from Robert and ushered him toward the beach. "We'd better get out of here," he said, his voice so low only Jimmy could hear. "You can talk to me on the boat."

Just the night before, Jimmy had made up his mind that he would stay here forever. The irony wasn't lost on him. He nodded and went along with Constable Giles, unsure if he was cowardly or wise. Despite his conviction to stay, as he climbed into the rowboat, he realized it might be the last time he would set foot on the shores of Juniper Tickle.

Flory's bitter voice found him through the fog. "I hate you, Jimmy Bailor. Do you hear me? I hate you."

Though he didn't think her the type to revel in his anguish, it gave him peace of mind to know she didn't despise him half as much as he loathed himself. To make matters worse, it had been his own doing. What else could he expect to become of a liar and a coward?

27

Jimmy stepping onto the pier in Spigot Harbour was as much a surprise to him as it was to the onlookers. Immediately the talk started.

That's Jimmy Bailor.

It can't be. He's dead and buried.

It's the spit of him.

It's his fetch.

That's young Jimmy. Not so young anymore.

"Come on," Constable Giles said as he nudged Jimmy with his shoulder. "I'll bring you home to your mother."

Jimmy felt Terry Hardy's fist before he saw him. "You killed my father," he roared as he jumped on top of him.

The constable pulled Terry clear and held him back to allow Jimmy to get up. Jimmy brushed off Bart White's pants and faced his accuser as Terry wrestled the lawman to get another swing at him.

"I'm sorry about your father," Jimmy said. "I heard he was lost with mine."

The commotion drew a crowd from the wharf and nearby houses. They pressed in on Jimmy, but he disregarded their questions. He was telling his story only once more, and that was to his mother.

Giles shouted a warning at Terry and handed him off to a couple of fishermen. Terry settled down and pulled clear. "I'll get you, Bailor," he warned as he turned away. "Sleep with your eyes open."

Jimmy ignored him and strode home accompanied by Giles. Nothing about the house looked right. The curtains were closed, there was no activity in the shop, and the storm door was drawn in. It looked bleak. He glanced at Giles.

"She's home. Sad, that's all," the constable said. "She'll be happy to see you."

Jimmy didn't doubt that. His mother had always stood by him and protected him from bullies—including his father. He was ragged and unshaven, he had an aching jaw, and now he felt a bruise that would lead to a black eye.

Pulling the latch on the storm door, he hooked it open to let light in through the door pane. He paused, cleared his throat, and turned the knob.

"Abe, is that you?" his mother called, her voice infused with despair.

Jimmy stepped from the feeble light of the porch into the bright kitchen. His mother sat in the rocking chair by the stove. Her dishevelled appearance was unlike her. Until now, she had always dressed properly and kept her hair just so in case somebody came in.

"Mother." He paused and let her take in the situation. "Mother."

She stopped the rocker but didn't look up. Then she tilted her ear to the sound of his voice. As she met his eyes, her hand flew to her mouth. She gasped and pushed herself slowly from the chair, as if reluctant to move too quickly for fear her son would vanish again.

"Jimmy," she said breathlessly. His answering nod launched her across the room. "My boy is home," she wailed as she held his face with her fingers."Is it really you, Jimmy?" She pushed him away and looked him up and down before pulling him into her embrace. "My Jimmy, you came home."

Giles made a sound, reminding them of his presence. "We got him here as quick as possible," he said.

Jimmy's mother reached out for Giles's hand and squeezed it. "Thank you, Abe, for bringing my son home."

"I'll leave you alone for the time being," the constable said. "Jimmy, I'll be back tomorrow." When Jimmy gave him a questioning look, Giles added, "In case you remember something else."

Jimmy wasn't sure what he hadn't said yet.

Giles left, and his mother took his hands, threw her arms around him, and bawled afresh. He waited until she was done before he led her to the rocker.

"Did those people hurt you?" she asked as she motioned for him to pull up a chair and sit. She wouldn't let him go. He tipped the chair with his fingertips and dragged it to the stove.

Jimmy didn't realize he was cold until he sat in the heat. He believed all emotion might have left him, because he wasn't as happy as he should have been to see his mother and to be home. As he thought about it, he felt nothing. He was nothing.

"Jimmy, what happened to your father and the rest of them? How did you escape? Where have you been?"

Jimmy held up his hand for his mother to slow down. "Father didn't come back for me."

"Dan went to the camp, and you weren't there. I thought you'd been killed along with your father."

"I left there and wandered for days and ended up finding the boat. The people there took me in."

"But I thought they were all arrested," his mother said.

"The men were."

"Did those bullies mistreat you?" she asked. "My poor boy, what you must have gone through."

Jimmy told his mother about Juniper Tickle. He left out the part about the newborn baby and the bear, because he didn't think she could accept it. She certainly didn't believe him when he gave her the basics, and the truth might do her in.

"Why didn't you come home? You knew I was here."

"How was I getting home?"

"You got there, didn't you?" she pointed out, exasperation rising in her voice.

"If somebody had come check on the women like the constables promised," he argued, "I would have been home earlier."

"Jimmy, you must understand, we thought they killed you," she said. Her scolding tone agitated him. He didn't want to get in a shouting match with his mother, so he simply nodded. "We have to get you out of those clothes. Get you into the tub and something to eat."

She took control of him. He let her. It was easier that way.

"Your father's boat will be here in a few days," his mother said as she boiled the kettle. She went to the pantry and brought out a cherry cake. "Dan Acreman said he'd captain her for me. You won't have to go out on that ocean ever again."

Jimmy was going to mention he had travelled on a boat for two days and hadn't gotten sick, but that wouldn't mean anything to his mother. As she went on, talking about how they were going to live, he let his mind conjure Flory's face and her last words to him. If he was going to be tortured, he wanted it to count.

28

Flory gave Lizzy a grateful look. Bart was enamoured with his new little girl and hated to leave her alone. Daddy was elated when he learned her name. However, for now, Lizzy insisted Caroline needed a nap and the men should talk outside.

This should have been her happiest day, but instead, she was seething. She made an excuse that she would start supper as Lizzy led the men from the house. Flory dearly wanted to enjoy their return, but she was too mad.

Jimmy Bailor. How could they not have seen that he had come from the vessel? They had been kind to him, and he kept that secret. After all, they wouldn't have turned him away. There was nowhere else for him to go.

Flory grabbed the kettle and jumped back when water splashed and the stove hissed its disapproval. She closed her eyes. How could she muster the discipline to forget Jimmy and what he had done? Since Daddy was taken away, she had been pressured by circumstance and everything about the crush of Juniper Tickle. Now that the ordeal was over, she should be thrilled to heave off that mantle. Instead, she was vexed because she had been duped.

Maybe that's what hurt the most. She had trusted Jimmy, and he hadn't reciprocated.

From the porch she listened to Lizzy talk about the bear. Lizzy laid her hands over her son's ears when she spoke about how she thought they were all going to die. Flory wondered why she hadn't mentioned that before. But it was a bear—why should she be surprised? Flory had had those thoughts, that they were all going to die. She could only attribute why they hadn't to Jimmy's involvement. Alternative outcomes pressed on her mind. She shuddered.

"Now tell me about you," Lizzy said. "How did you get here? What happened? How did you get freed?"

"Hold on, now," Bart said as he pulled her close and kissed the top of her ear. "One thing at a time."

"Okay, okay," she said. "We're just happy to have you home."

"Believe me," Daddy said, "no happier than we are. We lived on bread and water and little else the whole winter."

"Nearly froze to death there, too," Bart said. "But it's behind us now."

"How is it behind you?" Lizzy asked.

"The judge said there was no evidence to convict. We didn't have a trial until a few weeks ago."

"Something about delays with that constable getting there," Daddy said. "The ice was shocking thick and moved into St. John's and stayed."

"We were sentenced for larceny, for stealing the axe," Tommy said. "Judge said that the time served made up for it."

"Really?" Lizzy asked. "I'm so sorry."

"You have nothing to be sorry about," Bart said. "It wasn't your fault."

"I'd like to know where that boy came from," Daddy said, changing the subject. "Tell me again."

Lizzy told him how she and Flory had found Jimmy.

"Do you think he came off the *Annie May*?" he replied. "Would be strange if he didn't."

"He was at death's door when we found him. I don't know how he made it here, but after the winter we had, I can't help but be glad he did."

Flory joined them. "I'm not glad, then," she said. "He's a Bailor, and I hope we never tread the ground he walks on."

"Until the boat is gone from the point," Daddy said, "I don't think we should go handy to it. That thing's brought us nothing but bad luck."

"When will it be gone?" Flory asked.

"According to that constable, they'll be back in a few days." Daddy coughed. His whole body shook. "Good to be home to get better. We'll have to go easy on the grub until we get used to eating again."

"You're all so thin," Lizzy observed. "Flory will have you fattened in no time." She looked at her sister-in-law and smiled. "Won't you, girl?"

"Yes," Flory said. "Come get a mug-up. We still have molasses and raisins. I have buns in the oven, and the teapot is ready."

"We spared what we could," Lizzy said. "We only lost eggs for a little bit. Isobel and Jack will have kids soon, so the milk will be in good supply."

"You took care of everything," Daddy said.

"Not me. We wouldn't have made it without Flory."

"I could lay out that constable for not coming to check on you," Bart said as he kissed Lizzy's hand. "I was afraid of what we'd find when we got here."

"There would have been a murder in Juniper Tickle if anything had to happen to you," Daddy vowed. "Jail would have meant nothing to me."

"That's why the constable lingered with the others in the boat. I think he might have been afraid and was ready to run." Bart got up, hugged Flory, and twirled her around. "I'm proud of you."

Daddy pulled her toward him from his seat on the chopping block. "That's my girl," he said. Flory joined in the revelry, but the joy didn't reach her heart. Jimmy had taken that from her.

A week later, the rhythm of Juniper Tickle was slowly adjusting, and Flory eagerly joined in the workload to take her mind off her troubles. Daddy, Tommy, and Bart mended nets, readying them for the bark pot, which she set to simmering on the beach. Flory and Lizzy had spent the last few days gathering birchbark and boiling it in linseed oil to get the concoction just right. Every spring, Daddy would dip the nets to keep them from rotting before the men went fishing.

Lizzy spotted activity on the point and alerted them just before Constable Giles showed up.

"Begging your pardon," he said as he rounded the house.

"What do you want?" Daddy asked, not missing a beat with the mending needle.

Giles gave them an update. The boat rudder would be fixed so the *Annie May* could return to home port. The herring barrels were stinking with rotted fish and would be dumped.

"Not here. We won't live with the flies if you do."

Constable Giles agreed. Daddy didn't look up.

"I have a parcel for Miss Flory," the constable said.

Daddy grunted and kept at his work while Giles laid a package on the step.

"Tell me about the boy," Daddy said, pausing to fill his needle. "Was he on the boat?"

"Young Jimmy fished with his father. That's all I can tell you."

"So, what happened to the men you were so eager to blame us for murdering?"

"We don't know. That's the truth."

"Was there a murderer here with my daughter and my son's wife?" Daddy asked. "You owe us that much."

Giles sighed. He stared at Robert White, then cast his gaze toward the ocean. "Young Jimmy was put ashore a few days before," he said. "He has no account of what happened to his father."

"Put ashore? Where?"

"About fifteen miles north of here," the constable said. "There's a summer tilt."

"It was far from summer," Daddy said.

"Yes. It's a wonder Jimmy made it here."

"Your sure he wasn't on the boat?"

"As sure as I can be," Giles said.

"As sure as you were of our guilt?" Daddy muttered as he turned to mending once again.

Giles walked away.

Flory and Lizzy waited at the far corner of the house until Giles left. They joined Daddy.

"What did he want?" Flory asked, though she had heard most of the conversation. She kept silent on her question about whether Jimmy had been with them, though she was fairly certain he hadn't.

Daddy relayed the information as he worked. "There's a package for you," he said as his eyes met his daughter's.

"For me? What could the constable have for me?"

"Open it and find out," Daddy said as he gestured toward the step. "It's right there."

Flory untied the line and unwrapped the brown paper. Inside were a bunch of items.

"What is it?"

Flory rooted around and called out what she found—a wooden toy for Bobby, a rattle for Caroline, pencils, paper, and a couple of candy bars. Two hair combs. Bart's pants, the ones Jimmy had worn the day he left. The last item was also wrapped in brown paper and rested at the bottom. She took it out and untied the knot.

"A tin of peaches." Flory sighed. Unsure if she should laugh or cry, her mind raced to the morning after Caroline was born. How things had changed since then.

"Did you say peaches?" Daddy asked.

"Yes," she said as she sat the step. A tremor fought to escape her. Once released, it incited a riot of emotions. She shuddered silently and wept into her palms.

29

For two reasons, Jimmy had been tempted to go with the crew when they brought home the *Annie May*. One was to test his sea-worthiness. He had come all the way from Juniper Tickle without the least bit of queasiness, something he hadn't realized until he arrived in Spigot Harbour. But in case thinking about being on the water were to resurrect that misery, he decided to stay put.

His second reason had all to do with his doting mother. Jimmy was sick of it already. He couldn't imagine what the coming summer would be like.

The worst part was that she hadn't changed. His mother was exactly the same as he remembered her. The more he protested her devotion to him, the worse she got.

Jimmy, let me do that. You'll hurt yourself.

Jimmy, put on a hat. You'll get cold.

Jimmy, you must be hungry. I'll fix you something.

Jimmy, eat. You're too thin.

Jimmy, Jimmy, Jimmy. No wonder his father wanted to call him James. He was probably tired of hearing *Jimmy*.

His mind raced as he strolled toward the dock to greet the

schooner, which was now his property. He wondered if his father would turn over in his watery grave if he knew it was Jimmy's boat. As for Jimmy, he was both terrified and excited about the prospect. It was a possibility so new, he had no idea how he would deal with it.

Raymond Blythe and George Dolan smoked their pipes on a bench overlooking the wharf as Jimmy approached.

"New spot, I see," Jimmy said by way of greeting.

Both men turned, and their faces lit up at the same time. "Jimmy, it's you," Mr. George said, his feeble hands pushed on the bench to get up.

Jimmy stopped him and sat down between the two.

"The town had you given up for lost," Raymond said.

"Not us, though," Mr. George said as they both nodded as vigorously as their generous years would allow. "We knew you'd come out of it."

Raymond sucked on the pipestem. "Heard you came across a bear," he said as he leaned back and puffed clouds of smoke around his face. "Let me tell you about the time I was chased by a bear. Not much older than you, I was."

Jimmy grinned and listened to Raymond's tale before he told them about the polar bear and Juniper Tickle. Raymond's five days in the woods lengthened, though he let Jimmy have an extra day in case Raymond had miscounted. Jimmy told them how their advice had kept him alive. They both blew smoke in accord and sat a bit straighter on the bench.

"You must miss your father," Mr. George said, his solemnity genuine. "A sad loss for Spigot Harbour."

Jimmy wasn't sure how to respond to that. He stayed quiet and let silence speak its own answers.

"William got a hard name in later years, but he was a good

man. A hard worker, that one," Mr. George said after several draws on the pipe. "The *Annie May* will soon arrive in port, and her sister vessel, *Annie May II*, is sitting right over there."

Jimmy's eyes followed Mr. George's pointing finger. The *Annie May II*? He searched the recesses of his memory for any mention of it but came up short.

"Who owns her?" he asked as he squinted toward the boat.

"You do," Raymond said. "Your father told us about it last year. Told us not to tell you. It was delivered after the ice left. All paid for, too, according to talk."

"You must be putting me on," Jimmy said. "Mother didn't tell me." He stared at them, studying their expressions. "Are you fooling?"

"No, no." Raymond and Mr. George were sincere.

"She's two-masted," Mr. George said. "William said you could work your way up."

"As in my father, William Bailor?"

"Yes," both men said at once.

"But why?" Jimmy asked. It was directed more to himself than to the men.

"He said he wanted to start you off right," Mr. George said.

"Told us himself one day when he was mending nets the winter before last." Raymond looked at Mr. George and then at Jimmy.

"You were with my father?"

"All the time. He'd listen to these two old codgers all day, he would," Raymond said. "You were in school, and the shed was warm. We kept the fire going for him."

"He'd have a special bottle of whiskey for us," Mr. George added. "To ease the ache in these old bones, you understand."

"Always full," Raymond said. "Now, we'd only have a drop, and he wouldn't touch it himself." His conspiratorial look led

Jimmy to believe he would swear to that as fact if asked. Jimmy laughed at Raymond's seriousness.

"He was proud of you, son," Mr. George said as he patted Jimmy's leg.

"Mighty proud," Raymond said as he patted the other.

"I must have come back to another Spigot Harbour where another William Bailor lived," Jimmy said. "We can't be talking about the same man."

Both men eyed one another and shook their heads.

"Your father was hard on you," Raymond said. "He said you were coddled too much. He said there was a good man in there if he could get past the boy."

"There's the *Annie May* now," Mr. George said as he pointed to the harbour. "Thought we'd never see her again."

The men leaned on their canes and watched the boat approach. Their eyes watered as she drew closer.

"You said the *Annie May II*," Jimmy said. "Odd that both vessels have the same name."

"Named after his mother, he told us," Mr. George said absently as he stared out the bay.

"Died when his sister was born," Raymond said. "Sarah was her name, I believe."

"A bachelor uncle took them, made your father work too hard, too young. Mind you, he didn't say that," Mr. George said. "He didn't know what happened to his sister after—if she married, or where she went."

Jimmy, stupefied, rose from the bench. He felt ashamed for not knowing. Certainly he felt he had earned the good-for-nothing title. There was no doubt in his mind.

"I'm sorry, Father," he whispered skyward. "I know that's not enough."

30

Jimmy's thoughts tumbled as he made his way to the dock. The word *proud* stood out. *There's a good man in there*. But there was an odd thing about pride. A person could have too much and sometimes not enough. In those cases, pride was worn like a coat—either too big or too small. Jimmy had always thought his father's was too big and there was no coat for him. That's where he fit—he didn't know enough about what he should be proud of to *have* any pride. He hadn't seen the *good man* in himself, and certainly not in his father.

He was still reeling from his conversation with Raymond and Mr. George when the gangway lowered. Dan Acreman stretched out his hand as Jimmy stepped onto the *Annie May*.

"Good to see you, son," he said. "Real good."

Jimmy shook his hand and met Dan's eyes.

"We were lucky," Dan said, his voice kind. Jimmy recalled his father dismissing Dan just before that fateful day. "Real lucky."

Jimmy closed his eyes. The *Annie May* didn't hold good memories for him. He left Dan and wandered, pulling his fingertips across the rails along the schooner's side. Of course, he had spent many hours hung over those same railings.

He drifted into the house and put his hand upon the wheel. Feeling like a stranger to this part of the boat, today he felt like an outsider to it all. He had been oblivious to the fact he had been an outcast among the crew because he was William Bailor's son. But saw it now—sitting on the nets while they worked. Not pulling his weight. Eating the best food. His father's heightened ire while in his presence. He smiled wryly at the thought of how his father had always brought home the tinned fruit, leaving the rest of the men without any. And when he didn't bring it home, it was because they were late and he had shared it with them.

"Remembering something, son?" Constable Giles asked as he stood beside him.

Jimmy flinched. "Just that my father was a good man." It was the first time he had spoken that out loud, and he meant it. William Bailor was a good man.

"He didn't deserve to die," Constable Giles said. "Would you know anything about that?"

"No," Jimmy whispered.

"What did you say?"

"I said no." Jimmy turned to the constable. "I told you I wasn't there."

"Looks like you are eager to take over," Giles said.

Jimmy pulled his shoulders back and stared at him. "That's not your business, now, is it?"

"You're right. I was merely wondering if you'd remembered anything else."

"I told you I wasn't there," Jimmy repeated. "I was at the summer tilt. You can check."

"We did." Constable Giles eyed Jimmy's expression. "The tilt was destroyed."

"That can't be right. I left it a bit torn up, but *destroyed* is a bit much." When Giles offered no further information, Jimmy asked, "How?"

"Fire. Didn't look recent."

"What's that supposed to mean?"

"Just doing my job. Questions came from St. John's."

"I wouldn't know about any fire. There was no wood." Jimmy tried to remember how he had left the tilt. Could there have been a spark? He didn't see how, but then again, he hadn't been the most observant.

"What about the Whites?"

"What about them?" Jimmy asked.

"Any sign of your father or the crew coming ashore there?" the lawman asked as he scribbled something in a small ringed notebook and flipped the page. "You were there all winter. Surely you saw something."

"No, they said the boat came in like that," Jimmy said.

"And you believed them?"

"The Whites are good people, Constable."

"That's not what I asked," Giles said as he continued to regard Jimmy, his pencil resting against the notebook.

"Whether I liked them or didn't like them wouldn't change the answer. There was no sign of my father or the crew." Jimmy hoped his tone of finality would put this to rest, but Giles continued.

"So, you didn't like them?"

"That has nothing to do with it. When I got there, there were two women and one child stranded—by you, I might add—in a tiny village without any help from the outside."

"And you helped them?" the constable pressed.

"When I was well enough," Jimmy said. "I'd been starved for several days. I was cold. I was tired. I wasn't much help in the beginning. Then I did my share."

"Did you harm either one of them?" Giles asked with a raised eyebrow.

"What's that supposed to mean?"

"Is there any reason to suspect that either of the men from Juniper Tickle would come looking for you?"

"No," Jimmy said. "What would they want me for?"

"Oh, I don't know," Giles said. "You never know what kind of tales those girls will tell."

"There's nothing to tell. Like I said, they are good people."

"What about if those good people found out you'd be the owner of not just one but two enterprises?" Giles inquired as he turned and swept his hand toward the *Annie May II*. "Would they say you did something inappropriate?"

"I don't know what you're hinting at," Jimmy said. He struck the tiller with the heel of his hand.

"Not hinting at anything. Just trying to protect you and your mother's interests."

"It doesn't sound like it. Flory and Lizzy will have nothing to say about me that would be of interest to you. I'm sure of that."

The women had taken him in and saved his life. They weren't bad people. Especially Flory. A smile threatened at the thought of her, but Jimmy held it back so Giles would leave him alone.

"If you remember anything at all, be sure to tell me," the constable said.

"If you're finished, Abe," Dan said, "I want to show Jimmy the *Annie May II*."

Constable Abraham Giles nodded, and Dan stepped away to let him out of the wheelhouse. His distaste for Giles was plain to see.

"Sorry about that," Dan said, laying a hand on Jimmy's shoulder. "I saw him too late to warn you."

Jimmy nodded his thanks and followed Dan to the other vessel, preoccupied by thoughts of his father and the questions from Giles. He missed two questions from Dan and asked him to repeat them.

"Sorry, Dan. I've got a lot on my mind."

"Understandable," Dan said as he clapped Jimmy on the back. "Another time."

Jimmy nodded, shook his hand, and headed back to the wharf, taking a right instead of going straight home. He had questions for his mother and things he wanted to work out about his father, and he needed time to think. All was not as it seemed. Perhaps, for him, it was more appropriate to say all seemed not as it was.

He strolled by the schoolhouse and kept going. Cutting through the woods, he smiled at the memory of his intentional delays while taking this route, always trying to get home without anyone noticing. Jimmy had distanced himself from everyone. He had no friends in school, and he isolated himself as a means to survive. The irony struck him that he had been more alone in a community of hundreds than he had been with two women and two children in Juniper Tickle.

He spied the chimney smoke from his house and grimaced. As he raised a foot to step onto the track, he heard a noise behind him. As he turned, something big and hard struck him alongside the head. Blood spattered on his clothes and across his face as he fell to his knees. Something knocked against him, and he heard his arm snap, followed by several whacks across his back as his face hit the dirt. He couldn't move.

Footsteps faded. So did Jimmy. Blood flowed across his brow and over his cheek. His nostrils filled. The thick, hot liquid parted his lips and took his breath as he heard his mother scream.

31

“Someone’s here,” Daddy said as he scampered from the daybed and rested his forearms on the windowsill. “Four men rowing in.”

Tommy ran to the window by the table and peered out. “Looks like that Constable Giles fellow is one of them,” he said as he pulled back and looked from his father to Flory.

“Tommy, get Bart,” Daddy said.

“No need. Bart and Lizzy just went around back,” Tommy said as the door opened in the porch.

Lizzy looked terrified as she came in ahead of Bart with the baby in her arms.

“What do they want now?” Bart asked as he laid his son down. “There’ll be no peace, it seems. They believe us to be criminals.” He pulled off his cap by the bib and scratched his head and put it back on.

“They’re on the beach,” Flory said.

“You stay here,” Daddy said. “We’ll handle this.” He nodded at Flory’s brothers, and they went out on the gallery. They kept the advantage of higher ground, forcing Giles and the others to look up.

"What do you suppose they want?" Lizzy asked.

"Shush," Flory whispered as she cracked the door. Her heart thundered when the salty breeze brushed her face and she saw Bart's back through the slit. Lizzy craned over her, and Bobby bustled in front of her while she held the knob.

"We have a few questions for you," Constable Giles said. "Want to come down here? No need to bother the women."

"We'll stay here," Daddy said. "Say your piece and then get out of here."

"I'm afraid it's not that simple, sir," Giles said.

"Simple enough," Bart put in "What do you want?"

"Young Jimmy Bailor was attacked a few days ago," the constable said. "Some folks think you might be responsible."

Flory gasped and pulled open the door. She stepped around her nephew and pushed past her brothers. "Is he all right?" Daddy held her arm to keep her on the step.

"Don't know, miss. He was in a bad way when we left."

Flory's hand went to her mouth as her stomach pushed bile into her throat. "You mean he could die?"

"Could already be so, miss." Giles gave a slight nod. "A real bad way."

Flory turned on her heel and ran back inside. Lizzy caught hold of her hands. "I'm so sorry," she said.

"I didn't want anything to happen to him," Flory said. "I really didn't."

"I know," Lizzy said as she patted Flory's shoulders. "I know you didn't."

Flory lowered her palm to cover her face. "Poor Jimmy," she said. She moved back to the door to listen, her mind and her heart in turmoil. "I feel bad for Jimmy, but what has that got to do with us?"

"We need to know your whereabouts," Giles said. "Were you in Spigot Harbour three days ago?"

Flory rushed out on the step again. "The collector boat was here three days ago."

"That's right," Daddy said.

"Can you prove that?" Giles asked.

"O'Rielly on the collector can," Daddy said.

"I can get the bill," Flory offered.

"No need. O'Rielly has a good memory. We'll stop there on the way back."

"I don't know why you had to come all the way here," Bart said.

"Folks said about Jimmy being here all winter with the women," the constable said. He didn't finish the thought.

"Why, you . . ." Bart said as he jumped from the step. Giles backed up as two men pulled guns.

Lizzy screamed, "Bart, *no*!"

Her husband stopped at half-swing and dropped his fist, shoving it in his pocket.

"He's not worth it," Tommy said.

"Leave it," Daddy said.

Bart stayed put, his chest puffed out, but he was red-faced and fidgety. He reminded Flory of a hungry fox eyeing the chickens, ready to devour them.

"We don't take kindly to people talking about our women," Bart said through clenched teeth.

"I'm sorry," Giles said. "No offence meant. I'm just doing my job." He seemed genuine enough for Bart, which was probably the only reason the chickens weren't destroyed.

"Well," Bart said as he slowly deflated. "Leave the women out of it."

"I understand," the constable replied as he motioned for the men to fall out. "No need to disturb you folks any further. We'll check with O'Rielly. If all is as you say, we won't be back."

Flory stopped herself from asking them to tell Jimmy she was thinking about him. Instead, she turned and went back inside ahead of the men. She scurried to the pantry and found the tin of peaches before returning to the gallery.

"Constable," she shouted. "Constable." She chased them to the beach. Giles stopped and waited for her.

"Can you give this to Jimmy," she asked breathlessly.

The constable cocked his head and smiled at her. It was a look of compassion. "I will indeed, miss," he said.

"Tell him Flory sent it."

Giles reached out and took the tin from her, gently cupping it in both hands. "I will straight away," he said. "Straight away."

"Tell him not to send any more," Flory said. "If he wants to live up to his promise, he should bring them himself." She turned away and stopped herself from sprinting to the house. Instead, she walked with dignity, her chin up, stiff, while looking straight ahead.

Daddy and Tommy watched from the windows as the boat pulled away. Flory saw Lizzy shooing them away when she glanced up. When she entered the kitchen, the men left. They scattered to the outdoors without saying a word. Bobby wanted molasses buns before going home. Flory eyed Lizzy and knew she had put him up to it. She took a bowl from the pantry and went to work.

Lizzy laid her hand on Flory's arm as her sister-in-law stirred the butter and sugar. "He'll be all right," she whispered. "So will you." Clearing her throat, she said, "I have a craving for a molasses bun, myself. Want a cup of tea while we wait?"

Flory sighed before combining eggs and molasses into the mixture. She asked her nephew to add the baking soda and watched it bubble. Bobby giggled as Flory met Lizzy's gaze. This was what she needed.

She hoped Jimmy would be okay. Yes, she was still mad, but she didn't want to carry that forever. If anything happened to him, she feared she just might. She wasn't letting him have that—nor would she eat that unlucky tin of peaches.

Anger and fear volleyed for rank over her emotions. Fear slowly rooted and bloomed.

32

Jimmy's eyelids fluttered but refused to open. Pain pounded at his head, sending pulses down his back and along his legs. It hurt when he moved his toes. He attempted to lift his arm to relieve the pressure of something wrapped around it, but his fingers only twitched in response.

No words came when he tried to speak. Or perhaps he had made a noise—he felt a touch at the side of his neck in response. He gulped and then coughed as the hand pushed him downward.

Whispers came and went, and he believed he was spinning but couldn't stop. His lips were dry and his mouth coarse.

"I can assure you, Loretta," a familiar voice drifted around him, "I checked with the collector boat. It wasn't the Whites."

"It had to be those murderers. Who else would it be?" That was his mother's voice. "You better find out. Check with O'Rielly again."

"He had the receipts with the dates." It was Giles. Yes, that was who he heard. "We checked his logbooks to be sure. There's no mistake. The Whites weren't involved."

"Flory." The word squeezed out of his aching throat. "Flory."

"Doctor," Loretta called. "Doctor, he's awake."

Fingers pinched and prodded him as he went in and out of reality. He was floating, like the ocean was beneath him and he was drowning. But Flory was there. Sometimes she was holding his hand and other times bolstering his head above the waves. She was always kind. When he felt the bed beneath him again, her words came through the fog. *I hate you, Jimmy Bailor.*

One version of Flory battled the other in his mind. Then they joined, and his eyelids obeyed the call to open his eyes. He peered through a white mesh as he stirred, and pain fired through him. Jimmy laid his head back again, but the pain remained.

It was bearable now, and he was awake. He moaned.

"Jimmy. Jimmy, honey, it's me, Mom."

"Mother," he rasped.

"Oh, Jimmy," she said. Her voice came closer. "You're going to be just fine."

Her lips pecked somewhere under his eye. Jimmy saw her face, distorted by gauze, as she bent toward him. Her hand hovered around his forehead before she returned it to her side.

"I can't lose you," she whispered.

There was a ruckus somewhere near his feet. "He knows me," she said as she turned away.

"Mother," he said again.

"See? He knows I'm here."

The gauze came away from his eyes. "Swelling is gone down." Jimmy followed a light and the white sleeve of the man standing over him.

"I'm Dr. Sullivan. It's good to have you back."

Over the next few days, his pain subsided to an ache. He gained more mobility and was able to move his head. One arm had been broken and was mending. Jimmy had been in the hospital for nine days by the time he woke up.

"Recovery will take time," Dr. Sullivan said a week later. "Time and lots of rest."

"I'll be sure he won't have to do a thing," his mother said. "He'll be well looked after. I hired a nurse, too."

Two weeks passed before he could venture outside and let the air blow on him. His mother put the stool out at the urging of the nurse. Mr. George and Raymond kept him company. Sometimes they stayed silent, if he was struggling to stay awake, and sometimes the gentlemen were full of stories about the times they had recovered from one thing or another. Jimmy's mother didn't approve, but he enjoyed the regaling.

Emma Winsor came by one day. "Heard you were doing, better," she said. She looked from Mr. George to Raymond.

"Better be getting on home," Mr. George said. "You going?" he asked Raymond. Both men dodged away, and Emma sat.

"We're all worried about you, Jimmy," she said as she sat stiffly beside him. "Truly, we are."

"Thank you, Emma," Jimmy replied. "I'm doing better."

"Jimmy," she said nervously, "Terry didn't do this. He was with me." Her words came hurriedly, her face pinched as she laid her hand on his.

"I don't understand," Jimmy said. Emma's outburst caught him off guard, and he didn't know what to do. "What do you mean?"

Emma wiped her face with a kerchief she took from her pocket. "I know you and Terry have had your differences."

Jimmy held up a hand. "I know it wasn't Terry. He wouldn't have hit me from behind. That's not his kind."

"So, you'll tell them you were mistaken?" she asked.

"Tell who?"

"The constables. They arrested him last week."

"What?" Jimmy said as he stood up. "What? You must be mistaken."

"They said you identified Terry." Emma's face was as confused as his.

"I did not," Jimmy argued. "I didn't see who it was."

"Emma Winsor." Loretta Bailor's raised voice was stern and condescending. "You go on home out of it. We don't want no more trouble here."

"Yes, ma'am," Emma said as she scrambled to get up, her eyes cast downward. "I didn't mean any harm, Mrs. Bailor. Just seeing how Jimmy was, that's all."

"Go on home."

"Mother," Jimmy said. "Emma is a friend."

"No friend of yours," she yelled back, her disdain apparent. "Terry Hardy is a menace. Her being here will bring trouble."

Emma caught Jimmy's eye. "Please," she mouthed before she turned and ran away.

"Mother, why was Terry Hardy arrested?" Jimmy asked as he made his way to where she stood in the doorway.

"I don't know. You'll have to ask the constables."

Jimmy could tell she knew something.

"I will do that," he said. "Terry Hardy would have faced me and beat me. That's his kind. He doesn't do things any other way."

"Well, that's not my affair," his mother said as she ushered him inside. "Hester, make Jimmy something to eat before he lies down."

Jimmy stood in the hall. He was tired, but he didn't like what was happening and didn't know what he could do about it.

"Mother, why is the boat called the *Annie May*?" His voice was quiet as he watched an answer play out on her face.

"That's an odd question. What does it matter?"

"I'd like to know." Jimmy stared at her. "After all, Father named two of them the same."

"He might have told me one time. A sister or something." His mother made circles in the air as if trying to summon the answer from her memory. "I don't know, Jimmy."

"Like you said," he replied. "I guess it doesn't matter."

"Right." She guided him to the kitchen. "The past is better left where it is. There's no need to relive it today."

33

"I'm not eating, Mother," Jimmy said. "Tell me what you've done."

"Why, nothing," Loretta said, obviously perturbed by her son's words. She got up from the table and leaned on the back of the chair. "Eat," she ordered. "You need your strength."

"I need the truth," he countered. He pointed to the chair. "Please sit."

"I won't be attacked or questioned in my own home, Jimmy Bailor. I didn't tolerate it from your father, and I certainly won't tolerate it from you." She huffed and quickly exited the room.

Jimmy waited a moment before he followed her to the kitchen. "I'm not questioning you. Nor do I want you to be mad," he said as he stood behind her and touched her arm. "I want to know what you know."

His mother turned and laid the dishtowel on the cupboard before letting out a heavy sigh. "I merely suggested that Terry Hardy always thought you were chasing Emma Winsor. He beat you constantly and wouldn't have any scruples about doing it again." She hugged him.

Jimmy slowly lifted his arm to pat her back. He stared at the wall. She had done it. She had manipulated the situation and was the reason Terry Hardy was jailed.

"He blames you for the death of his father."

"I didn't see his father," Jimmy said. "I keep telling everyone I was in that cursed camp for at least a week and then wandered for days, maybe weeks, before finding my way to Juniper Tickle."

Loretta pushed back and stared at him. "That can't be right." She shook her head.

"Mother, I should know how long I was there. I'm not an idiot," Jimmy said, his tone harsh.

"No, no," she said. She began counting on her fingers. "Abe told me that you had gone from the camp."

"Yes," Jimmy said. "I didn't see anyone. Maybe if I'd stayed I could have been rescued."

He thought about his choice of words. Rescued. It was Flory and Lizzy who had rescued him. They had saved him, physically, but his time with them in Juniper Tickle had saved him in other ways. He couldn't imagine himself as the old Jimmy now.

"You aren't even listening to me," Loretta said.

"Sorry," Jimmy said. He gave her a pensive look. "Really." He stared at her and took her hands.

"Like I was saying, Abe told me two days after your father didn't return that you were with them."

"Okay. He wouldn't have known."

"That's just it. He told me the tilt was gone with no sign of you anywhere."

"He might have been sparing your feelings," Jimmy offered.

"No, he was adamant that they checked. I made him go back the next week to be sure, and he personally guaranteed the place had burned."

"Maybe they looked in the wrong place. I'm sure there are tilts everywhere."

"I was afraid of that, so I asked Dan to go with him," Loretta said. "Dan confirmed you weren't there and that it had burned."

"Well, I was there for about a week," he said. "I ran out of food and wood and couldn't wait any longer." Jimmy thought about that time and how naive he had been.

"Oh, honey, I wish I'd have gone," Loretta said with such sincerity it made him laugh.

"You, on the water?" he quipped. He shook his head as his imagination took over.

"What? I mean it, Jimmy. If I had known you were there, I'd have gone."

"You remind me of Lizzy. She wanted the bear to eat her to save the rest of us."

"Bear?" Loretta stared at him. "What about a bear?"

Reluctantly, Jimmy told his mother about their encounter.

"That's what mothers do, Jimmy," she said once she got over the shock. "We protect our own."

"You know, I didn't believe that Father had just left me," he said. "I was right."

"When Abe comes over this evening, I'll be asking about not finding you." She wagged her finger in the air. "He'd better have an answer for me."

Jimmy laughed. "I have no doubt."

Dan Acreman's voice interrupted them. "Sorry, don't mean to listen in."

"Come in," Mother said. She turned to Jimmy. "Dan's been looking after the business of the *Annie May*, for you, for us."

Jimmy nodded. "Maybe I'll go out sometime," he said. "Give you a hand."

"*Wisht*," Loretta said to quash any such thoughts. "No more fishing trips for you."

"Now, Mother," Jimmy said. "I'm not a boy. I have to make a living."

"Not like that," she protested. "Isn't that right Dan?"

"Leave me out of it," Dan said as he grinned at Jimmy. "I'll be going. I just wanted to let you know that we're back."

Dan tipped his head to Loretta, gave Jimmy a flaccid smile, and left.

"He was in a hurry," Loretta said dryly.

Jimmy enjoyed a piece of cake and a cup of tea with his mother. She really was a wonder. Not many women could take on running a store and all it entailed. It was hard work. Well, Flory might, he supposed. Flory would tackle anything.

"What are you smiling at?" Loretta asked. "You haven't been listening to a thing I've been saying." She began to clear the dishes and raised a hand when he offered to help. "I don't know what those women were teaching you, Jimmy Bailor, but in my house, I clear the table."

"All right, Mother," he said as he circumvented her and laid the dishes in the pan, anyway. "I'll remember for next time." He pecked her cheek and jumped back to avoid a flick with the towel.

"Either it's getting dark earlier or Abe is late," Mother said as she glanced through the window. "I thought he'd be here by now."

"Something might have come up," Jimmy said. "Lots of crime, it seems, in Spigot Harbour."

"Don't you dare joke about that. Abe's been good to me and you since your father died."

Jimmy thought his mother was a bit fierce in her defence of

Constable Giles, but he said nothing. He wouldn't dare risk her wrath. His father had often been on the receiving end of her ire. Jimmy had seen her throw plates at him, lock him out, and who knows what else, but his father hadn't raised a hand or his voice to her. If there was anything he could say with certainty, it was that Loretta Bailor got her own way. She was such a different person than Flory—he wasn't sure why he was comparing.

He scolded himself each time he thought of Flory White. She occupied his thoughts more often than not. He guessed time would take away the horrible feeling he carried after betraying her. Her shattered spirit when she learned his name was etched on his heart. He wondered how things would have turned out if only Giles hadn't been there. After all, he had planned to stay. But he was blaming Giles for his cowardly secret. He hoped Flory would forgive the lout who had made that choice and recognize the better person he had become.

His mother's words penetrated his thoughts. "Are you getting your coat?"

Jimmy scrambled from the chair and hurried to her.

"Only for you got a smack on the head that might excuse your inattention," Loretta said as she jammed her arms into her coat, "I think I'd clobber you myself."

Jimmy laughed at her earnestness. "Where are we going?"

"To confront Abe, of course," she said. "I want to know why he said he checked for you when you were obviously at the tilt."

"Oh, that," Jimmy said. "Like I said, maybe he wasn't familiar with the area where I was left."

"He can tell me that, himself," she said as she pitched his coat at him. "Come on. It's getting dark." Absently, she added, "I should have asked Dan when he was here."

Jimmy was more interested in why Terry Hardy had been

arrested. What did Giles know that he didn't? Unless a lot had changed with Terry, he would have met Jimmy head-on instead of attacking him from behind. Then again, fair and Terry didn't go together. Terry's only goal was winning. But he couldn't think that Jimmy would get the best of him. There was no way. And besides, Emma said he was with her.

Thinking and keeping pace with his mother was hard. He ran to catch up with her as she strode out to the road with purpose, stony faced and arms swinging.

"Poor Giles," Jimmy whispered. "You're under Loretta Bailor's scrutiny."

34

"Abe mustn't be home," Loretta said as she stopped by his door. "Perhaps you were right, Jimmy. He must be dealing with something else."

"Do you want to keep going as far as the jailhouse to see if he's there?" Jimmy asked, stepping up beside her.

His mother looked to the horizon. "It will be dark before we get back," she said. "Perhaps it can wait."

Jimmy heard a crash inside the house. His mother's head turned to the door, then back to him. He had seen that questioning look more than once.

"His cat?" she ventured. "He'd have a lamp lit by now."

She walloped Jimmy when he mentioned cats could see in the dark. "Not funny," she said. "You know what I mean."

Loretta turned the knob and pushed the door inward. "Abe," she called. "Are you home?" She took one step inside before Jimmy pulled her back.

"I smell kerosene," he said. "Something's not right."

The words had no sooner left his mouth than a rumble followed by a *whoosh* indicated a fire had ignited. Jimmy saw light flickering through the window and flame somewhere in the back of the house. He caught a glimpse of a darker outline that could have been furniture, but instinct told him otherwise.

His mother grabbed onto his jacket, stopping him as he tried to run inside. "There's somebody on the floor," he Jimmy as strings of smoke floated toward him. He coughed and pulled clear of her grip, then dragged his coat upward to cover his mouth and nose as he went forward. Unfamiliar with the big house, he didn't want to trip and need rescue. He kept low as fire roared to life somewhere in a room he hadn't yet located. There were doors everywhere in the large porch. Smoke blinded and disoriented him.

A flickering sliver of light near the floor beckoned him onward. He pushed the door and was met by a burst of flame. It gorged itself on the curtains and walls. Hungry, white, hot tentacles spread along the ceiling on all sides of the fiery room. Jimmy lowered himself to a crawl and groped his way along the floor. Panic awakened within him, but he fought it back. His breath was shallow as heat and smoke clawed for entry. His lungs demanded more air. He was about to retreat when his hand brushed a sock-covered foot.

Jimmy crawled closer, but he couldn't rouse Constable Giles. He wasn't moving. Remnants of a lamp engorged by flame lay beyond his hand, and his shirt sleeve had caught fire. Jimmy curled his hands around the man's legs and yanked him toward the door. A blazing trail followed them. Snatching a cushion from the daybed, he beat at the flame. He coughed and sputtered as he pulled the body from the inferno. The man's weight slowed their progress.

When he backed into the porch, Dan Acreman and a neighbour rushed in, grabbed them both, and pulled them outside with ease. Jimmy collapsed and crawled away. He threw up smoke and spit and all that he had eaten for supper before scrambling a few steps farther and rolling onto his back, exhausted and panting. His mother ran to him and used her coat to wipe the soot from his face and eyes. She kissed his head several times and repeated what an idiot he was, how scared she was, and how glad she was that he was safe.

Within minutes the community had gathered, and they splashed buckets of water from the closest stream onto the house. The night was afire with sparks and raging flames as the engulfed house plundered the darkness. The delicate starlight surrendered to the smoke. Jimmy dug in his heels to put more distance between him and the blaze. When he managed to regain his breath, he stood on wobbly legs and prepared to join the water line.

Spigot Harbour's nurse, Mary Fields, who had mended and sewn almost every man, woman, and child in the community, took charge over Abe Giles, who had been lifted out of the way. She saw to Jimmy before he got up and added to the scolding his mother had given him. Then she squeezed his shoulder and told him how brave he was before declaring that Giles was dead, and that more than likely he had died before Jimmy reached him.

The night was a whirlwind after that. The neighbours worked as one as they tapped the river to save the surrounding houses and sheds. By the time dawn breached the sky, the smouldering ashes of the house had been doused with water. Smoke and steam collided, thinned, and disappeared in wisps before the fire was declared extinguished just at sunrise.

Community members, embittered over the goings-on, had been so bold as to say that Jimmy had killed Giles in a fit of rage. They believed he had been caught by his mother, who was now covering up the whole affair, and had tried to save the man instead. But Henrietta Jenkins quickly dismissed this, as she had walked home ahead of the pair and had seen them from her window. Though some discredited her account because the Bailors had recently employed her, others quashed the gossip as simply untrue. Jimmy Bailor wouldn't have been able to overpower Constable Giles.

"Pride and courage are not good bedfellows," Loretta said. "Leave gossip to gossips, and let your dealings speak for themselves." She was also quick to point out she would do away with Jimmy if he ever did anything so foolish again. But he could tell she was impressed by his actions when she gave her account to the constables two days later.

"Did you see anyone or anything?" Constable Grayson asked. He and Constable Morgan sat across from Jimmy and his mother.

"No," Loretta replied. "I've been trying to figure it out since it happened."

"What about you?" the constable asked. He read a note in his hand and looked up at Jimmy. "James."

"Jimmy is the hero in all this," Loretta said. "He tried to save Abe. He must have heard us at the door, got up, and tripped when he lit the lamp. If I hadn't gone there, this wouldn't have happened."

"Not unless he tripped three times," Grayson said. "He had suffered at least three blows to the head from behind. He didn't see them coming."

Loretta gasped. She swooned onto the chesterfield, and Jimmy went to her aid.

"What's going on in Spigot Harbour?" Jimmy asked in astonishment as he helped his mother to a chair and fetched a glass of water.

"That's what we mean to find out," Grayson said. "What was your business with Constable Giles?"

"I had a couple of questions about Terry Hardy, why he was being held for attacking me."

"And I wanted to know about something relating to my husband's disappearance," Loretta finished as she took a sip of water.

"So, you didn't get to ask him?" Grayson questioned.

Loretta was firm. "No. We told you. Jimmy went in after the fire started."

"That's not entirely true," Jimmy said. "Mother opened the door. I smelled kerosene and pulled her back."

"Yes, son," she said. "But that had nothing to do with Abe."

"It has everything to do with it," Grayson said. "Was there fire when you opened the door?"

"Not at first," Jimmy replied. "We heard it start."

"But you saw nobody?"

"No. I thought I saw a shadow, but I could be mistaken."

"You probably interrupted the killer," Grayson said. "A few minutes earlier and you might have met the same fate."

"Or we might have stopped him," Jimmy countered.

Constable Grayson's eyes pierced him. "There's somebody on the loose in Spigot Harbour who will stop at nothing to get what he wants. Do you have any idea what that could be?"

"No idea. Could it be linked to the *Annie May*?"

"Those files are in St. John's. We'll have to check the notes Constable Giles has on your case."

"Terry Hardy didn't do this. He's in jail," Jimmy said. "I'm certain it wasn't him who attacked me, either."

"Hardy was released," Grayson informed him.

"What?" Jimmy and his mother said in unison.

"When?" Loretta asked.

"We don't know. The cell is empty." Grayson looked at his notes. "We'll check against what Constable Giles has written."

"We found this on the desk at the jailhouse," Constable Morgan said as he offered a small brown paper package to Jimmy. "It has your name on it."

"For me? That's odd."

"Abe brought that back from Juniper Tickle," Loretta said dismissively. "I told him to get rid of it."

"From Juniper Tickle?" Jimmy felt dazed. He undid the knot and found a can of peaches.

Loretta explained to him and the lawmen that Constable Giles had gone to Juniper Tickle to inquire as to the whereabouts of the Whites at the time Jimmy was attacked.

"Upon his return, he had this from one of the women," she said. "The youngest one, Fanny."

"Flory," Jimmy corrected her.

"That's what I said," his mother interjected. "She said if Jimmy wanted her to have it, he'd have to bring it himself."

"She said that?" Jimmy stammered.

"You are missing the point, Jimmy. She obviously knows you own two boats and wants you to take her out of that wretched place."

"Mother," Jimmy said reproachfully. "How could you even think that?"

Constable Grayson raised his voice. "Can we get back to the issue? You're saying that Constable Giles, in his investigation, cleared the Whites?"

"I didn't believe him, of course," Loretta said, her voice

laced with venom. "But he did say that the O'Rielly man who collects fish could vouch for all of them. He was probably in on it, too. Write that down. I want them investigated."

"That's not how this works," Grayson said. "We tend to believe people unless they give us reason not to."

"Exactly," Jimmy said. "I don't believe Terry Hardy attacked me, and I wanted to know why Giles thought he did."

"We'll confirm that," Grayson replied.

"I may have told him that the Hardy fellow always had it out for Jimmy," Loretta admitted.

"*Mother*!" Jimmy looked at her and then the constables. "Terry Hardy would have faced me, more than likely beat me, and would have strutted around Spigot Harbour saying so. He doesn't do things through back doors—he goes through the front." Jimmy couldn't believe he was defending Terry Hardy. "I know he didn't do this, nor did he attack me."

"Do you have any idea who might have?" Constable Morgan asked.

"No. I honestly don't."

35

Flory sat on a rock where the *Annie May* had been. She told herself it was coincidence and nothing more. It was her new place to think. She was grounded here, anger and all. With her arms wrapped tightly around her legs and her head resting on her knees, she gazed out over the satiny vista. The dusting of clouds above turned the water silver. Cool, she thought. Cool, like her mood.

Despite the gloom that hung over the tickle, she contemplated her resolve to put up with it. The ocean sounds lapping the rock beneath her was a balm on an incurable suffering. It smoothed the edges, though the wound still hurt. Some days, tremendously. Maybe her anger would resolve itself over the winter, though she doubted she would recover.

How silly she was to be affected so deeply. But knowing that and making her heart agree with it was not a goal she would attempt to reach. She liked the anger because it made sense. The anger kept her head down over the summer, kept the fish drying, the meals on the table, and the washing done.

A scuff of rocks and a soft rustle of a skirt alerted Flory to Lizzy's presence long before she spoke.

"What are you doing?" Lizzy asked her. "Feeling sorry for yourself?"

"No," Flory replied. "Just minding my own business."

"Oh. And is that a hint for me to mind mine?"

Lizzy laughed when her sister-in-law didn't answer. She pushed Flory over on the rock and climbed up beside her. Wrapping her arms around her knees, she aligned herself with Flory.

Flory sighed when the silence stretched on. "I'm okay," she said. "No need to worry about me."

"I'm not worried," Lizzy said. "Unless you tell me there's a reason to be."

Flory stared at her. Lizzy smiled.

"What's wrong?"

An overwhelming sense of misery filled her, and tears pushed for release. She swallowed several times. "Nothing," Flory said simply.

"Don't give me that. You haven't been yourself since the men came back. Or should I say since Jimmy left."

"I can't help it. I'm so mad."

"What would have been different if he had told us who he was?" Lizzy asked her.

"I don't know. That's just it. I really don't know." Flory lowered her head. She watched the watermark on the shoreline. Closer to the ocean's reach, areas out there didn't get a chance to dry before the waves breached again, however fierce or gently they came. That was how her anger and disappointment felt. Always wet. Always fresh.

"Sometimes people have no choice but to hide themselves. Sometimes in plain sight," Lizzy said. "You asked me one time how I met Bart. I was living as a boy on the streets in St. John's when we met. I tried to rob him."

Flory swung around to face Lizzy, her eyes wide. "That can't be true." She studied Lizzy's face. "Can it?"

"It is true. I had no choice." Lizzy gave her a condensed version of how she had met Bart. Flory sensed she wasn't telling her a lie, but she sensed Lizzy wasn't telling her everything, either. "To reveal myself would have been the end of me."

"You had no friends?" Flory asked.

"Nobody. I slept outside or in barns or wherever I could be safe for a night."

"No wonder you were useless when you came here," Flory said with a grin. She rolled her eyes.

"Exactly," Lizzy said as she pushed Flory from the rock. "I had nowhere to learn anything."

"I had no idea. I still can't believe it."

"So," Lizzy said, "do you hate me now?"

"Hate you? Why would I hate you?"

"Because I didn't tell you."

Flory drew back, then shook her head. "It's different, though," she said. "I told you I couldn't explain it."

"We all hold things back," Lizzy said. "One time or another. Sometimes it's to help people, sometimes it's so you don't hurt them."

Deep in thought, Flory dragged her foot across the dirt.

"Do you know that though we got married, it wasn't Bart who rescued me?" Lizzy said as she pulled Flory into a hug. "That was you, Florence Alice White. You became my friend, and you saved my life."

Flory squeezed Lizzy in her arms and let her tears flow.

"I'm so mad with him."

"That's not anger. I'm afraid that's something more complicated."

Flory moved out of Lizzy's arms. "Who said we were friends?" she said as she chortled through tears and hiccoughs.

"I know you like me," Lizzy said as she wiped at her own tears. She threw her arm over Flory's shoulder. "Now that that's out of the way, I have something to tell you."

A flash of fear went through Flory, but Lizzy squeezed her shoulders reassuringly. "We're having another baby. That's all."

"A baby," Flory said simply. Then her smile faded. "A baby. Lizzy, you can't stay here."

"That's what I came to tell you." Lizzy released Flory's shoulders and took her hands. "I can't put you through that again."

"Never mind me. It's you who can't go through that again."

"See, I knew you liked me," Lizzy said, wiping away more tears. "Oh, I hate these darn things," she said with a grimace. "But I can't stop them."

"Tell me what you're planning."

Lizzy explained that she and Bart had talked about wintering in Twillingate. Medical help would be available there if anything happened. They'd had a good summer, weather-wise, and lots of fish to barter. Daddy had saved money to help get them settled. They would be back in the spring with the newest White and spend the summer in Juniper Tickle.

"I'll be counting the days," Flory said. She meant it. Lizzy was a friend, not just family.

Three weeks later, she stood on the shore with Daddy as the supply boat took Bart and his family to a new life. Flory and Lizzy had cried most of the day, away from everyone. She stood with her back straight as the breeze teased her hair.

"At least Bart won't die from starvation," she called. "Now that you can make bread."

"See you in the spring," Lizzy called back. "I know you can't wait."

Flory grinned and waved furiously, shouting goodbyes. Tommy had gone, too. He was heading for St. John's. Flory was destined to spend the winter alone with Daddy in Juniper Tickle.

36

Robert White looked across the tickle just as the sun announced the day. He eyed the glass. It would be a fine day, and a fine day was a better day than any to tell the truth. It was time.

Flory's eyes had lost their shine. Robert couldn't abide by that. Not with knowing what he knew. Once he told her, Flory could run off and take it all in on this fine day. Then it would be her decision what came next.

He couldn't hold on to her forever. That wasn't right. She had already seen enough unfairness, and he couldn't let his taste of it and his choices be the end of her. The truth, however it was fashioned, was a hard place to begin, but he would have to start there for it to make sense.

Flory came from people who forgave—at least on her mother's side. Robert had to remember that. He would start with his name and go from there. In that regard, he was no different than Jimmy Bailor. He couldn't pretend to be, and he certainly couldn't judge Jimmy harshly for it.

Flory's mother was somebody who understood, who accepted, and moved on. Somebody who didn't hold grudges. He counted on this to be a quality to have passed on to her. She came from people who left, like his sons had done, like he had done. That was the part he would have the most trouble with. Flory's leaving would hurt him the most, but it wasn't his place to make her stay. If he didn't tell her, he had no doubt she would stay. He wouldn't do that to his little girl. She deserved better.

Flory also came from people who were liars like him—and maybe it was time she came from people who owned up to the truth. It could, and would, start with him.

Robert White was born Philip Hender, in a place across the sea, that of which he had forgotten the name. He didn't rightly know his age when he had been picked up on the streets and brought to the Dominion of Newfoundland to work. However, he did know he wasn't much older than Flory when she lost her mother. He was promised a wage, which didn't come, a place to stay, which he had as long as he worked, a bite to eat, which was always meagre, and that he would be free to do what he wanted after a few summers.

As he grew up, he dreamed of owning his own house, starting a family, and being a proper man. But the few seasons turned into more, the money didn't come, and when the merchant pulled out after four summers, he promised them the same on the other side of the ocean, from where they had first come. They were beaten and starved, as they had been on the voyage when he was younger.

On the second night, he stole a dory and rowed east from the five-masted schooner. To where, beyond east? He had no idea. Would he live to see land? He had no idea. Having no idea was far better than the prospect of the slavery he had endured at the whims of the rich.

He stole the merchant's food and money and didn't look

back. If he weren't swift and careful, he knew he would be found. When the sun was setting on the third day, he made landfall. He rested and foraged but was wary of being discovered. So, he stayed for two days to replenish and moved on. He skirted the coast, between islands, through inlets and coves, and after a week, he came upon the little tickle.

As he rowed to the hidden, innermost shore to spend the night sheltered by a multitude of islands, he saw a single juniper tree that looked as out of place as he felt. That tree was his inspiration, and he decided he would stay. He had an axe—the one that was still nowhere to be found—and he built a shelter. Exploring the coast, he came upon a town called Spigot Harbour. He bargained for salt and fishing gear, afraid to spend the merchant's money for fear of being found out.

Philip met a young girl there. Caroline Clark tended the store for the owner. He went back several weeks later with salt cod and traded for goods, and he talked to Caroline. She asked him his name.

A boyhood friend who had died on the ship taking them to Newfoundland came to mind. "Robert." He would be sure to remember his mate and that name.

Her expectant look made him pause. Last name! He needed a last name. Her collar lace drew his eye.

Robert White.

Whereabouts are you from?

Juniper Tickle. That rolled off his tongue as if he had been born and raised there, as if Whites had settled and prospered there since the time of his great-grandparents. From that moment on, that was his truth.

Robert White spent the winter in Juniper Tickle chopping logs to build a house. When spring came, he saw Caroline. By the following spring, he was as close to certain as certain could be that he would be safe, so he used a portion of the stolen money to buy windows, livestock, a stove, and a few pieces of furniture.

He brought Caroline home with him that fall. The shopkeeper's daughter was taking over the store, and she was no longer needed. Caroline was willing to try Juniper Tickle and had no immediate ties to anyone local to dissuade her.

They wed, started a family, and she was happy. He treated her as well as he could. Robert closed his eyes and pictured her smiling face. He talked about her grace in making a home for them despite the tough times.

Memories of their final words to each other caused him to wince. While she lay dying, he told her his birth name and what he had done. She forgave him. That was Caroline.

"Daddy, why are you telling me this?" Flory asked, her wide eyes focused on him, her body tense as she shifted on the bench.

"I wanted you to know that I was afraid to leave here," he said. "I was jammed by the truth."

In many ways, being taken off to jail—and being accepted by the law as Robert White from Juniper Tickle—had freed him. It solidified the certainty of his lie on legal papers, though not in the way he would have imagined. Perhaps as Philip Hender, yes, and as a thief and much sooner.

"I don't understand. All my life I was Flory White, but I'm not her?"

"Oh, Flory, of course you're her. You've always been her. You'll always be her," Robert said. He pulled her into his arms. "You're my Flory. Nothing can change that."

She pulled back and stared at her father. He swept the tears from her cheeks with the pad of his thumb.

"What I'm trying to tell you is that I understand Jimmy," he said, his voice softer than before. "I may not like what he did, but he was caught up in a mess not of his doing. He was trapped."

"But he didn't tell me," Flory said. "I feel so foolish."

"Truth is, the moment I heard his name, I could have killed him," Robert said. "I'm sure if I had a gun I'd probably have shot him. I was mad with the Bailors. We did nothing to those people. I thought they were all alive and we were left to rot, that you weren't safe. But once we heard what happened to him, he was as much without blame as we were. I was too stubborn to see it."

"He should have trusted me to tell me," Flory insisted.

"I know what you're saying. I should have told your mother," Robert said. "But I didn't. It had nothing to do with trust. I know you don't understand that. Some things should stay hidden, that's all. Especially if you know it might hurt somebody more by knowing. Or maybe that's an excuse I tell myself to make it easier."

Robert stood and looked out the window, then at the glass.

"It's funny how what is supposed to make things easier is harder to accept." He chuckled as he tapped the barometer with his finger. "My staying cooped up in Juniper Tickle was selfish. I was looking out for myself. Maybe your mother would have gotten the help she needed if she weren't tied to this place. Tied to me."

"That's different."

"Don't fool yourself," Robert continued. "There's not one thing different. But that's mine to carry."

Flory sighed.

"Bart and Lizzy leaving, that was the right thing," he said. "They shouldn't be trapped here because of me."

"That's different, too," Flory said.

Robert shook his head. "It's not. Look, Flory, don't let what happened come between you. Be forgiving like your mother, not a coward like me."

"Aww, Daddy, I don't think you're a coward. I don't plan to go anywhere." Flory hugged him.

"I don't want you to shackle yourself to my past, Flory. You're brave and humble, but you're also a young woman who deserves a life beyond that of her father. Especially that of her father's lies."

Flory let him go, then leaned in and kissed his forehead.

"Remember, Flory, you deserve a good life. One better than the hardship of Juniper Tickle."

"Being here with you is no hardship," she whispered as she closed the door.

Robert watched her walk out to the point. For a long time after she had gone out of his sight, his stare focused on the trail. He swallowed the uneasy feeling of being left alone in Juniper Tickle after all these years. Flory would be on the rock where she did her best thinking by now. He would support her in whatever she wanted. In the meantime, there was an axe he had to find.

37

Jimmy was torn. Was he daring to hope that Flory wanted him to come to her, or was he plain stupid? Bring it to her himself. What did that mean?

He couldn't ask his mother. She was angry with him for being angry with her. Jimmy had come to understand that his mother only allowed people around who supported her way of thinking. He would have believed that to be fortunate at one time. Maybe he was giving his younger self too much credit. He had always aligned with his mother because there was always something in it for him.

"Jimmy, believe me when I say that people want what they can get from you," Loretta said. "I don't want you to have your heart broken like I had mine."

He didn't know what that meant, but he was sure it was Mother drawing attention to herself. She bossed others around, and she could because she had leverage on them. Jimmy had often heard that many would starve if Loretta Bailor wasn't right. He was older when he discovered that truth. She stopped giving credit to the Hardys after she learned about Terry beating him up. When he found out about that, Jimmy stopped telling her. Then Father had taken Terry's father aboard with the crew, and Mother had no choice but give them credit. Jimmy chuckled at how his father had gotten the better of her. In his own way, by not telling, he had, too.

Mother's spite, and her know-it-all attitude, didn't work with him since his return, and she didn't know how to deal with that. She had always been able to control her son by showering him with cakes and candies and things that others didn't have. Jimmy had been too young to know and too spoiled to care.

Until Flory.

Mother had gone to bed in a huff, and he had gone to Raymond and Mr. George's bench by the shop door to ponder his predicament. Flory White was a complication, all right, but she sure was a pretty one.

Jimmy looked up at the stars. They were the same here as in Juniper Tickle. He wondered if she was seeing what he was seeing. Did she think of him? How would he find out?

Pain rattled his jaw before he realized he was moving and seeing different stars. A hand over his mouth prevented him from sucking air. He kicked. The hand that smothered him muffled his shouts. He was dragged around the corner of the house, where even the frailty of the starlight and the moon were made dimmer. It was also away from his mother's bedroom window.

When his eyes adjusted, he had just about passed out from lack of air. He went limp on purpose and the hand loosened, allowing him to take a breath. Jimmy tried to scream, but the hand clamped tight again.

"Shut up," Terry Hardy said. "Shut up or I'll kill you."

Jimmy nodded.

"I have nothing to lose," Terry said.

Jimmy heard desperation in his voice. He nodded, and Terry let him go. Jimmy fell on his back, and Terry pounced on top of him.

"Get clear of me," Jimmy demanded, his heart pounding.

Terry stood up and pulled Jimmy up with him. "Look, Bailor. I had nothing to do with any of this. You hear me?"

"I know," Jimmy said quickly. "I know."

Terry leaned over. "Emma said you believed me," he said. "I couldn't be sure."

"Where did you come from? And why are you here?"

"I don't know," Terry said. "I honestly don't know. I can't go home. I can't go to Emma's, and I don't think they'd look for me here."

"Who's looking for you?"

"Them two constables."

"What for?"

"Killing Giles," Terry said. "I know I got a hard name, and that's of my own doing. But killing people—how did it come to people thinking I'd do that?"

"How did you get out?" Jimmy asked, keeping his voice a little above a whisper.

"Giles came and said I was free to go. He said he was looking at somebody else."

"Did he say who?"

"No." Terry shook his head. "I wish he did."

"Why are you here? What do you want from me?"

"I know I wasn't nice to you. But you deserved it."

Jimmy chuckled. "Nothing like honesty. You're right," he said. "I had a few hard months to think about that."

"I know you had nothing to do with the boat. I always knew. I was just mad and all. I suppose you were, too."

"Yes," Jimmy said softly. He was seeing a lot of things differently. Even missing his father was different. In a way, he had been responsible for Terry being fatherless—like him.

"I need a place to hide," Terry said. "They won't look here."

"I can let you down the cellar." He wondered if it was an offence, but he hadn't heard that Terry was being questioned. That might not happen until the constables came back in the morning. "Nobody goes down there but Mother and me. I'll make sure she doesn't."

Jimmy believed it was the right thing to do. He sneaked Terry in and gave him a few items that he wished he'd had when he found the tilt. Once Terry was settled, Jimmy went to bed as if it were any other night.

Dreams about bears and fire and Flory screaming she hated him all mixed into one nightmare that made for a fitful sleep. Loretta made breakfast, but he could tell by her silence she was still mad. She sipped her tea, sighing audibly and often, as if a great inevitability had befallen her for which she had no blame. Jimmy smiled into the hot porcelain cup and didn't respond.

A rap on the door brought his mother on her feet and into the porch before Jimmy had laid his cup down.

"Tea?" she offered the constables. To his surprise, the officers said yes.

"Mr. Hardy hasn't been found but is wanted for questioning." Jimmy had almost forgotten about Terry hiding below them until Constable Grayson said his name.

"I told you, he wouldn't have done it," Jimmy insisted, a little louder than he meant.

"He's a likely suspect and the only one we have."

"There must be somebody else," Jimmy said. "If it wasn't Terry, where would you focus the investigation?"

"We have nobody else," Morgan, the second constable, said.

"What if this was somehow linked with my father's disappearance?" Jimmy asked them as he sat forward.

"We have no indication of that," Grayson said. "Those records were sent to St. John's and filed after court was finished."

"Constable Giles said he checked the tilt where I was and that I wasn't there," Jimmy said. "That wasn't true. I was there for almost a week."

Loretta piped up and told them about her conversation with Giles. She mentioned that was why she had wanted to see him the evening he died, to clear that up.

"He said there was no sign of me," Jimmy repeated. "They went back a second time and it was burnt, which also doesn't make sense."

"Could they have been in the wrong place?" Grayson said. "How well did Constable Giles know the area?"

"Not well, I would imagine," Jimmy said as he stared at his hands. "We just wanted to clear it up. I guess now we'll never know."

The men stayed until they finished their tea and then went back on the hunt for Terry.

Jimmy waited for an opportunity to go to the cellar. He told his mother he wanted to check on some stock Raymond Blythe had asked about.

"Why the Bailor men cater to those two old fogeys, I'll

never know," she said as she busied herself with a dusting cloth on the store shelf.

In the cellar, Terry gripped Jimmy's shirt and steered him toward the wall. "I thought you'd given me up," he said. "Good thing for yourself you didn't."

Jimmy pushed him away. "I told you I believed you." He brushed and smoothed his shirt's cotton fabric.

Terry's apology was barely audible. "I know. I feel trapped since all this business began. I know it's my own doing, my big mouth and all. Emma keeps telling me that's what gets me in trouble." Terry blushed when he spoke of his sweetheart. "I'm just not so good at listening."

Jimmy wanted to say at least he knew where he stood with Emma, but he left it alone.

"I overheard the constables talking," Terry told him. "Something you said wasn't right."

"What was that?"

"Dan brought Giles to the camp that first time."

"Dan Acreman?"

"Do you know another Dan?" Terry asked gruffly. Then he became apologetic again. "Yes. He would have known exactly where you were."

"Why would Dan not pick me up?" Jimmy asked aloud, more to himself.

"He'd been talking about buttering you up for something your father had planned. Then that new schooner came . . ."

"You think he wanted to go over on the other schooner with me?"

Terry rolled his eyes. "You really are dumb."

"Enough with the insults," Jimmy said. "Tell me."

"He was laying the notion of being schooner master on the

new one," Terry said irritably. He stared at Jimmy as if he could force him to see what was right in front of him.

Jimmy still didn't get it. "But what would that have to do with not picking me up?"

"You'd be out of the way," Terry said. "He used to say the baby was aboard. My father said that's what he called you."

Jimmy fell back on an oat sack as if Terry had punched him. His mother would depend on Dan, and with Jimmy not around, he could do what he liked. Even with Jimmy around—at least the old Jimmy—Dan would have it better on the *Annie May II* than he would have it under William Bailor's command. Jimmy would have been eating right out of Dan's hands.

"Do you think he did anything with the crew of the *Annie May*?" Jimmy asked quietly, dumbstruck. "Your dad? My father?"

"I think it was convenient. But he was ashore that day," Terry said. "I saw him myself."

"Dan was here the night Giles was murdered," Jimmy remembered. "He heard Mother saying she had to ask Giles about finding me. I can't believe this. I really can't believe this." Jimmy shook his head.

Dan was his friend. At least he had thought so. *The baby is aboard*. Jimmy was a means to an end—a bitter end for Constable Abraham Giles. It was hard to fathom such a thing.

"This can't be right," Jimmy said. "Not Dan."

"Did you know he was sweet on your mother one time?" Terry asked him.

Jimmy shook his head.

"So was Giles."

"What? How am I only hearing about this now?"

"Do you think my mother told me who she was sweet on

before my dad?" Terry asked, then answered his own question. "No. You got eyes, don't you?"

Terry stared at him, his eyes big. When Jimmy didn't respond, he shook his head and leaned against a foundation post.

"There was some kind of a racket back then, but I don't know much about it. Only heard my father say that if your father knew Dan Acreman had been his wife's beau and what he'd done, he wouldn't be on the *Annie May*."

"I still can't believe Dan would murder Giles. Why would he try to kill me?"

Terry sighed. "Killing you would leave a wife and mother alone, one who had two ships and a mercantile, and they had a previous relationship."

Jimmy made a clicking sound with his tongue. "Money," he said. "Mother says it's the root of all evil. I guess she's right. I'll go get the constables to sort this out."

"Forget the constables," Terry said as he darted for the stairs. "I'll be finding out right now."

Jimmy heard his mother scream. Footsteps pounded above him, and the front door slammed before he could bring himself to move.

"Jimmy, are you all right?" his mother shouted as she raced toward him, "Did he hurt you?"

Jimmy shook his head and backed away from her. "It was Dan," he uttered.

"Dan? What was Dan? What are you blabbering about? Did that Hardy boy hurt you?"

Jimmy took a deep breath. "Dan almost killed me, and he

killed Giles," he said matter-of-factly. He still had trouble believing it.

"Dan Acreman?" Loretta asked She laughed as she took in Jimmy's expression. Her hand flew to her mouth. "Not Dan."

"Yes, Dan. I have to catch Terry before he gets to him. You get the constables."

He raced away from his mother and hoped she would get the policemen. Dan's house was closer to the path he had used when he took the long way home from school. Terry wouldn't go that way. He could stop Terry before he reached Dan. Jimmy sprinted toward the gap in the trees and into the woods.

He didn't slow until he saw Terry's body lying on the ground below his vantage point on the rise. Jimmy stopped and called his name, but Terry didn't move.

"Dan," he shouted as he turned all the way around. "Dan, we know it was you."

"You know nothing," Dan said as he pounced from behind a tree and swung a spruce limb at Jimmy's head.

Jimmy ducked and heard the air as the stick passed over him. He edged toward Terry.

"You should have stayed dead, you little baby," Dan spat. "None of this would have happened if you had stayed in Juniper Tickle."

Dan swung again, and this time Jimmy ducked into a roll, moving out of the way. The limb splintered on a tree and broke in two. Dan's hand bled, and rage filled his eyes. Just like the bear.

"I knew you were there," Dan said. "Giles sent me out to check on the women." He punched at Jimmy, but the blood oozing from a cut on his forehead partially blinded him, and Jimmy danced out of range. Dan was out of breath, panting.

"Terry got a jab in before you struck him with the stick," Jimmy said as he circled behind a tree.

"You were playing house," Dan said absently. "Bringing in water or milk or something. I couldn't believe you found your way there. I went back to the boat and told Giles the women wanted to be left alone. I figured the winter would get you all."

Dan was frothing at the mouth when he dropped the stick and tackled Jimmy, driving the two of them head over heels down the steep grade. He perched atop Jimmy when they came to a stop at the base of a knotty var. Jimmy's wind was knocked out of him, but he managed to pull away from another poorly aimed punch. He rolled quickly to the other side and knocked Dan off balance. Pushing against the man's chest with both hands, he threw Dan sideways. Jimmy scrambled to his feet.

Dan came at him, swinging furiously. Before Jimmy could react, Dan's fist caught him below the ear, then in the gut, sending him reeling. Dan jumped at him again, and Jimmy sidestepped, more in a fumble as opposed to calculation, sending Dan shoulder first into a tree. Jimmy heard a crack before Dan cursed and turned on him again.

This time Jimmy was ready. He pulled back, threw a punch, and caught Dan above his good eye. Another punch, delivered in quick succession, folded Dan over at the waist. Dan spat blood and glared at Jimmy. Jimmy's hand was throbbing.

"You think you're better than me. Like your mother. Well, your not."

He flew at Jimmy, wild and animal-like, and they both hit the ground with a thump, Dan on top of him again. Jimmy bucked before Dan could catch himself, and he sailed over Jimmy's head and down the embankment.

Suddenly, two constables scrambled up the slope and accosted Dan. Jimmy lay on his back, panting while every single inch of him pained. Mary Fields came into his peripheral vision through a fattening eye, and he waved her away from him and toward Terry. Jimmy's mother fell to her knees by his side and cried as she rested her forehead against his.

As her tears spilled over his face, Jimmy surprised himself. He felt no urge to cry. He grinned instead. He couldn't help it.

38

In the beginning, obstacles couldn't discourage him no matter how hard they tried. But that sentiment was getting old for him now that he was running out of options. He had found nothing in three other church registries. This was his last chance. Jimmy pulled opened the enormous doors to the Basilica of St. John the Baptist and entered.

He wasn't a holy man in any sense, but he was an admirer of great work. The church's interior was even more magnificent than the exterior. It was impressive and stunning. Great painted windows told stories in coloured glass. High arched and ornate ceilings were intricately crafted. Polished wood and granite gleamed from every angle. Everything was a feast for the eyes. If he wasn't on an undertaking, he might have devoted more time to savour the elaborate marble statues and woodwork. Craftsmen had all to do with this place. Jimmy hoped the records had been kept as meticulously.

Quiescence and solemnity were displaced, or perhaps enhanced, by whispers of the dozen or so women and men who faced the walls at intervals, moving slowly around the great cathedral. Like cogs, one replaced the other as they went. Several figures occupied the front pews with beads clutched to their breasts, heads bowed before the exquisite white altar.

Off to one side, somebody exited one of the many doors while somebody else went in. A line of dowdy souls waited patiently, and Jimmy joined behind the last person, hoping his questions would find answers.

Once inside, he knelt. He heard murmurs through a panelled wall before the sound of wood on wood captured his attention and a hatch opened to reveal a small meshed opening by Jimmy's ear.

"What would you like to confess?" came a voice with a soft timbre.

"Confess?" Jimmy stammered, caught unawares. His thoughts raced.

"This is the confessional, my son," came the reply.

The silence stretched on as Jimmy's emotions bubbled like thick pea soup on a reddened stove. The priest, as unaware of the scorching turbulence seeking release as Jimmy, cleared his throat on the other side of the panel.

"I killed my father."

Jimmy's whispered stammer surprised him as it left his mouth. The words circled the tiny room, surrounded him, until they strangled him. Gradually, the thumping in his chest slowed.

"I killed my father," Jimmy said again. Silence lingered as he examined his claim.

"How did he die?" the priest asked.

"I wasn't there . . . I don't know . . . but it was me that killed him." Jimmy's eyes watered. He dabbed at the tears with his coat's lapel.

"How could you have killed him if you weren't there?" the

compassionate voice from the tiny window prodded. "Help me understand."

Jimmy told him everything.

"Perhaps you have to forgive yourself for the boy's actions you see through the eyes of the better man you've become."

Jimmy tried to let that sink in. "I don't know how."

"You're doing it. Why did you come here in the first place?"

"I'm trying to find my father's sister."

"For what purpose?"

"I didn't know my father like I should have," Jimmy replied.

"What will finding his sister do?"

"I don't know," he admitted. It was true. He hadn't gotten that far in his thinking. "I'd like to find out."

"That's a noble undertaking," the priest said. "I pray you're successful."

The priest directed him to the parish records office, said a prayer for him, and closed the shutter to bring an epiphany and forgiveness to the next soul in the lineup. Jimmy rose and stumbled into the nave and sought the nearest exit. His steps were lighter as he pushed through the Basilica doors and out into the sunshine.

Jimmy sat on the step, fatigued but lifted. He debated whether he would try to find his aunt or not. His mother wouldn't be pleased. But he had come this far.

At the parish's records office, Jimmy inquired about William Bailor, knowing generally the year in which his father was born. He breathed a sigh when he was rewarded with an entry for a William James Bailor, born to a James and Annabella Mary Bailor, née Faraday. Sarah Jane Bailor was born almost three years later. Annabella Bailor's death certificate showed she died the same day Sarah was born. James was lost at sea two years later. How terrible that must have been for Jimmy's father.

The talkative lady was helpful and tracked Sarah to a birth record for an Elizabeth Anabella Faraday, though no father was listed. Sarah was unmarried, but she might have named the child after the father, or the child might have been documented by her mother's maiden name. There were no other entries for Sarah Faraday or Sarah Bailor.

"That's not uncommon," the lady said. "We are diligent with the records, but sometimes people move away and get married, and those records would be in another parish."

Jimmy nodded. Mr. George had mentioned an uncle had taken the children in. That could have been his mother's brother, hence Sarah might have gone by Faraday.

"Sometimes nuptials are published in the St. John's *Telegram*. You could try there if you have the time."

Jimmy thanked her. As he was leaving, she called out to him. "Another place to ask is at the Mercy Convent."

She gave him directions. Jimmy hoped he was getting closer to discovering his father's family. It pressed on him. It felt important.

The convent was nearby. Upon inquiry there, he learned that Sarah Bailor, or Faraday, might have perished about ten years before. One of the older nuns remembered a Sarah but not the last name, though Faraday did sound familiar. She told Jimmy where she was buried but doubted there would be a stone.

Jimmy's family research was limited to one woman who might be the daughter of a prostitute, possibly a prostitute herself, and for all he knew could be dead by now, too. His outlook was less than promising.

The newspaper office was on his way to the St. John's docks. He wasn't expecting much when he got there, but he didn't want to leave St. John's without exploring all possibilities. The place was small. Tied stacks of newsprint were piled high around the door.

A tiny man wearing spectacles—Nathanial Spears, according to the wooden sign on the desk—moved about behind a counter. Once they got the greetings out of the way, Jimmy mentioned he was looking for Elizabeth Faraday.

"So is the entire city," Mr. Spears said. "Her and the Topsail Star."

"That can't be right," Jimmy said. "Elizabeth Faraday? You're sure? And who's the Topsail Star?"

"Of course I'm sure, and the Topsail Star is a *what*, not a *who*," Mr. Spears said. "An article has been posted in the papers once every six months or so. It's near that time for another one. A reward is offered for her whereabouts. Do you know her?" The man put aside the paper he was reading and stared at Jimmy.

"It's an odd tale, really," Jimmy replied. "More of an unlikelihood."

"Want it on the record?" Mr. Spears asked as he leaned forward and grabbed a pencil. "We pay for stories that are newsworthy."

"No, nothing like that," Jimmy said, fighting the urge to step back and get out of there. "She might be a relative, that's all. By the sounds of it, I hope not. What did she do?"

"Just a second. I'll get the story. There's even a sketch of her."

Jimmy read the articles. The last one had the artist's pencil rendering. Jimmy's eyes bulged.

"You know her? Where she is?" Mr. Spears queried. A catlike grin had formed on his reddening face.

"Nothing like that," Jimmy said quickly. "Just surprised she's so young, that's all. She's not who I'm looking for. The age is wrong."

Jimmy left the office and headed for the *Annie May II*. His mind raced.

39

Like Daddy had predicted, the snowstorm struck mid-afternoon. The brooding sky and calm sea of the morning stood in sharp contrast to the raging turbulence that left the panes rattling in the window frames.

Daddy was snoozing on the daybed when Flory cocked her ear. The knocking she heard was not the windows in the sash. She nudged Daddy's shoulder on her way to the pantry. He jolted and sat up.

"What did you do that for?" he called to her before he heard it, too. He met her coming from the pantry with the shotgun and cartridges. The wind was on the front and the knocking was coming from the rear, where the storm door had been barred in.

"Who the blazes is there? Let them in, child." Daddy clutched the loaded gun loosely, but his stance was that of somebody who was prepared to use it at the first sign of trouble.

Flory opened the back door and unhooked the second latch. She held the handle so the wind wouldn't blow it from its hinges. Two figures, encrusted in snow, backed off the step to let the storm door swing wide, then stepped into the porch. She pulled the door closed and set the latch as she ushered the two figures ahead to allow the door to close.

The two stomped the snow from their boots and parted to let her by. As they peeled off their clothes, she didn't recognize the first one, but the second was Jimmy Bailor. Her face lit up, and her heart raced at the sight of him. "Jimmy," she gasped. "It's you." She resisted the urge to run to him.

"Where did you come from?" Daddy asked.

"We were on the way here when the storm came upon us," Jimmy said.

"Coming here?" Flory asked, her eyes big.

"I've got things to take care of," Jimmy replied. He pulled the sack from his back before he noticed Robert White and the gun. "Sir, do you mind if we stay here until the storm passes? Or the barn, if that's more suitable."

With a nod, Robert handed Flory the gun and indicated with his head for her to return it to the pantry.

"What's your business?" he asked.

"I have to speak to Lizzy, sir," Jimmy said. "We tried their house before coming here."

"Lizzy?" Flory asked. "What for?"

"I'm afraid I can't tell you. I must speak to Lizzy. Is she here?"

"No," Robert said.

Jimmy's pallor changed and his brows shot upward.

"Nothing like that," Flory said. "She's fine."

"I don't mean her any harm," Jimmy said. He pointed to his companion. "This is Terry Hardy."

"Hello," Terry said. He stopped shedding his outerwear and reached out a mitted hand to shake Robert's.

"You can stay," Robert said as he eyed the glass. "I wouldn't turn a dog out in this. Looks like it might be a while."

Terry continued to strip his mitts and hat, as did Jimmy. He grinned at Flory, and her heart exploded.

"I'm glad you're alive," she said. "No worse for wear."

Jimmy picked up the broom and swept out the snow they had tracked in.

"No fault of his own," Terry said.

Flory carried the teapot to the table. "Tell us more."

They sat around the table, where Terry and Jimmy relayed the news from Spigot Harbour. Robert was on his second cup as they regaled them with tales of how they had caught the murderer.

"Like the bear," Jimmy said. "It's all true."

"I don't know about any bear," Terry said.

Flory and Jimmy proceeded to tell him of their brush with death.

"You really are looking for Lizzy?" Flory asked.

Jimmy nodded and bit his lip.

"Won't tell me why, either," Terry said. "But I owe it to him to help. He saved my life."

"We don't need to know," Robert said. "That business is between Jimmy and Lizzy. As long as Bart doesn't get arrested, it's fine by me."

"He won't," Jimmy confirmed. "Where are they, anyway?"

"Twillingate," Flory said. "Tommy is gone to St. John's."

"I almost forgot," Jimmy said as he pulled at the pack he had brought. "I didn't get the message until a few weeks ago that you hadn't eaten the can of peaches with your father."

Flory blushed. "That's all right."

"No, it's not. I have them with me. I believe you said I was to bring them myself. And a promise made is a promise kept." He smiled and waited until her face reciprocated before he pulled two tins. "Enough to go around," he said as he got a knife from the pantry. Jimmy opened the first can and poured half in Flory's saucer, then her father's, and the second one he shared with Terry.

Flory was tentative at first. She took the spoon and stared at the plate. But after one bite, her eyes brightened. She hadn't tasted the like before. She grinned at Daddy first before turning the smile to Jimmy. He really had a good heart.

Flory swallowed a gasp as he turned. She had been curious to know why he wanted to see Lizzy, and just now, his facial features reminded her of her sister-in-law's. There must be a relation there, she thought. She had noticed *something* when he first came to Juniper Tickle but hadn't been able to gather just what. How had it taken her so long?

She wouldn't say, nor would she let it come between her and Lizzy. Friends didn't interfere, and Flory and Lizzy were friends. Besides, that might not have been the reason Jimmy wanted to talk to Lizzy, anyway.

Jimmy gave her a book he had bought in St. John's. "Just for you," he said. *Black Beauty* by Anna Sewell. Jimmy assured her it would be a good challenge for her but not too hard. She wanted to throw her arms around him for bringing such a beautiful gift, but she refrained. Her hand lingered on his as he passed over the book.

"Jimmy," Robert said. "I got a new axe from O'Rielly. I wanted to give you the one belonging to your father. It's still here. I left it in the shed so the handle wouldn't spoil in the heat."

"I'll pay you for it."

Robert shook his head. "It wasn't ours to begin with."

Jimmy thanked him and promised to collect it when they left. They hunkered down for the night once it got dark.

At daylight, Jimmy and Terry went to the barn, tended the animals, milked the goat, and collected the eggs. Once the snow stopped falling, the young men shovelled all the pathways, filled the water tank and kettles, and neither Robert nor Flory had to do a thing outside. Flory made pea soup and dumplings while they worked.

By evening of the second day, Robert watched the glass and said the next day was going to be a good one. Sure enough, dawn came cold but bright and calm. Jimmy and Terry tended the stable. Robert went to the shed and brought in the axe with the *WB* inscribed on the handle. He offered it to Jimmy.

Jimmy rubbed his fingers over the helve and gave him a wry smile. "I'll keep it on the *Annie May*, where it belongs," he said. "Thank you." He shook Robert's hand. "If you have no concerns, sir, I'd like to come back in the spring and see Flory."

"You're welcome here any time. But now, regarding seeing Flory, that's up to her." Robert looked at Terry. "Young man, can you help me get a few pairs of snowshoes from the barn loft? You might need them making your way to the point."

Jimmy had said they had rowed in from the *Annie May*, which was anchored with four others aboard in a sheltered cove behind the island out of the wind and snow. But they had travelled in from the point once the snow hit, so it would be tough getting back.

Terry followed him and nodded at Flory. "Be seeing you, ma'am."

"Flory, please," she said. "I'm too young to be ma'am."

"Flory," he said with a grin. "Hope you get to meet my Emma. She's tough and pretty like you."

She blushed as Terry left.

"Well, what do you say?" Jimmy asked.

"About what?" Flory replied innocently.

"About my coming back in the spring." He reached for her hand. Their fingers intertwined.

"Daddy told you that you were welcome," she said. Flory smiled as she stepped closer.

"That's how it's going to be," he said, and he inched ahead. "Well, Florence Elaine . . ."

"Alice," she corrected him.

"Well, Florence Alice White, would you mind if I came calling in the spring?"

"I'll think about it," Flory said as she beamed up at him. "I'll let you know in the spring." She laughed and threw her arms around him. "I really thought I'd never see you again. I can't wait until spring."

"I didn't think you'd want to see me again."

"I was mad. But Lizzy and Daddy helped me get over that. It was childish."

"I deserved it," Jimmy said. "I really am sorry."

"We don't go backward, Jimmy Bailor."

"James William Bailor," he said with a chuckle.

"Well, we don't go backward, James William Bailor, only forward from here."

"Forward from this," he said as he touched his lips to hers. It shocked them both. They pulled away and laughed. Then they kissed again until they heard Robert and Terry on the step.

"Forward," she said. "I don't hate you, Jimmy. Not at all."

"Good thing," he said. "Spring can't come soon enough."

40

With weather and ice conditions along the coast of Newfoundland well-known as unpredictable and treacherous, it took more than a month for Jimmy to make his way to Twillingate. He wasn't entirely sure what compelled him to go, even after examining what his motives might be, but he stepped off the *Annie May* on a cold February morning in search of Elizabeth White, née Faraday, his first cousin and only known family on his father's side.

It felt like he was finishing something, though to his knowledge, his father hadn't expressed interest. But since William had named his two vessels after his mother, Jimmy believed this would mean a great deal to him. That reason alone was good enough for him.

He spent the day making inquiries as to the whereabouts of the Whites. Jimmy was considering he had been led astray until he remembered Lizzy was having a child, which was why she was in Twillingate in the first place. He asked about a nurse, and after seeking her out, he was rewarded with directions.

It was coming on dark when he knocked at the door of a

small, single-storeyed house that squatted into the hillside behind another. He would have missed it if he hadn't been told it was there.

Lizzy answered the door and squealed when she saw him. "Jimmy Bailor, is that you?" she said. She hugged him, then pushed him away and held his shoulders. "More meat on you now," she said. "You're eating good somewhere."

Jimmy laughed. "My mother is taking good care of me. Is Bart home?"

"Yes. Come in out of the cold."

A small but neat interior greeted him. Diapers hung above the stove. Bart, who had been eating at a table he recognized from Juniper Tickle, stood alongside his wife as Jimmy stepped in. Jimmy extended his hand, but Bart wouldn't take it. His cold stare would have frightened Jimmy the fall before. However, he was certain that Bart wouldn't do him harm, at least not in front of the children.

Bobby looked up from where he sat by a cradle. He rushed to Jimmy and wrapped his arms around his legs. Jimmy tousled his hair and picked him up. The little fellow hugged him. Jimmy's heart thumped loudly, and he smiled.

"Sit, Bart," Lizzy commanded. "Jimmy means no harm."

Bart reluctantly moved to his stool and sat.

"New one?" Jimmy asked as he tilted his head toward the cradle.

"A little girl. We called her Sarah."

"After your mother," Jimmy said before he could stop himself.

"Yes," Lizzy stammered. "How do you know?" She looked from Jimmy to Bart. Fear flickered in her eyes along with the glow from the kerosene lamp.

"Just a guess. Caroline was named for Bart's mother, if I'm not mistaken."

Lizzy nodded.

"I came for Bart," Jimmy said. "I have a proposition for you." He noticed Bart's grip on the table loosen and the knuckles change from white to pink.

"What would that be? What would William Bailor's son want with me?"

Lizzy urged him to sit and poured a cup of tea. Bobby stayed anchored to Jimmy's neck despite his parents' attempts to make him leave Jimmy alone. Jimmy insisted to let the boy be—he wasn't a bother at all. He liked that the little fellow hadn't forgotten him.

"I don't know if you heard about all the goings-on in Spigot Harbour," Jimmy said. He quickly filled them in. "Unfortunately, we will never know what became of the crew of the *Annie May*." He stared into his teacup. "I've resigned myself to that."

Lizzy patted his shoulder. "We're sorry for all you've been through, Jimmy," she said softly. "But why are you here?"

"I have a need for a couple of good men," he said as he eyed Bart. "Shareman on the *Annie May* or captain on the *Annie May II*. You can pick."

Jimmy told Bart about the boats and the required crew. He had nobody else lined up except for a few younger fellows from Spigot Harbour, and had need of a few more.

"This can't be true," Bart said.

"I assure you it is. Unless you have something better. Your father might be convinced to show us younger ones a thing or two. I haven't asked him. I figure if you said yes, he might, too."

Lizzy's eyes shone. "We don't like it here," she said. "It's too big for us. But Juniper Tickle in the winter isn't the place for us, either."

"I'll let you work that out," Jimmy said, looking at Bart once more. "If you say yes, of course."

"I don't have a better offer," Bart said hesitantly. "You're not putting us on?"

"Why would I do that?" Jimmy asked simply. He'd learned that from Flory.

Bart's face changed. His sour expression livened, and a glint settled in his eye. "I don't know. We were just talking about next spring and what we'd do."

"The babies have us thinking," Lizzy added. "But it's hard to think when you have nothing to think about."

"I almost forgot. I had something for the children," Jimmy said. "I left it on the boat. Bart, if I keep Lizzy company and have another cup of tea, would you go get it? You could have a look around the *Annie May* on the water and see what you'd be getting yourself into. Terry Hardy is expecting you."

Bart turned a questioning eye to his wife. She nodded, and he retrieved his coat and left.

"Happiest time I've seen him all winter," Lizzy said. "We were trying to decide what to do. Bart wanted to go to St. John's, but it's too big for me. Here's too big, too." She frowned. "This is kind of you, Jimmy."

"Not kind. It's practical. Now I want to talk to you about the other reason I came."

"Other reason?" She eyed Jimmy. "You know, don't you? When you said my mother's name, I knew that you knew." She pushed back from the table and went to the stove.

"Lizzy, look at me," Jimmy said softly. "I do not mean any harm. Honest."

"So, you know everything," she said, flatly, her back to him. She shuddered and sniffed, and Bobby bolted from Jimmy's lap to encircle his mother's legs with his little arms.

"I know what the papers say. I don't believe it. But I'm the only one who knows anything at all," he said. "I promise." Jimmy stood behind her. "Come back to the table before Bart returns."

Lizzy's movements were slow as she joined him at the table and sat. "I knew this day would come," she said. "I guess it's here."

"I don't know what day you think it is, but I'm sure you're wrong. You're the daughter of my father's sister. That's all I wanted to tell you."

"That's not possible." Lizzie's eyes were wide.

"It is the truth." Jimmy informed her of what he had found. "As for the accusations, that's all they are. I've been accused of killing my father and his crew and the constable, and God knows what else. There are three sides to every story, and only one includes the truth. I don't want to know any of it."

"You don't? You won't tell Bart?"

"None of my business. If you want to tell him we're related, that's your business. If you don't, that's your business. I have enough to worry about keeping myself straight."

"Oh, Jimmy." Lizzy squeezed his hand. "You're such a good man. We'd all be dead if you hadn't come to Juniper Tickle."

"And I'd be dead if I hadn't," he was quick to reply.

"Now, speaking of Juniper Tickle," Lizzy said. "You know, there's this girl."

Jimmy held up his hands. "Just so we're clear. None of this has to do with Flory or getting on her good side," he said. "I already told her I'd be coming for her in the spring."

"That makes me so happy. You really are a good man. Bart will be all right with us being relatives."

"You'll tell him? Them?" Jimmy asked.

"Yes," she said. "Of course. I'd be proud to."

"Don't go to St. John's," Jimmy warned. "Ever."

"I know. Life is good with Bart and the Whites. Now with you added to that, I don't need anything else. Imagine, we're cousins. Who would have thought?"

41

"I know you," Loretta said. "I've met you before. I never forget a face."

"My wife worked here many years ago," Robert said. "For your father." He paused. "Caroline Clark."

"Caroline," Loretta repeated. "Yes, I remember her." She covered her face with her palms and whispered, "Did she have a good life?"

"I'd like to think so." Robert's eyes lost their glow. "Not hardly long enough."

Loretta nodded. "She left because of me. I thought Daddy thought more of her than he did of me. Thought my then beau, Dan, was interested in her. Saw things that weren't there. I was so mean to her. I was envious."

"I'd like to think she left because of me," Robert interrupted.

"You sure put the sparkle in her eye. That's what made me so jealous. She had what I didn't, until William."

"Let's leave it at that," Robert said with a grin. "Flory is like her, you know. Strong. Loving. Independent. She and Jimmy will have a good life together."

"He looks at her like William used to look at me," Loretta pined. "Oh, and don't worry, Jimmy has already told me about interfering. I don't know what you fed that boy in Juniper Tickle, but he left here a boy and came back a man."

"A good man," Robert agreed. "You are part of that. Don't forget it."

"I'll take that as a compliment, Mr. White."

"Robert. Please."

"Robert." She nodded. "Robert, would you do me the honour of escorting me to my seat before you walk your daughter down the aisle?"

"Mother," Jimmy said from behind her. "Come on and take your pew. We're almost ready."

Jimmy's red face moved from his mother to his soon-to-be father-in-law. "Hope everything is all right?"

Robert laughed. "You might need to sit down, by the look of you."

"Come on, Jimmy, bring your mother to her seat," Loretta said as she grinned at Robert. "I think you might need me to hold you up."

Jimmy laughed. "I thought you were having words, that's all."

"Everything is just fine, son," Robert replied. "I hear the bells. You'd better take your mother to her seat."

As if on cue, the horse bells jangled outside. Robert opened the church doors and welcomed his daughter.

"Flory, you are glowing," he said as he swallowed the lump that had suddenly filled his throat.

"She certainly is," Lizzy said as she fixed Flory's veil and brushed at the dress. "Jimmy will be beside himself."

"Stop fussing," Flory said. "I don't know how you talked me into having a wedding."

"I know, I know," Lizzy said. "See you inside."

"Go on," Flory said as she waved Lizzy away. Lizzy giggled as she left.

"All this fuss," Flory said as she looked back at her father.

"You deserve all this fuss. Don't ever forget that."

Flory smiled at him and looked at the door.

"You know, Flory," Robert said as he reached for her arm. "We can turn around and leave. You just say the word."

Flory glared at him. "You're serious?"

"I wouldn't have let you come here if I were serious." He stared at her and smiled. "Go make a life for yourself with that young man. Ready?"

"I've been ready since I first laid eyes on him, Daddy."

42

Present Day

Professor Faraday Cole stepped out of the dinghy and stood upon the shores of Juniper Tickle. He and ten students from Memorial University's archaeology department were to spend the next three weeks excavating the area of the former community and performing an environmental analysis. His students would leave here with credits for ARCH 3585 and ARCH 3586.

He told them that, by unearthing the foundations of this place and studying its heritage, they would develop the practice of archaeology and learn valuable skills in environmental archaeology, aids that could be brought into other career choices in traditional or social sciences.

While that was true for the students who would camp and work there, for him it held a deeper connection. He would fall asleep tonight in the birthplace of his four-times great-grandmother Florence, the youngest daughter of Robert and Caroline White. She had married a James Bailor from Spigot Harbour. Professor Cole learned he had been named after somebody who married one of Florence White's brothers, a Faraday from St. John's.

He'd had no idea there was a Juniper Tickle in Newfoundland

and Labrador until his daughter explored a family tree as part of Heritage Week in high school. She had traced her roots, and eventually they led here. There were also articles about a murder involving the Whites around the time they lived in Juniper Tickle.

Every family, he surmised, wouldn't have to go too far back to find a blemish that couldn't be righted or which was outrageous even by today's standards. That wasn't why he was here, though. He wasn't looking for skeletons, or answers, nor was he chasing ghosts—he just wanted to see the heavens and the earth as his ancestors would have seen them. Faraday was a facts man, a dig-in-the-dirt man, not a digging-*for*-dirt man. He had always been fascinated by the builders and the livyers and how they survived.

However, he couldn't deny that this place was personal. His own relatives had been accused of murdering a boatload of men right here. Interestingly, his five-times great-grandfather, William Bailor, had been one of the victims. Though there had been jail time for larceny on the Whites' side, there was no evidence that the Whites had ever seen the men they had allegedly murdered. So, it was personal, yes. He was anxious to start the dig in the morning.

Professor Cole ushered the students ashore and told them why they were there. The group set up camp in the clearing at the head of the tickle. They guessed, because of the mounds and dips in the terrain, that this was where the settlement had been. The earth tried its best to reclaim the squares and corners and perhaps would have succeeded in another hundred years if they didn't disturb it. Tomorrow they would find the foundation walls and begin unearthing his lineage.

After a week of digging and cataloguing, the professor looked out over the area and smiled at his students' work. They had found two houses, one on each side of the gut. They had discovered the remnants of a barn and, in the woods, skeletal remains believed to be those of a horse or a cow, and smaller bones believed to be sheep and possibly goats. These were typical finds for resettled places along these shores. But one bone structure was different. After much searching online, results suggested that the remains were those of a polar bear, which wouldn't have been native to this place. He wondered what the story was behind that. The animal might have wandered here and might never have seen the face of a human, but traces of ash on the bones suggested that perhaps it had made contact with people.

As near as he could determine after a cursory search, there had been no graveyard in Juniper Tickle. Regardless, if an official cemetery existed, they wouldn't disturb the dead on this trip. If they found an unofficial one, or mass grave, he would have involved the Royal Canadian Mounted Police, who had inherited the jurisdiction when Newfoundland and Labrador joined Canada.

In week two, they believed they had uncovered the foundations where they had first been laid. There were signs of rock chimneys, a few nails, and a Newfoundland penny dated 1898. The class was excited about that find. They had discovered it the old-fashioned way without the use of a metal detector. The instrument was the last thing they would use when their investigation was closer to completion.

There were no tools to be found, though the soil samples

showed evidence of an area where wood was piled, chopped, or sawed at the rear of both dwellings. They unearthed no stoves or bed frames. This indicated that the community had most likely moved, and Faraday's ancestors would have taken their possessions with them. His lineage traced back to the Twillingate and Bonavista areas, so that made the most sense.

History didn't record much before Juniper Tickle. There were no church records, no census, no last names available anywhere his daughter could find. He had gotten the name Faraday through an oral history, but even that was skeptical at best.

Things got interesting during week three. One of the students had taken the metal detector for a sweep of the area.

"Professor Cole, come have a look," Paulette called.

His mug stopped midway between his lap and mouth as he focused his attention toward the group. Paulette was flailing her arms. Faraday leaned forward on the stump he had claimed as his perch near the firepit and gulped the last dregs of his warm coffee. He signalled he was on his way and crossed the sandbar to the site now labelled Secondary Dwelling. Several of the students' shovels still penetrated the soil, and a rusted piece of metal lay beside the hole.

"We found an axe," Paulette said. "But there's something else beneath it."

"Interesting find," Faraday said.

"It was buried," she said as she nodded vigorously. "Like, not buried beneath a hundred years of soil buildup, but buried as in *buried*, and *then* there was a hundred years of soil buildup."

Paulette pointed out the natural layering evident at the side of the hole, then the axe they had found several inches beneath that.

"That is very interesting," Professor said with an approving nod. "Well done, class."

"There's more," Drake said as he brushed away loose soil from a ragged piece of cloth. He looked up at Faraday from where he was kneeling by the hole. "The metal detector still pinged, and we found this."

"Want to inspect it, sir?" another student asked.

"It's your find," Faraday said. "Finish it up."

The students excavated around the item. They placed markers, brushed, dug, and recorded as they went. Finally, they all sat on the ground, feet planted upon the layer they had dug, which circled a faded, possibly blue plaid fabric in the middle of the depression.

"Paulette." Faraday indicated for her to do the unveiling.

She waved the metal detector one more time. The device beeped loudly. While Drake filmed using the university-issued camera, Paulette handled the rotted cotton with great care. It was rolled in a bundle. As she unwound it, the fabric revealed several coins and jewellery. She and her classmates separated each piece to be documented.

Within the stash were several earrings and two necklaces. One was made from pearls, and the other was gold with a porcelain, patterned, oval amulet. The last item was a large brooch. Appreciative mumbles and whistles circulated in the group.

"Let me see that brooch," Faraday said as he gestured to Paulette to hand over the piece. "There is something vaguely familiar about this. Not sure from where."

The professor took the object and examined it. He wiped

away much of the century-old grime to reveal a yellow stone surrounded by diamonds in a star-shaped pattern.

"Star. Something about a star," Faraday said. He held it up for the others to see. "Anyone recall an article?"

"I'll do a search, sir," Drake said. He bent over his phone. A few others followed suit.

"That's it," Paulette said. "Nothing else left in this." She held up the ragged cotton. "It must have been a dress. Looks intact. Well, except for the tear here at the shoulder. I think it was put in the ground like that."

"The Topsail Star," Drake shouted as he hoisted his phone aloft and showed the picture around. "We've found the Topsail Star."

"What's its significance?" Faraday asked.

"Sir, you'll find this piece particularly interesting. Listen to this article from the *Telegram* in 1901.

"Mrs. Catherine Whiteway, wife of Prime Minister William Whiteway, offers a reward for the return of her rare brooch. The yellow and white diamond design was crafted by R. H. Trapnell Ltd. as a wedding gift from her husband in October 1872 and holds a high sentimental value. Mrs. Whiteway claims that a Miss Elizabeth Faraday, a maid in her employ, may know the whereabouts of the broach. She also states that she is not interested in any other pieces of jewellery or clothing. This reporter is led to believe that Miss Faraday absconded with more than just a brooch, though the Whiteways have not confirmed such conjecture."

"I found a different article in the MUN archives, sir," another student said. "It was a year later, according to the date, and there's a sketch of the girl." He showed the picture to Faraday, who read the article aloud.

"Seeking information on the whereabouts of one Elizabeth Faraday, pictured, in the disappearance of the priceless brooch, the Topsail Star, pictured. A significant reward is offered for information leading to her whereabouts or for the return of the jewellery. Owner is not seeking prosecution. Boston papers copy."

"Is that correct, Professor Cole?"

"I'm sorry, Harvey, what did you say?" Faraday asked him.

"Could this be a relative?" Harvey pointed to the pencil sketch from the article.

"Well," Faraday said with a grin, "there's this thing about history. It's either somebody's best guess based on what's before them, or it's tainted by the viewpoint of whoever recorded it at the time. The truth doesn't get in the way of that."

"Do you think she's your kin?"

"Things seem to point to that conclusion," Faraday said. "As for how this stuff got here," he said, "I'll leave that up to the history books to tell me what they think of that."

43

More than a century before

William Bailor ground his teeth to hold his tongue. Loretta wouldn't forgive him if she knew the truth. There was no way he was leaving Spigot Harbour in the evening to go straight for that good-for-nothing boy. It was a waste of his time. He certainly didn't intend to pay the crew for a frivolous sail to Thunder Cove for Jimmy. There was money to be made, a good run of herring to bait the trawl lines, and they might get to set this evening and twice tomorrow before retrieving Jimmy. He hoped the last few days would make a man out of the boy. William didn't know any other way to go about it.

"We'll stay at the summer camp tonight and be home late tomorrow," he said as he picked up his lunch pail.

"Here's a few extra tins of fruit," Loretta said.

"All these?" he said as he hefted the package.

"A couple for Jimmy. I'm sure he'll be hungry."

William sighed. "He's fine, Loretta. I know you're worried, but I'm sure he's fine."

Loretta kissed his cheek. "I miss him," she said.

"I wouldn't have left him if I thought something would happen." Jimmy would have to fend for himself for a change. Make in a fire, get himself a cup of tea, and other things William had been able to do when he was ten. He didn't understand the boy. James had turned out lazy and would surely amount to nothing if Loretta had her way.

William felt his cheeks redden. He knew he had better get out of the house before he said something that would widen the rift between them. He gave Loretta every advantage, and it didn't seem to matter. Their son was the only thing that counted for her. If William hadn't done something like this, the boy would be living off of them forever. He wasn't having it.

William stomped to the wharf and didn't answer anyone's greeting. He would be the talk of Spigot Harbour going out this late in the day. It was a good thing Dan didn't show up, because he wasn't having that backtalk, either. Maybe by spring he would calm down when he needed every hand he could get. But for today, he would do without him.

"Put the barrels aboard," William said. "Trap and trawl buckets, too. Hope you brought enough grub to do you until tomorrow evening."

The men grumbled as they readied to leave port. William knew who was doing the most complaining in the cluster by studying the steam rising in the freezing air. The winds had died out, and it promised to be a nice evening on the water. William added a cask of kerosene.

"Fill the lamps," he said. "We'll be catching herring tonight."

William could navigate his way into or out of Spigot Harbour day or night. Most mornings they would be well at sea when daylight broke, and it would be long after dark when he got home, even in the lingering daylight hours of summer. The men knew what they had signed on for, and he paid them enough to keep them coming back.

They had set the trap by the time the moon rose. Dave Hardy and his cousin, Frank, were out in the dory, one at each end, holding the lamps while two other lights hung on the rear of the *Annie May*. The boat creaked in the still night air as the black ocean lapped the sides. The tension among the crew was a stark contrast to the water's lulling sense of serenity. When the first lamp burned out, more than one grateful sigh pierced the air before a flurry of activity broke out and they hauled the trap.

Just before daylight, they had filled and capped twelve barrels, with pans of herring left over. They filled the lamps to warm their fingers as they set to work on the trawl lines. Frank cut the herring while the rest sat around the trawl tubs baiting the hooks with the cold fish pieces. Icy sea water and gore dripped around them. Even the heat from the lamp couldn't revive their fingers.

"There'll be plenty of time to eat and get warm when the hooks are in the water," William said as he inspected the tubs. "That trap needs to be put away." He dragged the mesh aside to get another tub of trawl lines. Salt water and pieces of herring covered the deck as the sun crested the ocean horizon.

"That's six tubs," Frank said.

"Three hundred hooks," William observed. "That'll do for the first try." He craned his neck to peer over the splitting table. "Enough herring for a second round?"

"Sure," Frank said. The others eyed him sourly. He shrugged at them when William left for the wheelhouse. "He was right here," he said. "What could I do?"

"Waste more of it than you are now," Dave said. "We'll never get home out of it if you don't."

They set the trawls and went below to eat before it was time to drag the lines in again and start over. Two of the four ate quickly and leaned against the ribbing to doze while Frank and Dave sat in silence at the table, too tired to nap.

William joined them and sent them back on deck to haul the trawls. Their spirits lifted as they saw nearly every hook had a codfish on. That excitement was short-lived, because the cod had to be gutted and put in the hold, and it still wasn't enough to fill the *Annie May*. The men were exhausted by the time the fish were stowed and the trawls baited and set back in the water.

Wearily, they went below, stripped off their oilskins, and sat. None bothered to eat. They leaned their backs against the hull to snooze before it was time to haul the trawls for what they hoped would be the last time for the day. But then again, William Bailor was a hard taskmaster.

"I'll be glad to have Jimmy aboard and get home out of this," Dave said under his breath. "That kid brings nothing but trouble."

Suddenly, the vessel lurched and heaved them from their seats. Frank and Dave picked themselves up off the floor as footsteps pounded on the ladder.

"A squall is upon us," William said. "We have to save the sails."

The ship heaved starboard, knocking them all off their feet again. They scrambled behind William on the ladder, two coatless and one bootless, and raced to the mast. Frank retrieved the axe and chopped the trawl lines. Hundreds of codfish dragging in all directions would make steering impossible and, worse than that, damage the rudder.

"What happened?" Dave screamed over the blinding storm.

"Never mind," William shouted. "We have to get out of this."

"He fell asleep," Frank roared as he let go the mast, "that's what. He bloody fell asleep."

William abandoned the wheel to confront him, but the boat jerked and rolled almost to the tipping point, sending Frank into the frigid water and out of sight. Dave reached for the gaff just as the nets came tumbling toward him. He was swept overboard behind Frank.

"Grab the trap," William barked. He tied the lead rope around the mast to keep the works from sliding in after the men and losing all chance of rescue.

Dick Freeland scrambled for the wheel. Mike Croke dragged the net toward the spar to allow William to tie off the line in hopes of pulling the two aboard. The squall intensified, whipping hail and snow into their eyes. It splattered and plastered a frozen shroud on every surface. Mike wrapped one arm around the mast to get his bearings as a barrel, weighed down by herring, broke loose, toppled, and rolled toward him. William shouted, but Mike couldn't get out of the way in time. He flailed in an attempt to grasp the slippery spar. The barrel clipped him and sent him sliding along the icy deck. He was crushed on the gunnel.

Dick left the steering to help his mate. The wheel spun and the ship twisted into the belly of the squall, sideways to the surging wave that would break on the *Annie May*. Dick grabbed hand over hand at the rail and struggled to get to his screaming comrade. William, sensing the sea's coming onslaught, used the rope to secure himself to the mast.

Freezing water crashed onto the deck as the bow genuflected into the Atlantic. When the foam cleared, Dick and Mike were gone. William saw the next wave surging and reached for the axe tangled in the sail. He would have time between the waves to clear himself from the net and mast and grab the wheel. He would have to steer out of the squall to have a chance of saving himself and looking for his men.

The wave broke above him, and his hands were too cold to grip the helve. The splintering sound didn't register with him until the mast snapped, the line peeled off the spar, and he was towed toward the gunnel by the hefty nets. He willed his hand to close on the axe handle and made a last-ditch effort to chop the line and free himself.

The raging wind caused the fallen mast to pull taut on the rigging. It recoiled and made a wide sweep of the deck. The shattered end drove toward William and struck him broadside. The axe flew from his hand into the galley, and his limp body spilled over the side as the net sank beneath the turbulent water.

As quickly as it had come, the squall passed. The *Annie May* bobbed to the wont of the ocean tides and Labrador currents. The winds drove her off the land for many miles, then back to drift into a channel and a bay full of islands. There she weaved for days before she drove ashore on the high tidal surge of an autumn full moon. She hooked on the rocks and waited on the point of land that snagged her.

The *Annie May* was found, abandoned with naught but a cracked mast and crooked rudder, by the Whites of Juniper Tickle.

The story told by the Whites was very different than the story told by the families waiting in Spigot Harbour. Both sides believed their version to be correct and factual. When the truth is unknown, like with the *Annie May*, sometimes what is speculated is what becomes factual—a story that aligns with what can be accepted or what can be believed by those without answers and those most impacted. The families of the crew were certain that their people were murdered—and that the deaths of their loved ones went unpunished.

As for the Whites, the men knew that they had been blamed in the wrong. Their accusers tarnished their good name. When the story was told and bonded to everything around it, when it passed to descendants of both families, its fate was sealed, though they were opposing accounts.

Like light refracted through a prism—altered but still light—truth can be constructed by people. Due to malicious intent and emotional ties, as refraction changes the optics of a prism and sometimes colours the output, truth is rarely as transparent or precise.

Though history unfolds as reasoned by the person telling it, the reality is long buried, and that which is speculated may resemble nothing of the truth that is passed on as family history.

First and foremost, Ida Linehan Young is a grandmother to the most precious little boys, Parker and Samuel, a mother to three adult children, Sharon, Stacey, and Shawna, and a wife to Thomas. In her busy daily life, Ida works in the information technology sector of the federal government of Canada, and she volunteers her time in the community of Conception Bay South with the Kiwanis Club of Kelligrews.

Ida had a fascination with writing in her high school days, when she dabbled in poetry and essays. In 2012, she became serious about her writing with a story to tell, and that led to her memoir, *No Turning Back: Surviving the Linehan Family Tragedy*, in 2014. Having found a passion for writing, and with a love of local history and lore, she published four works of historical fiction: *Being Mary Ro* (2018), *The Promise* (2019), *The Liars* (2020), and *The Stolen Ones* (2021). In June 2021, the first three novels were issued the Silver Medal for Best Series—Fiction by the Independent Publisher Book Awards. *(continued)*

The fourth novel in the series, *The Stolen Ones*, won the NL Reads 2022 competition and the Margaret Duley Award. The novel was also a 2022 Bronze Medal Winner (Historical Fiction) of the eLit Awards, presented by the Jenkins Group. Ida's second work of non-fiction, *If I Cry I'll Fill the Ocean*, appeared on the *Globe and Mail* bestsellers list. In 2023, Ida published her first work of speculative fiction, *The Room Upstairs*, which appeared on the *Atlantic Books Today* bestsellers list.

With strong influences from the familial art of storytelling passed down by her father, Ed Linehan, and her maternal grandfather, Frank Power, Ida writes stories about her beloved province, Newfoundland and Labrador. She enjoys researching events of the late nineteenth century and weaving fictional characters through historical tales that complement that cultural richness, renewing interest in the province's storied past. Sometimes she writes across different genres just to tell a story.

Follow Ida on Facebook, Twitter, or Instagram:
@idalinehanyoung
Or on her website:
www.idalinehanyoung.ca